EVERNIGHT PUBLISHING ®

www.evernightpublishing.com

Editor: Karyn White

Cover Art: Jay Aheer

ISBN: 978-0-3695-0043-4

FALLEN GLIDERS MC: VOLUME TWO

DEDICATION

For my lovies

FALLEN GLIDERS MC: VOLUME TWO

DIGGER

Fallen Gliders MC, 3

Lynn Burke

Copyright © 2018

Digger

I leaned down, eyeing the ball and lining up my cue. "Fourteen into the six, into the corner." Shutting out the eighties music overhead that Jonny insisted on playing in the club, I focused on my finger bridge and the balanced grip of my right hand. A gentle slide forward sent the cue ball right where I'd said, sinking the six into the corner pocket.

"Bastard," Hawk grumbled around his toothpick, and Janie laughed. She was on one of her manic highs where she infused everything and everybody with life. I'd seen her lows—Mother Mary bless the girl and Hawk for his dedication to her.

She'd started their relationship on lies, but turned her back on her own father to prove her loyalty to Hawk—and our club. Draped against Hawk's side, she snuggled against his much taller frame, her eyes sparkling and full of love as she gazed up at him. What a pair they made, always touching in some way, both looking at each other as though the whole world existed in the other's eyes.

Got my poetic side going every damn time I hung out with them. Also brought on the beginnings of depression.

To find a love like that...

I turned back toward the table and lined up my next shot, breathing easy, focused like a laser even though my stomach twisted with longing for what they shared. I wasn't about to find it with any of the club whores. I'd had them all, dozens of times and ways, but never felt anything more than the satisfaction of blowing my load and releasing tension for a while. Besides, I was a hideous motherfucker and found everyone and everything new suspicious.

Ball sunk, I meandered around the table, eying the few remaining. Only one clear shot, a combination that a novice would scratch on. Once more, I leaned down.

A shiver slid down my spine, standing the hairs of my neck on end. Brow furrowed, I called my shot and slid the stick forward.

I fucking scratched.

"Capone!" Hawk called, and I glanced over my shoulder with a scowl.

Capone, another of our Fallen Glider brothers, sauntered into the club, a woman tucked under his shoulder.

Long, pale hair like moonlight hung to her waist. Curves to kill for with just enough extra a huge man like myself wouldn't have to worry about splitting her in half while fucking his way to Elysium. My cock swelled in my jeans as I stared at her.

Pretty boy Capone led her to the bar and pulled her down sideways onto his lap as he sat. He whispered in her ear, bringing a blush to her cheeks and a smile to her generous lips.

Lucky fucking bastard.

"Digger."

I jerked my head around toward Hawk.

He smirked, and Janie laughed again. "Your shot," he said, glancing past me toward where I'd been staring.

Jaw clenched, I focused on the game—or tried to. Lining up my next shot put Capone and his woman directly in my line of sight. I glanced up from the cue ball. She turned, and our gazes collided. Hazel eyes, bright like the stars...

I missed the ball completely.

Hawk chuckled. "The fuck, Digger?"

Face heating, I shrugged and moved back, cue wrapped in both of my hands, the butt resting on the floor. Unable to help myself, I turned my attention back on the woman, fighting to not run my hand over my disfigurement. She continued to watch me as Capone talked to Jonny, our president, on the stool beside him.

I wished I remembered how to smile, but the scar down the side of my face to the left corner of my mouth made me look like the Joker. An ugly brute, built like a fucking bull was how my brothers described me.

Wasn't far from the truth. At six-foot-six and over two-hundred and seventy pounds of solid muscle, tatts covering my entire upper body, and that fucking scar my blond beard couldn't hide... I only got laid because women wanted my cock. Just shy of a foot long and girth enough to fill any woman's eyes with fear. No matter how wet or willing, most women couldn't handle it all, and I longed to find someone who could take me balls deep—and enjoy it.

My dick ached, and I shifted my stance as Hawk pocketed a couple.

One side of the woman's lips quirked, and she slid her gaze down over me. Took her damn time, too. My pecs jumped as though on their own. Quads flexed. At least I kept my hips still as the bulge in my jeans snagged her attention. She fucking licked her lips.

I groaned although my mind said she must need glasses.

"You playing?" Janie asked while hip-bumping me. She bounced back a ways, and I didn't budge. The little butterfly of Hawk's couldn't weigh more than one-twenty soaking wet, and like the moon-haired woman, hadn't given my scar a second glance when I'd first met her in Sturgis the summer before.

"Yeah." I cleared my throat and struggled to find my groove. I'd run the first table, but fuck if I could concentrate for shit.

"Capone!" Hawk hollered across the club. "That kid you got in the kitchen covering your ass can't caramelize onions worth a shit!"

A few of our other brothers laughed and yelled out their agreement.

"Can't be in that damn kitchen every night," Capone shot back with a grin, tightening his arms around the beauty on his lap.

Thursday night, and although the club wasn't packed, enough brothers and whores had come in for the burgers Capone had made famous. A few more busted his balls before dropping the ribbing and going back to whatever the fuck they'd been doing before he'd come in.

Hawk finished the game for me, and rather than play a third, he and Janie headed out, hands groping each other. Going home to fuck, most likely.

I grabbed a beer and sat in a corner where I could keep an eye on things. On Capone's woman of the night, really. For a half hour, I watched her, sipping my beer while imagining all the things I'd do to her if given the chance.

Capone and I had shared women before, but only on invite—never because of self-inclusion. Fuck, did I wish he'd give me the look, the tip of his head indicating he was in the mood for a threesome.

She glanced my way enough to make me think she'd be game, but when Capone whispered in her ear again, stood, and led her upstairs to the third-floor rooms, I got left behind.

I took off a few minutes later, driving through the freezing rain to the house I'd bought a couple months earlier where no one waited for me. Nothing but a cold shower and wide palm to ease the ache in my balls Capone's woman had caused.

For the first time, I wished I had a woman to bring home with me—one to stay rather than leave after being tied to my bed. My fucking defenses towered over my brain like an unscalable wall, though, so even if a woman truly gave me the time of day beyond wanting my cock, trust issues that festered inside of me would keep them locked out.

Fucking sucked ass, my shit for luck.

****

Couldn't catch a fucking break. Saturday night, the moon-haired girl hung on Capone's arm. Although she was hot as fuck with an ass made for pounding, I studied her actions. Where her gaze lingered when not on Capone or me.

When I'd shown up at the club earlier, a dark sedan sat two blocks down. Darkness had fallen so I couldn't make out more than two people sitting in the car, but that fact kept me alert, walking the edge of violence my mind often fell into. Hawk had taken over as

Sergeant at Arms earlier that year, but my personality fit the mold better than his. I let him deal with the talking since I sucked with communication, but if an altercation came to blows or knives, I took over.

Capone's girl seemed innocent enough, and for Jonny to give him the go-ahead to bring her to the club, she must have checked out all right. *Coincidence*, I told myself that the sedan with the tinted windows and the moon-haired girl showed up at the same time.

As with Thursday night, I sat nursing a beer in the dark corner furthest from the door, keeping an eye on things, all too aware of the near stranger in the club. My attention lingered on Capone's woman more often than not, her smile and lone dimple. The soft curve of her cheek. The deep cleavage between breasts hugged by a tight t-shirt.

Capone wrapped his hand in her hair, and I stared as he kissed her, my cock swelling. A whisper against her lips, a nod of her head, and they disappeared upstairs.

Fuck.

I glanced around the club, noting a woman fawning over an uninterested Jonny, and the other whores already spoken for. The stairwell drew my attention again. Head home or head upstairs?

Fuck it.

Setting my empty bottle on the table, I stood, mind made up on relieving my brewing balls to the sound of her cries. If I couldn't have a wet pussy or ass, my hand would have to do. Again. I hurried up the stairs after Capone, and caught sight of him disappearing into one of the hotel-like rooms on the third floor. A fucking perv, I let myself into the one beside them, knowing the thin-ass walls would let me hear every noise they made.

I unzipped my jeans, palmed my cock, and lay down on the bed. Lazily stroking myself while waiting, eyes closed and imagining myself in Capone's shoes as she went down on him. Lying back on the bed, legs spread, pussy dripping and needing to be stuffed.

A bead of pre-cum slickened my hand, and I clenched my jaw against the need to jerk faster.

Eventually, a moan sounded—female and breathy—drawing up my balls.

Goddamn…

Minutes later, the cheap bed in the room next door squeaked. Thumped with a set rhythm. Gasps, groans, and cries from her lips spurred me on, until I pumped down my length with a brutal grip, imagining her tight pussy squeezing me, milking me as Capone fucked her mouth.

"Oh, God!" she shrieked through the wall. "Yes! Fuck, yes!"

My body convulsed, and I cupped my free hand over the head of my dick and shot into my fist, groaning as I emptied myself. Hardly satisfactory, but better than fucking blue balls or a cold shower. Capone's deep groan came on the final thump.

Lucky fucking bastard.

I should have joined them at the bar. Dropped a few hints. Maybe he'd keep her around for a while or even offer to share next time.

Fucking hope stiffened my dick again.

Maci

Capone got the job done again, I'll give him that much at least. Not a mind-blowing orgasm, but good enough he scratched the itch I'd been dealing with since first seeing him a few weeks ago at the grocery store.

Thick black hair, vibrant blue eyes, and a sexy beard ... a solid six feet of pretty boy hotness any woman would love to fuck—even if he did sport a ring in both his eyebrow and lip. We'd struck up a conversation the third time running into each other at the store, and when he asked to take me out for a beer, I'd jumped on the chance to do something for myself for a change—even though I knew guilt would eat me alive later. I also agreed since he seemed the type who'd want to be balls deep inside of me before night's end, and it'd been one hell of a long time since I'd gotten laid.

He wasn't really my type personality-wise. Happy-go-lucky and vanilla is all good and well, but I preferred the broody, sullen man who needed a reason to smile, whose stare brought all sorts of fantasies to mind. Like the blond giant downstairs with the scar and scowl, both of which shone clearly through his light beard. The thought he might enjoy some rope play. Offer a little pain with the pleasure the huge bulge in his jeans promised. Hands wrapped around my neck, releasing endorphins to create an unforgettable climax I'd yet to experience. Make me forget the reality of my life for a while.

Damn. My pussy contracted at the thought of him. I'd yet to meet someone who could satisfy my cravings for ... a bit more in the sack. Not that I had much time to check out the fish in the sea with Mom being sick.

"Here ya go, darlin'." Capone handed me some tissues and collapsed onto the bed beside me.

"Pretty convenient," I said after cleaning up.

He turned his head toward me, his blue eyes rimmed by dark, thick lashes a woman would kill for. "The rooms?"

"Yeah."

"Lots of whores. Lots of brothers." He shrugged. "Need some place to go."

"You have a cleaning lady or something?"

"Jonny's cousin. She's in and out most of the day picking up after us."

I grimaced. Cleaning up after a bunch of bikers fucking their way through every club whore and date they could get up the stairs… "Can't say I envy her."

Capone laughed. "She's a sweetheart. A bit older, single, and motherly-type."

"Still." I huffed, taking in the simplistic room. Definitely made for fucking and little more. No pictures on the gray walls. No decoration or flair. A simple bathroom with hotel-style necessities and white, fluffy towels.

I turned my attention back on the muscled man-beef stretched out beside me. A right-nice slab, but… "You boys ever share?" I asked, wondering at maybe fulfilling one of my fantasies.

"Sometimes, yeah."

Damn. I bit on my lower lip, contemplating the conversation I'd had with a few other guys who got me into bed but weren't interested beyond a vanilla wham, bam, thank you, ma'am. "Spanking? Bondage?"

One of his brows rose. "You into that?"

My turn to shrug. "Thought about it. Haven't done it, no."

"Shit." He chuckled and rubbed a hand over one of his thick, tattoo-less pecs. "I should have invited Digger up here with us. Sounds like you two would get along."

"Digger?"

"One of my brothers. He's into that sort of shit. We've shared women a few times."

"You'll have to introduce us." I let the thought fly since Capone himself had told me he wasn't looking to get tied down. A player if ever I'd met one.

He laughed again, his gaze sliding down over my nakedness. Rolling to his side, he reached out and pulled me close. "Next time." A few brushes of lips, and he deepened the kiss. The man knew how to use his lips and tongue—no fucking doubt. My engine considered turning over again, but I couldn't get my damn mind off the blond I stared at both times Capone had brought me to the club.

I pulled back, licking my lips. "I could go for a beer."

His smile and twinkling eyes should have melted my heart. "Sure."

"Up for a game of pool?" I asked while grabbing my jeans off the floor.

"I'll kick your ass."

I snorted a laugh while checking my cell phone for calls, relieved to not find any. "You can try."

Two minutes later, I followed Capone back down to the club. I swung my gaze toward the pool tables, but same as Thursday night, no Blondy. A quick glance around the club revealed he must have left when we'd gone upstairs. Or, else he went upstairs with one of the club whores.

A slither of jealousy twisted my stomach, but I pursed my lips. I had no right or reason to be jealous seeing as how I'd never said two words to the hot man-beef and had just fucked one of his brothers again. Beers in hand, we made for the only available pool table.

Capone grabbed a handful of my ass as he passed me. "Gotta get me more of this," he whispered in my ear.

I smiled, wishing his words turned on my pussy juice faucet rather than just made me tingle. *Not cutting it...*

Heaving a sigh, I swigged from my beer and sat it on one of the bistro tables beside the cue rack. While I was no pool shark, I could sink a ball or two—as long as they weren't combo or bank shots. Who was I kidding? I sucked at pool and only suggested playing because of Blondy—and the fact the thought of another round with Capone didn't tickle my clit.

Blowing a breath between my lips, I grabbed a stick. That tingle of awareness I'd felt when we first walked into the club Thursday night licked at my skin. I turned around.

Blondy stood in the stairwell. Alone. Staring at me as though he wanted to devour every inch of me and then some.

Hot damn and hallelujah, my faucet squeaked open, and I squeezed my thighs together. *Yes, please, and then a little more.* I smiled and shifted my weight onto one leg to pop my hip out. Might as well work my curves, right?

I cast a glance at Capone, who racked the balls, and Blondy started toward us. My heartbeat kicked up a few paces, sending jitters clear through to my toes.

"Capone," the non-jolly blond giant said, his deep voice sending a spasm through my pussy.

My date for the night lifted his head and grinned. "Wondered where you got to. Someone you need to meet." Capone nodded toward me. "Maci, this is Digger. Digger, Maci."

Well tie me up and fuck me upside down. I tried not to grin like an idiot and probably failed.

Digger moved close and stuck his hand out.

The fresh scent of laundry detergent wafted off him with enough maleness to make my mouth water. "Nice to meet you," I said, my voice breathless and hand shaking as I peered way up into his face.

He didn't smile, but the lust in those dark eyes weakened my knees. His warm palm swallowed my hand, sending an unfamiliar flicker of flames up over my arm and down to my nipples. "You, too."

We lingered in our physical connection, the lousy choice of music from the overheads muffled in my brain. Digger. Blondy.

My night was about to get a hell of a lot better. Fuck the guilt eating at my stomach.

Digger

Her damn cell rang, and I released my hold on her hand so she could pull the phone from her back pocket.

She glanced down at the screen, her brow furrowing. "Excuse me for a minute."

I nodded, gaze glued to her swaying hips as she made for the bathroom.

Capone groaned. "Fine piece of ass right there."

Some sort of agreeing noise escaped my throat. A simple touch of her hand had swelled my cock again to the point I felt sure a zipper imprint would tattoo my length. That's what I got for going commando.

"So, what's up with Maci?" I asked as the bathroom door closed behind her. "You liking this one?"

"Not sure." Capone leaned on the pool table, arms and ankles crossed. "She's easygoing—low maintenance. Wants to have a good time." He shrugged. "I'll keep her around a while."

I scowled while running a hand down over the whiskers I grew in an attempt to hide my scar.

"Why?" Brow cocked, he peered at me.

"She's fucking hot," I said while dropping my hand, my attention once more swinging toward where she'd disappeared.

"She's also up for a threesome if you are."

I jerked my head toward Capone. "No shit."

He grinned and glanced at the bathroom. "She's more your type than mine, really—wants to get tied up and spanked."

"Goddamn."

His grin widened at my groaned word, but his smile quickly faded. "Here she comes. Doesn't look happy, though."

Maci strode across the club, a frown marring the

smooth skin of her forehead. A few of the club whores—Shelly especially with her limp, blondish hair—shot daggers at her with their eyes. Jealousy, plain and simple. She outshone each and every one of those bitches with her moonlight-like locks and unlined face.

"I gotta get going," Maci said, glancing at Capone then me. "My mom is sick. Long story." She expelled a long breath as my excitement deflated.

"I'll take you home, darlin'." Capone grabbed her hand.

"See you later, Digger," Maci murmured, a question and hope in her star-lit eyes.

"Definitely." Hands shoved in my pockets, I stood and watched the two of them head out the door. I wouldn't get to touch her body that night, but the future sure as fuck sounded promising.

****

"Fucking FBI is watching my shop." Hawk tossed a wrench to the workbench with a scowl.

"The fuck?"

He nodded toward the garage door closing us off from the rainy fall day. "Down a block. Other side of the street."

"Same assholes watching the club?" I strode toward the door and peered through the dreariness. Sure enough, a dark sedan like the one that had been outside of the club over the weekend sat facing Hawk's garage, the shadow of two people in the front seats.

"Same fucking *car*."

"Sure it's the FBI?"

"Who else would be watching us from a fucking sedan for Christ's sake?"

I couldn't make out the two men for shit through the tinted windows. "Fuckers."

"The club is understandable with the questionable

shit we pull, but here?" He tossed another tool onto the workbench. "I don't deal jack shit outta here."

I turned and leaned against the garage door, arms crossed. "If it is the FBI and they had anything on you, they'd have already nabbed your ass."

"Yeah." Hawk wiped his greasy hands on a rag and moved my way, glancing out the window with a scowl. He used his tongue to roll his toothpick from one corner of his mouth to the other. "Freaks me the fuck out, though."

"My past is ten times dirtier than yours. You got nothing to worry about." Even though Hawk was our Sergeant at Arms, I tended to do away with the threats that needed to disappear. He'd never taken a life, and as long as I was around, he wouldn't have to. Gun, knife ... hell, bare hands worked just fine if a fucker needed to be done in.

I'd only been fifteen when I learned the truth about the night my mom got pregnant with me. First time I'd held a knife with the intent to kill, I told the fucker he'd gotten my mom pregnant with me the night he'd raped her. Three years later, I knocked off the other two involved in the gangbang just to be sure I ended the life of the man who had sired me.

Silent Demons. All three of the bastards. The final one at least got a slash of his own knife in, slicing me from ear to mouth. Even though his body rotted in a deep grave out in the middle of nowhere, my fucking brain always whispered that I'd somehow lost that fight. Marred for life, ugly as shit ... that's why I spent so much damn time in the club's gym. Making myself stronger. Harder. Closing myself off to vulnerability.

Fitting that a man who could possibly be my father sliced my face the way the Joker's had. Fitting too, that I would join the SD's arch rivals a few years afterward. The Fallen Gliders didn't rape. Didn't kill for shits and giggles or deal in sex trafficking we'd heard whispers the Demons dabbled in. Sure, we dealt drugs, but if we didn't, someone else would. Might as well make a buck.

I glanced at the sedan again. "Think Nicky would talk?"

Hawk glared at me. "You on crack?"

I shrugged. "He left—"

"Because his sister OD'ed on the shit we deal, not because he's a fucking snitch."

A heavy exhale, and I nodded. Nicky had been our Sergeant at Arms before Hawk had taken over the spring before, and we both missed the fuck out of him. He'd rarely smiled—same as me. Had taken care of business without hesitation—same as me. "Think he's happy?"

"Wouldn't know. Bastard doesn't return my calls or texts."

"Same." Scowling, I went back to work on an old '46 Knucklehead I'd picked up a few months earlier. I hung out at Hawk's shop more than I did the club, getting my hands greasy and shooting the shit. Made the late morning hours go by before I opened my tattoo shop a few blocks from the club.

Nicky had found a younger woman after handing in his colors and never returned. At least Hawk hadn't taken off after he'd hooked up with Janie. Leaving the Gliders wasn't in the cards for me. No woman—or fucking FBI agent—would tear me away from my brothers. Lifer with the "67" tattooed on my neck, I would be working on bikes and inking people until I breathed my last.

A couple hours later, I held onto the office door jam and leaned into the room. "Want to hit the club for a burger?"

"Heading home to Janie." Hawk leaned back in his old black swivel chair that didn't swivel anymore.

"She okay?"

"Crashed again."

"Damn." The poor girl had been riding a high for close to a month, repainting every room in Hawk's house when she should have been sleeping.

"New meds don't seem to be working with the swings, but at least there weren't any tears this morning."

"You're a good man, Hawk," I said, not for the first time.

He huffed a sarcastic laugh. "Just love the woman. Has nothing to do with being good."

Jonny had publicly accepted Janie as Hawk's old lady the morning after the whole run-in with her father, so she now sat beneath my protection. "Still. Tell her I asked about her."

"Will do."

I strode out the shop's door, shoulders hunched against the rain, noting the black sedan in my periphery. The fucking car pulled out behind me as I drove off. "Motherfuckers." I grabbed my cell and dialed Hawk. "They're on me, not you," I said when he answered.

"Like you said, if they had anything on you…"

"Yeah. Better keep my nose clean for a while."

Hawk chuckled, and I hung up. My past didn't have loose ends—I made sure as fuck of that. The one man who'd thought to blackmail me a few years back ended up as shark bait, teeth and all. Hadn't been a clean kill, but it wasn't Gliders' business, and no one had been around to witness it.

I glanced in my rearview. Sure enough, the sedan followed. Didn't keep me from heading to the club, though, since the FBI—if that's who they were—already had an eye on the place.

Scowling and soaked from the downpour, I entered the club while the sedan that had followed me took up its place where the fuckers had been over the weekend.

Same fucking car, Hawk had said...

"'Sup, Digger?" Capone grinned at me from behind the bar. "Burger and beer?"

I nodded and made my way toward Jonny's office door which stood open at the club's far end.

"What's on your mind?" Jonny asked as I strode in, sure my thunderous scowl gave my shit mood away.

"Got a tail."

One of his eyebrows rose, and he sat back in his chair. "Fuck."

"As far as the law knows, I'm clean as a fucking whistle."

"No loose ends," Jonny murmured my usual statement after cleaning up a brother's mess.

"Not one." I sat in the chair across from him. "Think they're just fishing, hoping to get lucky?"

A muscle in his jaw flexed as he glanced at the open door behind me. "I think it's the FBI, and I also think they have someone inside."

I straightened, my brow furrowing. "What?"

"The shipment we sent up north this morning?"

"Yeah?"

"Car got pulled over. Searched, and not by the cops whose pockets we grease."

"Fuck." I ground the word out. "No fucking way that was happenstance."

"Nope."

"Any idea who?"

Jonny shook his head. "I'd vouch for every single club member."

"One of the whores?"

"Only way they'd know jack shit is if one of the Gliders told them—something they know better than to do."

I nodded, remembering how I'd watched Nicky cut out a man's tongue for spilling club secrets before slicing him open ear to ear. Messy as shit, but the man had it coming, brother or not.

"What about those fuckers who left us earlier this year?"

"They hadn't been in long enough to know jack."

I nodded, wracking my brain. Two younger brothers had handed in their colors right before Nicky left, and three others while we'd been in Sturgis. No new initiates had come through our doors since the winter before. Numbers dwindled nation-wide, though, something the presidents had discussed while we'd been in Sturgis.

I expected—along with Jonny—that the motorcycle gangs had lost appeal. While the seventies and eighties pulled people in like flies to shit, the law cracking down had certainly put a damper on our ways. Sex trafficking had some of the mafia and other clubs raking in the cash, but our pockets and contacts didn't compare to theirs. Jonny would never deal in flesh, anyway.

"What can I do?" I asked, leaning forward, elbows on my knees.

"Just keep your fucking eyes and ears open."

"Always."

Lips pursed, Jonny dipped his head, and I returned to the bar a few minutes later.

Capone handed me a bottle of beer. "Just texted Maci."

The shit in my brain disappeared in a blink.

"Yeah?"

"Asked if she wanted to hang out tomorrow night."

"And?"

"She hasn't texted me back yet."

I took a long pull from my beer. It'd been too long since I'd enjoyed a little pussy. Been even longer since Capone and I had shared a woman.

Fuck the no self-invite rule. "You up for a threesome?" I asked, leaning my folded arms onto the bar.

He grinned, his pearly whites flashing from the beard he'd started growing a few weeks earlier. "Always." Still grinning, he moved off to refill another brother's beer.

Pretty boy Capone with his baby blues and black hair—the whores swooned over his young ass when he'd joined the Gliders five years earlier. Still sent them into a tizzy when he smiled their way.

Ten minutes later, Capone set my burger in front of me. "Heard back from Maci."

"And?"

"Her mom's not doing well. Said she'd get in touch with me sometime next week."

"Fuck. I'd been hoping for some good news. Haven't had any for a few days."

Still grinning—I swear that's all the fucker did—Capone ambled off to grab someone else a beer.

I dug into my burger, the caramelized onions melting in my mouth. If his pretty face couldn't land him an old lady, his cooking skills sure as fuck would.

Maci

I sat beside my mom's bed. She lay unmoving, same as the previous five days. ALS was a bitch—a royal asshole that had been slowly taking her from me. One walk at a time. One smile. One word, until nothing remained of the woman I used to know.

She'd refused a ventilator early on, letting me know she would go when her body wanted to. Hospice had taken over, so it was only a matter of time before I would take care of her final wishes.

I'd cried all the tears. Dealt with the grief I'd been facing—dreading—since Mom's diagnosis years earlier. She'd lasted a hell of a lot longer than expected, for which I was glad, but...

I needed a fucking break, and the guilt over my selfish thought twisted my stomach.

Hanging with Capone the week before had been rejuvenating, a couple nights that had given me hope life would go on once Mom died. Not just the fucking, but the promise I'd seen in his friend's eyes. The connection I'd felt to a man I didn't even know.

Capone had texted me a handful of times wanting to hook up again, but without going into detail beyond Mom being sick, I'd turned him down.

Being a caretaker sucked ass. Bad enough Dad had been taken from us years earlier than expected. My sister found herself a wealthy young Californian. She had lit out for the west coast once I'd assured her I could care for Mom on my own.

At least one of us could have a happy, carefree life. I'd made the call a few days earlier, telling her to come home if she wanted to have the chance to tell Mom goodbye.

I slid my gaze down over Mom's supine,

shrunken form. Pink fluffy, her favorite fleece blanket lay over her legs and tucked around her waist. Gurgling noises sounded as her chest struggled to rise. Blue lips parted, she let out little exhales of breath her body managed to suck in. Morphined as much as possible, she wouldn't feel death settle over her. At least she lay in her own bed, in the apartment that I would soon find lonesome—especially since her passing would offer me freedom.

Again, the guilt festered. Ate away at my stomach.

I prayed to fucking God that I didn't end up like her when my time came, an invalid in need of constant care. A burden, stealing someone else's life along with mine. A grimace twisted my mouth—stealing? My head sure knew how to be a selfish bitch sometimes. And, a burden? My eyes burned, and I whispered an apology to Mom in my mind.

I held her thin, cold hand, my gaze on her chest. Time between breaths lengthened as I fought off my demons. I glanced over at my younger sister, who held Mom's other hand. At least she had a fiancé to see her through the grief on our horizon.

"I'm going to get some coffee," she murmured. "Want some?"

"Nah."

A spitting image of me, Mari had been mistaken for my twin more often than not even though I had five years on her. Once she quietly shut the bedroom door, I squeezed Mom's hand and leaned down to talk in her ear.

"Quit fighting, Mom." I struggled for a smile even though she hadn't opened her eyes in over five days. Damn woman defined the word stubborn. "Mari and I will be all right. We'll get through together." Swallowing against the tears, I shifted on the chair, needing to tell her what I'd been holding in until Mari left me alone with her. My sister wouldn't have agreed with my thoughts. "It's okay to go," I whispered, my gaze caressing Mom's face, knowing my words didn't come out of selfishness. "I love you."

A shuddering sigh rippled past her lips. I stared at her chest for a full minute before drawing a breath of my own and leaning down to kiss her cool forehead. "Fly free, Mom."

I inhaled until it hurt. "Mari?" My voice broke as I called out for my sister.

She rushed into the room, her gaze flying to our mother. "Oh, Mom…" Tears coursed down her cheeks, and I stood to pull her into my arms.

****

The coroner took Mom's body away. She wanted to be cremated, her ashes scattered around the lake where we'd gone camping as a family before cancer had taken Dad ten years earlier. I'd promised to do as she'd asked, but didn't think Mari would be up for a camping trip. With it being so damn cold, we'd have to wait on those plans anyway.

Six on a Friday night, and I sat alone in the apartment I'd shared with Mom for the previous five years since her diagnosis. Every trace of medical equipment had been sent off, all of Mom's things boxed up by the front door, ready to be donated to the Red Cross.

My first moment to myself in a long damn time. A moment to breathe.

An incoming text dinged my phone, and I lifted my head off the back of the couch.

Capone: **Got any plans for tonight?**

I snorted. **Getting drunk and forgetting life.**

Capone: **Sounds like fun!!**

I chewed the inside of my lip, contemplating. Less than a week after Mom's death, and all I wanted to do was party the night away in hopes of numbing the grief shrouding my life. "As if anyone would care," I muttered, my fingers flying over the screen. **Care to join me?**

Capone: **I already have plans. How about you join ME?**

What kind of plans, I texted.

Capone: **The secretive type**

A lick of adrenaline seeped into my blood stream, reminding me I still lived. **Count me in.**

Capone: **I'll pick you up at 8**

Me: **CU then**

Tossing my phone onto the couch, I pulled myself off the cushion, thrilled to have something other than sadness to focus on. A glass of wine in the bath tub, a few swipes of makeup, skinny jeans, and boots... I couldn't be more ready for a break.

****

Capone knocked on the door right at eight. My panties didn't melt at his smile—if I'd been wearing any. I wished like hell I felt *something* as he grabbed me around the waist and planted one on me.

His eyes twinkled in the hallway's light. "Hey."

"Hey back," I said with a smile, pulling the door shut behind me. "Where we headed tonight?"

Capone took my hand and pulled me down the apartment building's stoop and into the frigid night. "To fulfill a couple of your fantasies."

One of my eyebrows popped up as another lick of adrenaline kicked in, warming me through. "Oh?"

He pulled open the passenger door of his truck, his grin widening. "Remember Digger?"

Do I. "Yes."

"We're heading to his place."

"A Gliders party?" I asked while sliding onto the seat.

"Nope." The smile dissolved as lust replaced the twinkle in his eyes. "Party of three—if you're interested."

My nipples tightened, and I squeezed my thighs together, my grief taking a backseat. "Hell, yes."

"Thank fuck," Capone said with a wink. He shut the door and rounded the front of the truck.

I smiled for real while clicking in the seatbelt. *Fuck, yes.* Blondy with the body. Blondy with the intense gaze, the sexy scar keeping a badass scowl etched on his face.

Party of three...

Threesome, for sure. Ropes? A little spanking? I wracked my brain for what else I might have told Capone about the fantasies in my head, but couldn't remember for the life of me.

"Ready to party?" he asked, climbing into the cab and flooding the air with the spice of his cologne.

"You have no idea." And he didn't. I hadn't told him the specifics about Mom's illness or even about her death. Wasn't about to put a damper on the night by letting out all the shit of the previous five years. "What's on the agenda for the night?"

He glanced my way, his gaze serious. "Trust me?"

"I barely know you."

"You spilled a few secrets on our last date. Figured now that I finally got you to go out with me again, I'd show you that I know how to satisfy a woman's cravings."

"Awfully confident."

Capone shrugged.

"So," I said. "Digger."

"What about him?"

I angled on the seat as far as the seatbelt allowed. "You tell me."

"Whatcha want to know?"

"He's your brother, so I'm sure you trust him."

"I do."

I chewed on the inside of my lip for a few seconds while studying his face in the passing street lights. "You've shared women before, you said. That ever cause problems?"

"Like what?"

"You both fall for the same woman."

He chuckled. "No need to worry about that. Digger won't ever tie himself down to one woman."

Wasn't exactly the answer I'd been looking for.

"What's on your mind, Maci?"

I heaved a breath. "Just thinking about the dynamic of a threesome. Honestly, I have no fucking clue how to think or act."

"You won't have to do anything, and as for thinking, we'll take good care of you. Make you forget your own name."

I huffed a nervous laugh. "Awfully confident," I said again.

"Damn right." He winked, sending a pulse through my pussy.

Shit. How I wished it was his action that had caused my arousal, but it was the thought of the man waiting for us. "Digger knows we're coming?"

"Was his idea."

"Damn," I whispered.

Capone shot a glance across the cab as a street light illuminated his face. "Hot for my brother?"

I bit back a smirk and shrugged one shoulder.

"I know you want him. Could tell that night I introduced you two at the club." No hint of jealousy laced his voice—thank God. If he didn't mind sharing, I sure as fuck was ready to go.

Digger

My knee bounced as I sat on the edge of my couch waiting for them. I'd cleaned up my place, had some quiet music playing, and a case of beer in the fridge. Condoms, lube ... had it all laid out in the top drawer of the bed stand and one rubber in my pocket just in case.

Fuck. I stood and paced to the kitchen, grabbed a beer, and guzzled half of it down before sucking in a breath. I didn't get nervous. I didn't get butterflies. *The fuck?* Scowling, I strode to the window overlooking my driveway. Flexed my bare toes. Walked back to the couch while running a hand down over my whiskered jaw.

Headlights swung across the front of the house, sending light shimmering across my living room wall.

My fucking heart leaped into my throat, and I hurried to the front door like a kid about to meet his new puppy.

Maci climbed out of Capone's truck, catching my breath. Skin-tight jeans and boots—she looked like a woman who belonged on the back of a bike. *My* bike. Pale hair hanging down her back like a wave of moonlight. Her smile lit as my floodlights atop the garage kicked on.

My dick forgot I'd jerked off a half hour earlier. Fucker swelled, impressing my zipper against the tender skin.

I pulled open the door as she drew near, Capone on her heels. Trying for a smile would only have made me uglier, but I at least let her know with my eyes that I was happy to see her. "Come on in."

Slight purple smudges under her eyes didn't detract from her beauty as she lifted her head to keep my gaze while walking into the house. "Thanks."

If I hadn't known any better, I'd have thought Capone had already gotten a taste of her before coming over. Exhaustion lined her face and dimmed the sparkle I'd seen in her eyes the last time she'd come into the club. Clothing and hair weren't rumpled, though. No telltale flush on her face or bruised lips.

I glanced at Capone. He grinned—same as always. Certainly wasn't the most observant of my brothers. Probably why he worked the bar and kitchen.

"Can I get you a beer? Wine?" I asked, holding out my hand for Maci's coat.

"Beer would be great, thanks." Our hands brushed as she handed me her leather coat, sending a shot of pure lust straight to my already straining dick.

"Capone?" I asked, my attention sliding down over her tight t-shirt and the nipples tightening beneath.

"Gotta ask?" He chuckled, and I turned without a word, making for the kitchen, my mind obsessing over the fact Maci hadn't worn a bra. Pert, generous tits lay bare beneath that shirt, making my fingers itch and mouth water.

I grabbed a couple beers from the fridge and listened while they went into the living room, their voices barely heard through the wall separating us.

"Nice place," Maci said from her perch on the couch as I joined them.

Capone sat across from her in the only chair—my chair—his way of giving me control for the night even though he had first dibs on her.

"Thanks," I replied, handing Capone his beer. Brushing my fingers against Maci's again while turning over her drink sent another prickle of awareness of her through my body, straight to my dick. I sprawled into the corner of the couch, not bothering to hide the obvious bulge in my jeans.

She glanced down, pink flushing her cheeks. Her tongue flicked out over her lower lip before she sipped her beer.

I wasn't one for words—usually left that to Capone, but the heaviness over Maci pulled at my eyebrows. "You okay?" I asked, studying her face.

Lips tight, she nodded, but her eyes lied. Not fear, but definite sadness.

She didn't want to share, so I wouldn't press. "You know Capone brought you here to fulfill a couple of those fantasies you told him about."

She swallowed, but didn't turn away as I studied her face "Yes." The pulse in her neck kicked into a higher gear, her nipples hardening to tight nubs as I slid my gaze down over her body.

"Neither of us will push for more if you'd rather just have a few beers and hang out tonight," I said.

Maci put her almost full bottle of beer on the coffee table and climbed over the couch toward me— without looking at Capone first. If she didn't feel the need to seek his permission before straddling my thighs...

A quick glance in his direction showed his attention glued to her ass without a hint of jealousy. Satisfaction sizzled through my veins. I slid my hands to her waist as she settled onto my lap, her gaze on my lips. I fought off the self-consciousness her study of my scar brought on.

"Capone said you could make me forget my own name," she whispered while running her hands up over my chest.

My pecs flexed on their own beneath her firm touch. "Is that what you want?"

Lower lip sucking between her teeth, she nodded.

Wetness coated her eyes, and fuck the goddamn ache that knifed through my chest. "You're sure?"

"Yes," she whispered, pressing closer so her pussy rested against my straining cock.

Fuck, did she tempt me like no other woman I'd gotten my hands on. What she needed was rest, strong arms to hold her close as she slept.

I slipped my hand up over the back of her tight t-shirt, beneath her silken hair to hold her nape. "If you want to stop, just say so, and you have my word that we will."

She leaned in and kissed me.

Mind fucking blown.

Soft and pliant, sweet yet minty ... goddamn did I fall under the beautiful witch's spell. Rather than take control and plunder the ever-loving shit out of her mouth, I held back, tracing my tongue along her lips rather than fucking her mouth. She opened to me with a sigh, and I gently threaded my fingers through her hair, angling her head.

My arm banded around her back, tugging her closer until her pert tits pressed against me. Slow rolls of my hips against her pussy tightened my balls and made her whimper against my lips.

Two pairs of fucking jeans in our way—and my brother I'd forgotten about.

I tore my mouth from Maci's. Eyes hazed over, she stared at me, swollen lips parted.

Capone sat back in my chair, legs spread, hand sliding over his bulge, a smirk on his face. Fucker loved to watch almost as much as he loved to get his dick wet.

I massaged the back of Maci's head and wiped the moisture off her lower lip with my thumb, torn over doing the right thing by taking a rain check until she was in a better frame of mind.

She flicked her tongue out, and I slid my thumb into her mouth without thought. *Goddamn.* I groaned as she swirled her tongue and sucked. My cock jerked, and she ground her pussy against me. "Christ, woman." Swallowing back another groan, I grabbed her ass in my palm and stood. Fuck it. I'd give her exactly what she wanted and then some. I just had to trust she'd stop us if it was too much.

Maci wrapped her legs around me as though they belonged there.

I nodded toward the hallway, and Capone hopped out of his chair to lead the way. He dimmed the lights as I knelt on the bed, sliding Maci to the center. She clung to me, but I pulled back onto my haunches.

Pale hair spread over my pillows, pulse in her neck fluttering, eyes wide and filled with need. The desire to see her like that every day of my fucking life welled over me like a nine-foot wave.

Should have freaked me the fuck out. Shouldn't have enjoyed the satisfaction sizzling through my blood. Mentally, I pulled back, telling myself to keep my suspicions in place. Keep myself safe from rejection.

"You're fucking perfect," I said, running my fingers up her thighs, over her hip bones, under her shirt. Her nipples pressed against the thin fabric, tight buds calling out for attention. I palmed her tits beneath her shirt, and she arched into my touch, lower lip once more between her teeth.

"You like my hands on you."

"God, yes." She gasped as I rolled both nipples between my fingers.

"Capone?" I scooted back and flicked the button on her jeans as my brother climbed onto the bed and took over where I'd left off with her tits.

Maci gasped as he closed his mouth over her

nipple, t-shirt and all, grasping the back of his head to hold him close.

A muscle in my jaw flinched to see his mouth on her, but our time together was for her pleasure, fulfilling one of her fantasies—not getting my balls twisted with jealousy.

She doesn't belong to you, I told myself while sliding down her zipper.

Yet, another voice whispered in my head, clenching my jaw. I told the voice to shut the fuck up as I moved off the bed, pulling her jeans down her legs as I went. Bra-less ... and panty-less.

"Christ." I groaned the word as my attention snagged on her bare mound and the peek of her swollen clit.

I tore my clothes off as I stared, my mouth watering. Dick leaking. I fished a condom from the back pocket of my jeans before tossing them aside.

Maci's legs parted as I climbed back onto the bed. Pink and soaked, her cunt called to me. I needed a fucking taste before sinking deep between those plump lips.

I palmed her ass and lifted her. One slow, long lick from her tight rosebud to her clit brought moaned curses to her lips and her legs around my shoulders.

Tangy and sweet, her musk overrode my senses. I fucking devoured every inch. Lapped up every trace of her arousal, dipping my tongue in for more, needing so much more. Eyes closed, I breathed her in. I drowned in her taste, my balls clenching and ready to explode.

Forget my usual restraint. My control. I needed to be deep inside of her, needed to have her pussy clench around me as she cried out.

"Fuck." I tore my mouth from her sweet cunt.

Capone had taken off Maci's shirt, and she lay

gasping for breath, chest heaving as he backed off to free his cock from his leathers. He palmed his dick, smearing pre-cum over his length. She eyed his movements, licked her lower lip, and glanced at me.

Fucking looked at me for permission.

Another knife to my chest.

I dipped my head once, and Capone moved closer, touching the head of his dick to her lips. She opened to him, and he groaned as his length slowly disappeared between her lips.

My cock jerked, and forcing my jealousy aside, I tore open the condom and rolled it on with shaking fingers.

Thank fuck for the rubber, because the heat of her pussy as I slid up through her soaked folds would have done me in before I buried myself inside her. Teeth clenched, I spread her legs wider, grabbed my cock, and pressed it against her opening.

Maci whimpered around Capone's cock, and I flexed my hips.

Tight. Hot.

I fought to keep my eyes from rolling back into my head as I slowly worked my way into Maci's body. Like a fucking vise, her pussy squeezed my dick, pulling me in deeper. Deeper.

Fuck me. I groaned as my balls came to rest against her ass. No frown furrowed her brow, no wince or shying away from my length.

"Goddamn. You took every fucking inch of my cock."

"So good," she whispered on a moan while wiggling her hips before Capone slid into her mouth again.

I bit on my lower lip while dragging my cock back out of her, every flutter of her pussy walls tempting me to thrust like a fucking dog until I blew my load. Her wetness coated my throbbing dick, and I pressed in for more, running my hands down her thighs, thumbs spreading her lips wider. Her clit protruded, ripe like a summertime peach I wanted to sink my teeth into.

Buried to my balls, I rubbed one thumb pad over her nub. She jerked, and Capone groaned. She deep-throated him, his balls resting against her chin.

Fuck.

I rubbed my other thumb over her clit.

"Fuck, Maci." Capone swore while she hollowed her cheeks and backed off. He grasped her hair and pushed back in while I slid out to the tip.

My dick ached, but I held myself in check, reminding myself the night was for her.

Maci

So damn big...

Digger's cock stretched me beyond what I'd ever felt before. Filled me to the point I wanted to cry at how perfect he felt inside of me. Slow and maddening, the both of them worked in opposition with their thrusts, the friction sheer torture, erasing my mind of everything except the need to come.

The sting of Capone's fingers pulling my hair. The glide of his cock deep into my throat as I swallowed around him. The warm hand pulling at one of my nipples. The thick cock pushing into me ... the thumbs on my clit.

My pulse raced, stomach tingled as I lingered on the edge. I pressed my heels into Digger's ass, and thank fuck he finally upped his pace. Catching his gaze, I tried to tell him with my eyes how badly I needed to come, how badly I wanted them to go over with me.

"Not yet, beautiful," he murmured with his deep voice, the fire in his eyes lighting one inside of me.

So fucking hot. So damn sexy.

Capone groaned and backed off completely, squeezing the base of his cock. Gasping for breath, I lay back, my gaze snagged by Digger's rippling muscles, the flexing of his abs as he filled me with his cock. The veins popped from his forearms from the grip he had on my hipbones, the bulge of muscles in his shoulders, his straining neck ... parted lips.

He pulled out, his huge cock jerking up to bounce on his abs as he backed off the bed.

I swallowed, but didn't get a chance to ask what the fuck, because Capone crawled on top of me—naked as a jay, sheathed and ready to fuck. He captured my mouth, and my eyes fluttered closed as he sank into my body, balls deep.

He dragged in and out twice before wrapping his arms around me and rolling.

My hair fell around us, the cool air licking along my sweat-dampened back, my ass on display for Digger.

"Christ." He let out a few more curses while palming my backside. He pulled my cheeks apart and shoved his tongue into my asshole.

I groaned, eyes closed and forehead resting on Capone's as he moved beneath me. "Relax, baby," he murmured, his hands sliding down my back to hold my hips still. "Let him make you feel good."

Capone's hands replaced Digger's on my cheeks, holding me open. A cap snapped open, and my ass clenched involuntarily.

"I'm going to fill this tight, little hole," Digger said, his voice half-growling the words as he rimmed me with a lubed fingertip.

I gasped as he pressed past the ring of muscle, and Capone kissed me again, his tongue taking my attention off the sting in my ass. Digger pressed in another inch or so, and I fought to relax. He slid his finger out to the tip, and when he pressed back in, the slight pain morphed into pleasure, drawing me back toward him as he retreated again.

"More," I heard myself whisper, pressing toward him as Capone slid back into me.

A second finger worked alongside the first, and Digger moved in opposition of Capone, his fingers fucking my ass.

Fullness unlike I'd ever known—I felt like a cock-hungry whore, but damn, did I want more.

"Please," I said with a moan as my climax hovered, my fingers clenching the comforter alongside Capone's head.

"Feel good, beautiful?" Digger asked, shoving his fingers in to the knuckles.

"God, yes."

He dragged his fingertips along the thin wall separating him from Capone's cock, and all three of us groaned.

"Fuck, Digger." Capone's blue eyes hazed over, his brow furrowed. "Take her before I blow my load."

Digger's fingers disappeared from my ass, but before I could moan a complaint, something much broader pressed against my opening.

"Oh, God." I bit down on my lip at the memory of the size of his cock.

"Relax, and press back," Capone crooned and swept his mouth over mine.

I forced my body to do as he said, and the head of Digger's cock slipped past my ring sending a zing of pain up through my body. *Holy shit.*

"Fuck, Maci," Digger said, his low voice sending a shudder down over my spine.

A deep groan escaped my lungs as the pain faded, and Capone swallowed it down as Digger pushed in a little further.

Oh, God... Oh, God... The chant went on in my head as Digger backed off and worked his way in.

"Christ, are you tight." The strain in Digger's voice matched the tension in Capone's body beneath me. Both held me in a bruising grip, and I gave over to them as the edge of my climax once more drew near.

Digger bottomed out with a low groan.

Capone pulled out of my pussy to the head. He thrust back in at the same time Digger retreated.

Fireworks exploded behind my eyes. "Oh ... fuck. Yes, more..." Grunted words, animalistic sounds flew past my lips as they moved together. Faster.

Sweeping me away in a vortex of pleasure I'd only dreamed about. "Going. To. Come." I whimpered with every thrust of their hard cocks. "Please."

Digger leaned over my back, reached between our bodies, and found my throbbing clit. "Take what you need, beautiful. Take us with you." He pinched, and I pitched over the cliff, my body trying to arch between their steel-like hold on me.

I shrieked, gasping for breath as they slammed into me over and over.

Capone followed me, smothering his groan in my neck.

Digger clamped his teeth onto my shoulder, and I came a second time as his cock pulsed deep in my ass. He swore between his teeth, pumping a few more times as I shuddered beneath him.

My ears rang as I fought for breath between the two men. The scent of soap, sweat, and sex filled my lungs, and I went boneless against the muscle beneath me.

Digger pushed my hair to the side where Capone still buried his face, and trailed kisses along the opposite side of my neck, down my spine and lower as he pulled out. A shuddering sigh rippled through me as his heat disappeared from my back, his huge cock from my ass, leaving me emptier than I'd ever felt.

I couldn't move. Capone didn't so much as twitch a muscle.

Running water sounded, and a few seconds later, it switched over to a shower.

Warm, calloused palms ran down over my skin and lifted me off Capone. Digger cradled me in his arms, and I relaxed against his warm, rock-hard chest, unable to move if I'd wanted to.

"You okay?" he asked, his voice rumbling

beneath my ear.

"God, yes."

Another rumble in his chest without definite words, something that sounded like relief and satisfaction, brought a smile to my lips.

He strode across the room, leaving Capone behind. Steam filled the bathroom, and he stepped into the hot shower with me still in his arms. I slung mine around his neck and scooted my body from his hold to wrap my jelly-like legs around his waist.

He peered down at me, unsmiling as always, his cock swelling as I rested my pussy against him.

The climax of a lifetime had just rocked my world, and I wanted another one already.

One of his brows cocked. "Most women would be done in for the night."

"Guess I'm not most women." I smirked up at him, heat curling in my belly.

"You're insatiable."

"You're fucking awesome," I shot back.

A hint of a smile twitched the unscarred corner of his lips.

The shower door pulled open, and a tousled-haired Capone joined us, grinning enough for the both of them.

Digger turned, putting his back to the spray, and Capone crowded close against me, gathering my hair in one hand, his mouth and tongue mapping my spine.

Massaging hands … wandering mouths.

I sighed, losing myself in their hold again, soaking in caresses, their gentle touches as they took their time washing every inch of my body.

Capone held me from behind, one hand splayed on my stomach, the other palming one of my breasts as Digger tipped his head back into the spray, water running in rivulets down over his face and tattooed chest.

His cock hung heavy between his thighs, drawing my gaze.

"I think you should show my brother what a talented mouth you have," Capone said in my ear, his hot breath tickling me. As though of the same mind, they traded places without a word, putting Capone into the shower's spray. He released his hold on me and pushed on my shoulder.

Warmth sprang to life between my thighs again, and I slipped to my knees, Digger's cock swelling in front of my face. I glanced up at him.

God, the heat in his dark eyes... I wanted nothing more than to put my mouth on him and suck him deep until he coated my tongue with his cum. Keeping my eyes locked on his gaze, I wrapped my hand around the base of his cock and tilted it toward me. I flicked my tongue over the head, gliding through the slit. He groaned and tangled his hands in my sopping hair, taking control from me.

My mouth stretched wide, I relaxed my throat and took him deep, satin-encased steel filling me, nudging the back of my throat and sliding further until my nose brushed his pelvis.

"Little fucking witch." He cursed a few times. "No woman has taken every inch of me like this." I smiled around his girth, and he pulled out, my hollowed cheeks drawing another curse from his lips. "Goddamn, woman."

Capone chuckled from behind me.

"I thought her ass felt like heaven." Digger thrust into my mouth, deep enough again I fought off my gag reflex. "So fucking hot."

He slid in and out while I lashed at his length with my tongue, dragging my teeth along his tender skin.

Cupping his balls in one of my hands brought a growl from his chest, tightening his abs.

I kept my attention on his face so far above me, soaking in his riveting gaze that made me feel like the queen of his world. Rippling muscles, water-beaded skin inked across his chest and arms ... he looked so damn badass that I felt myself drawing near another climax without even being touched. Giving head hadn't ever gotten me so damn worked up.

With a groan, he backed off and lifted me into his arms. "We'll finish this in the bedroom."

Soaking wet, he trailed out of the bathroom and to his bedroom where he lay back on his comforter, pulling me along with him. "I'm going to shoot my cum down your throat," he said as I settled between his powerful thighs and wrapped my lips around him again. He groaned as I took him deep. "Fuck, that's good."

Hands once more fisting in my hair, he took control again, thrusting his cock against the back of my throat.

The bed dipped behind me, and I widened my legs as Capone drew closer. He spread my cheeks wide and licked me from clit to ass.

I fought to keep my eyes on Digger as Capone worked me over with his talented tongue. Until he slipped two fingers into my soaked pussy, I panted for breath around Digger's cock. I wiggled, inviting more, needing more.

Capone must have gotten the hint, because he disappeared for a few seconds. The tearing of a condom wrapper had my pussy clenching. He grasped my hips and shoved in with one thrust.

I grunted around Digger, my eyes finally closing.

"Look at me while he fucks you," Digger said, his commanding voice pulling my eyelids back up. "Do you like his cock in your pussy?"

Not as much as yours. I nodded while swirling my tongue around the swollen head in my mouth.

"Goddamn," Capone moaned the word, thrusting harder.

"You should feel her ass," Digger said without taking his gaze off my face. He caressed my cheekbone with a thumb while thrusting into my throat. "I'm going to come in your mouth."

I begged him with my eyes to do it.

"You're going to swallow down every drop I give you."

Yes, please, fuck, yes.

His lips pursed, his dark eyes swallowed by his pupils. "Now." His cock swelled, and I swallowed around him. "Fuck…"

Capone pistoned into me from behind as spurts of hot cum shot down my throat. Without a single touch to my clit, I tumbled headlong into my climax, swallowing down every drop Digger offered, moaning around his length as my pussy spasmed.

Capone hollered and slammed into me, his cock pulsing. "Holy *fuck*." He ground the words out while sliding in and out of me, milking himself with my tightened walls.

I popped my mouth off Digger and went boneless again, resting my cheek on his thigh, my hips still held tight by his brother. Springy blond hair tickled my face, but I couldn't move as after sex tingles swept over my skin, depleting me of energy.

Digger

Capone crawled off the bed and went to the bathroom to clean up.

I couldn't tear my gaze off Maci and the mess of pale hair spread over me. Lips parted, eyes closed, she relaxed between my legs, one hand under my thigh, the other arm crooked over her head, hand on my pelvis beside my limp dick. She'd fucking drained me dry, and all I wanted to do was curl up with her on my bed and close my eyes.

Capone returned and used a wet towel to wipe between her thighs.

She didn't move except to sigh.

Once he finished, I yanked back the covers beside me, pulled her up over my body and settled her against the clean sheets. She pressed her face against my pillow, breathing deep and smiling.

Possessiveness swooped in, and even though the night was still young, I knew without doubt I wouldn't share her again. "Rest for a while," I said and kissed her forehead.

"'K," she murmured, probably half asleep already.

I caught Capone's attention, nodded toward his clothes, and pointed toward the door. I tugged on my jeans as he picked his clothes up off the floor, and I followed him out, quietly shut the door behind us.

"Poor woman needs to sleep," I said, keeping my voice low as we walked down the hallway. "Did you notice how exhausted she was when you picked her up?"

He glanced over her shoulder. "No."

I shook my head. Unobservant little fucker. I pitied the woman who ended up being the one to sink her claws into him.

Capone dressed in the living room while I dumped the warm beers down the drain and grabbed a couple new ones.

Sprawled in my chair, cold beer in hand, I peered down the hall at my closed bedroom door.

"Got it bad for her, huh?" Capone asked and took a long pull.

I did, and the thought didn't sit well with me. "Yeah," I admitted while scrubbing a hand down my face. "You?"

He shrugged in his casual, Capone way. "I told her I was just looking for a good time the first time I asked her out, so I'll step out of the picture if that's what you want."

I met his blue-eyed gaze, thankful to find zero trace of jealousy or anger. Keeping Capone around meant I wouldn't have to be vulnerable. Open myself up to the beautiful witch. But keeping him around meant he'd have his hands and mouth on her.

He grinned when I didn't answer and finished the rest of his beer, his throat bobbing as he sucked it down. "I'm never going to get a taste of her again, am I?"

"No chance in hell," I muttered even though I thought I'd made up my mind. Maybe the kid wasn't as unobservant as I'd thought.

"No point in my hanging out, then." Chuckling, he stood and stretched his back, plunking the empty beer bottle on the coffee table. "What if you aren't what she wants?"

His words fucking stung, and I lifted my beer, needing the cool liquid sliding down my throat.

Still chuckling, he tugged on his boots. "Pretty sure she fell for you the second she laid eyes on you in the club that first time, so don't worry."

My brow rose.

"I fucked her that night, but she didn't light up until you laid your hands on her two hours ago."

"She's fucking amazing," I said, my gaze trailing to the hallway again, thinking about how she'd taken all of me, in every way.

"You're welcome." Capone winked at me and grabbed his coat.

"You're really going to head out without telling her?" I asked as he strode toward my front door.

"I'm sure she won't mind waking to find me gone."

"You're a bastard."

"She won't be the last I fuck and leave without saying goodbye. At least I'm leaving her in capable hands."

I glared at him as he shrugged his coat on. "Someday a woman is going to break your heart, Capone."

"Not gonna happen." Grinning, he escaped into the cold, leaving me to finish my beer alone.

Within ten seconds, I put the beer aside and ambled back down the hallway.

Maci lay right where I'd left her, breathing deep. Passed out. In my fucking bed.

I turned off the light, pushed my unbuttoned jeans back off, and slid under the comforter beside her. She sighed and snuggled against my chest as I wrapped my arms around her. Her hair smelled like my shampoo. Her skin like my soap.

Every inch of her had been mapped out in my head, and even though I didn't know her last name, I sure as fuck wanted her to stay in my bed.

****

Someone cried. Wracking sobs that furrowed my brow.

I opened my eyes to darkness. Maci faced away from me, the sounds of grief I thought I'd dreamed pouring from her lips and shaking her body.

The fuck?

"Hey." I ran my hand down her arm, not sure if she was upset Capone was gone, or if we'd hurt her without my knowing it.

She rolled into me, burying her face in my chest, and I wrapped my arms around her as she sobbed.

"Shh…" I smoothed my hands down her back. Doing my damnedest to be gentle. "I've got you, Maci. It's okay." Similar words slipped past my lips as she continued to cry, and I wracked my brain for what the fuck had caused her break down.

Janie had done the same thing with Hawk not long after they'd met, but Maci didn't seem to have been on a manic high earlier—I doubted she struggled with the same episodes.

When she'd arrived earlier that night, I knew something had been bothering her, though. The fact she'd held it in while Capone and I had worked her over had me thinking whatever it was hadn't been such a big deal. My initial thoughts there was something wrong were spot on, I realized as she clung to me and cried until she had nothing left.

"I'm sorry," she whispered some time later, sniffling and pressing her cheek against my chest.

"Did I hurt you?"

"No." I waited, and she eventually inhaled a deep breath and pulled back enough to peer up at me in the darkness. "My mom passed away last week."

I blinked as her words processed. "Fuck. I'm so sorry. Did Capone know?" I asked, my brow furrowing at the thought he could be callous enough to bring her over to my place so soon after her mom's death.

"No," she whispered. "I—I never told him."

"You should have. What we did to you tonight—"

Maci pressed two fingers over my lips. "I wanted you to. I needed to escape the grief. I—I thought I'd finished with the tears, but guess not."

Unsure of what to say, I pulled her close again. Her warmth, her softness overrode my usual control, and I found my cock swelling regardless of the situation.

"Did Capone leave?" she asked a few minutes later, her voice muffled against my chest.

"A few hours ago. I'll take you home if you want to go."

"I'm glad Mom's suffering is over, but going back to the empty apartment ... it sucks, you know?" Her voice wobbled, and I squeezed her tight.

"You're welcome to stay the rest of the night with me if you want."

"I—I'd like that."

I know nothing about this woman... "Do you have to work in the morning?"

"I took some time off because of Mom. Making arrangements, that sort of thing. I'm off all next week, too."

"Anything I can do to help?"

She sighed. "Everything's done except for sprinkling her ashes around Pine River Pond."

"Wakefield?"

"Yeah. We used to rent a camp up there before my dad died awhile back." Her voice broke again, and I squeezed her close.

Fuck, this girl's past... "Do you like waffles?"

"As long as there's real maple syrup," she replied with a sniffle.

"And bacon," I added.

"Definitely." A hint of a smile coated the word.

I found my lips rising in a crooked grin, and I hugged Maci close again, glad she wouldn't be able to see my ugly face with how she pressed against me. "Coffee?"

"Sweet and blond, just like you."

A snorted, sarcastic laugh shook my shoulders.

"What?" Maci pulled back to peer up at me, and again, I thanked fuck she couldn't see my face clearly. "You're blond. You're sweet."

"Sweet?" I snorted again and ran a hand down over her shoulder into the dip of her waist and over the swell of her hip where I rested my palm.

"Sweet," she murmured again, leaning up to kiss me.

My dick jerked against her thigh, but I focused on her moist lips, her tongue, rather than the need to sink into her again.

She rolled on top of me, and I lay back, groaning as the wet lips of her cunt rubbed against my length. Guilt over wanting her again warred in my head, but the way she moved over me, sliding her slickness up and down my entire cock, tilting her hips to notch my flared head against her opening…

"Fuck," I mumbled against her mouth. "If you don't stop this, I'm going to take you again."

"Got another condom?" she whispered and bit my lower lip.

I grabbed her hips to keep her still. "You sure about this?"

She bit my lip again.

"Little witch." Leaning over, I swiped a condom out of the bed stand where I'd left them.

Maci grabbed it from me and sat up, tearing it open. My dick leaped at her touch as she slid it on, my teeth clenched. "Now…" She moved over my body, her tits soft against my chest. "Where were we?"

Palming her waist, I positioned her where I wanted her. "Right about here." My balls seized up as she pressed back, notching my dick inside of her again.

"Here?" she asked, leaning down to bite my nipple.

"Fuck, yes." My eyes clenched shut as she sank lower onto my cock, stretching herself, filling her tight, little cunt with every inch.

She let out a shuddered breath. "I can't believe you fit inside me."

I groaned, thankful as fuck that I *did*, and wrapped one of my hands in her hair. "Fuck me, beautiful witch."

Maci lifted and rotated her hips in steady rhythm, nipping my nipple, my lips, driving me out of my fucking mind.

With a growl, I flipped her onto her back and slammed balls deep back into her pussy. "Fuck, this pussy…" Her wrists in my hands, I lifted her arms over her head, driving into her in full thrusts, pulling out and burying to the hilt. "So fucking good."

"My God," she whispered, staring up into my eyes as I continued to flex my ass and retreat, fucking her as hard as I could. My bed slammed against the wall. Maci panted beneath me, our eyes locked in the darkness. I untwined my fingers from hers. "Keep your hands overhead."

She groaned as I slid my hands around her neck. Slight pressure brought another one to her lips as she arched her back, thrusting her tits at me.

"Like that?" I asked, squeezing a bit more.

"Fuck yes," she whispered as I held her immobile, my cock slamming into her.

"Come around my dick. Let me feel you let go." I captured her mouth, my tongue thrusting in time with my hips, tasting and taking how I wanted.

Maci fell apart beneath me, her body arching into mine as her cunt clenched down on my straining dick.

"That's right, beautiful." I grunted, one thrust away from blowing my load. "Milk me. Just like that…" My balls erupted, filling the condom as I groaned and sank my teeth into the tender skin of her neck, hard enough to leave a mark.

Maci

Digger served me waffles with real maple syrup, a pile of bacon, and coffee just like him, whether he would admit to being sweet or not. He scowled a hell of a lot, but tenderness ruled his insides. The looks he gave me, the gentle touches while moving past me. A brush of the fingers while passing me the syrup. One soft smooch on the top of my head while handing me my coffee.

A woman could fall hard for such a man. Big as an ox, badass tatts over his chest and arms, lush lips—even if a nasty scar disfigured one side. Add in his observant attention, and he created the perfect package. In my eyes, anyway.

He studied me while we ate, his gaze seeming to penetrate my soul and taking a good, long look into every corner.

"I'm eating breakfast with the most beautiful woman in the world—and I don't even know your last name," he said, his voice low and rumbling.

"Irving." I smiled, loving the softness in his dark eyes. "The hottest man on the planet cooked me waffles after the most mind-blowing evening of my life..." I arched an eyebrow. Surely, Digger wasn't his real name.

His lips pursed for a second. "Raymond Hearst, but I rarely go by anything other than Digger. Haven't for over fifteen years."

I licked a drip of syrup off my thumb, and his gaze zeroed in on the flick of my tongue. "Can I ask you something?"

"Anything."

"What's up with Capone?"

He tensed. "You tell me."

I shrugged. "Nice guy, but honestly, he's too pretty for me. Not really my type."

"So, why'd you go out with him in the first place?"

"I needed a break from taking care of Mom, and he offered, so..." I shrugged again.

"So you aren't upset he bailed on us last night?"

"Not at all."

Digger's gaze lit although he didn't smile. "Glad to hear it."

Smiling for both of us, I shoveled another forkful of waffles into my mouth and glanced around Digger's kitchen. A simple one-story house, definitely a bachelor's pad sorely lacking in personal items, but he kept it clean. No womanly touches anywhere ... the thought warmed me through.

"So." I returned my attention to him and pushed my plate away to wrap my hands around my coffee mug in front of me. "Now what?"

His gaze slid down over my neck, to the budding nipples beneath his t-shirt I'd grabbed to cover my nakedness. He lifted his gaze, a whole lot of lust in his eyes.

I pressed my thighs together.

"The 'now what' is up to you."

"Me?"

He nodded and bit a piece of bacon in half, chewed slowly without taking his attention from my face, kicking my pulse up a notch.

"Meaning?" I pressed when he didn't elaborate.

"I'm a Fallen Glider. Not the type of man most women would want in their life."

"Are you asking me if I want you in my life?"

His brow furrowed for a split second as though his mind warred. "Yes."

"Fuck me sideways," I said with a breathless laugh.

"I'd have to tie you up first, but I think I can manage."

Heat flooded through me, and I squeezed my thighs together, afraid of leaving a wet spot on his chair. That's what I got for nixing the panties...

"Well?" he asked, his body still as though ready to pounce like a mountain lion.

"I'm sure my goodie-two-shoes sister wouldn't approve, but I don't give a shit."

"Give it to me straight, Maci."

"You feel it, don't you?" I asked, motioning between us. "This ... connection, thing ... I can't explain it."

"I do."

So serious. I bit the inside of my lip to keep in my smile while studying his broody face. My type to a T. He needed a woman like me, someone to coerce his lips into smiling. Someone to ease the somber shroud over him.

I didn't want to burden him with my grief, though. Even though I drained the well in me during the night, I expected I'd do so a few times more before the sadness of losing Mom eased. My inside smile faded as my throat thickened.

My psychological needs to be appreciated, the desire to have purpose again now that she'd gone ... hell, the want for love swayed me toward him. "I want to explore whatever *this* is," I whispered. "See where it goes." The corner of his lip twitched, and I leaned forward onto the table. "Is that a smile?"

His brow furrowed. "I don't smile."

"You did last night in bed, but I couldn't see that well."

"It's not..." He turned away, his attention on the window over the sink. "It's not a pretty sight," he finally said.

"You're hot as fuck, Raymond Hearst, and nothing on this damn planet will change that fact."

He snorted. "You're blind."

"Think what you will," I said with an air of brushing him off and picking up my coffee. "I know the truth."

His lip twitched again, and I couldn't keep from smiling into my cup.

We cleaned the dishes together, me washing and Digger drying. Hips bumping, hands brushing as we talked about our childhoods and the normal shit new friends/fuck buddies discuss. He kissed the top of my head countless times, and I couldn't stop from smiling even if our conversation focused on surface things.

Twice, he walked to the front door and looked out the window.

"Something wrong?" I asked when he returned to my side the second time.

"Dark sedan is watching my house."

My eyes widened, and I paused in rinsing a mug. "As in FBI?"

He shrugged.

"Are you in trouble?"

"Haven't done anything to warrant their attention for years."

"But you've got a nasty past," I said, handing him the dripping mug.

He stared at me a long minute, his brow furrowed as though warring in his mind again while drying the cup. "I've broken the law a time or two." He didn't sound ashamed. Or scared. He put the mug away, hung up the damp towel, and leaned his ass against the counter right beside me.

I tilted my head back to keep eye contact as he loomed over me.

"Whoever it is," he said, his gaze piercing me, "they've been watching the club, too. Have for a couple weeks."

My eyes widened—over the fact he shared that information rather than the truth of it. "What's going on?"

He continued to study my face without moving. Me, a near stranger who had no business knowing the Gliders' business. I didn't expect him to answer. "Not sure, but Jonny thinks we might have someone inside spilling secrets," he finally said, holding my gaze as though testing me.

"Shit."

"Yeah."

A suspicious man—feeling out the near-stranger he'd had in his bed all night. My curiosity swelled, especially since I knew I had nothing to fear or hide. "Whose job is it to take care of that kind of situation?"

He peered at me for a time, and I held his gaze, letting him see he could trust me. "Hawk's the Sergeant at Arms, but I'm usually the one to deal with ... problems."

I nodded and returned to the dishes. While I should have been uneasy about hanging with such a man, the thought he bloodied his fists turned me the hell on. The type of man who would protect those he loved without hesitation. Without question. I glanced up at him through my lashes, thrilled he had shared such personal information.

He stared down at me as though reading my mind again. "That fact doesn't bother you, does it?"

"Quite the opposite, actually." I wrung out the wash rag and moved to wipe off the table. Smirking, I leaned forward, reaching across the table, exaggerating enough to lift his t-shirt to the middle of my ass cheeks.

His groan clenched my pussy and tightened my nipples.

"Damn, woman." He grabbed my waist, pulled me upright, and buried his face in my neck where he'd left a big-ass hickey. When I'd caught sight of his mark in the mirror earlier, a thrill I didn't understand had shot through me.

One of his hands crept up the front of his shirt, pulling me back into the moment. "No fucking panties."

"Nope." God, I sounded like a breathless whore. "Hardly ever wear the damn things."

He groaned in my ear and reached between my legs. "Already wet for me, too," he murmured, running his fingers through my folds. "You like that I'm a bad man."

I pressed my ass against him, feeling his cock swell against my lower back. "It would seem so."

"Tell me you aren't too sore from last night." His growled words sent a shiver through me, pebbling my skin.

"I'm not too sore."

He slid two fingers deep into my pussy. "Tell me I can keep you tied to my bed all day."

"Tie me up, Digger, and keep me there all day. Please."

He swept me up into his arms, and I tossed the rag over his shoulder at the sink while he started toward the hallway.

Digger

I didn't share personal or club shit with anyone who wasn't a brother. Hell, I wasn't even comfortable discussing business with Hawk when Janie hung out with us.

But, Maci... I'd been reading people for years, taught by the best, and there's no way in hell Maci worked for the law. 'Course, with my distrust of people in general, I wouldn't have shared shit had her mom not just passed. No fucking way she'd faked that grief.

Feeling her beneath my t-shirt had a second motive, but I wasn't surprised to find her bare of a listening device.

What if she planted bugs?

The whisper in the back of my mind twisted my stomach, and I decided I needed to make sure. I tossed her on the bed. "T-shirt off."

She obeyed and leaned back on her elbows, one leg crooked to the side, offering me a tempting view of her pink, glistening cunt.

I tore myself away and pulled a few lengths of rope from my closet.

Her pupils dilated as I crawled onto the bed between her thighs. "Scoot back against the headboard. Draw your knees up."

She did as told, and I bound her forearms from elbow to wrist.

"Grab the headboard."

Lips parted, she stared up at me while grasping the top bar and I tied her tight.

"Too tight?" I asked, settling back on my haunches and grabbing another length of rope.

"No," she whispered.

"If you want me to stop, just say the word,

okay?"

Maci nodded, not taking her gaze off my face.

Self-consciousness crept into my brain. Why the hell did she stare at me? Was she second guessing my ugly mug and the scar tilting my lips?

"You're hot," she murmured, a small smile tugging on her mouth.

"You're blind," I repeated my earlier statement.

A soft snort jiggled her tits. "Hardly."

I bound her right ankle tight to her thigh and worked a looping pattern up close to her knee before tying that to a corner of the headboard. "Okay?" I checked in with her again.

Her eyes had glazed over a bit, but the soft smile remained. "More than okay."

Once I tied off her second leg to the opposite corner, I sat back and feasted on the sight. Completely bound, spread open, and at my mercy, Maci peered at me with trust in her eyes—and a whole lot of lust. Her pulse beat in her neck. Nipples in tight buds. Glistening cunt with a droplet of arousal ready to slip down over her pink rosebud.

I slid my fingertip up through her wetness, and she moaned.

"You like my ropes?"

"I like everything about you."

Sliding one finger into her tight cunt, I lifted my gaze to her face. Lips parted, skin pebbling over her breasts, her eyelashes fluttered close to her cheekbones.

My dick strained up against my abs, pre-cum oozing down the side.

Maci reclined far enough that if I got onto my knees...

I grasped the base of my cock and smeared the pre-cum over her lips. She opened while lifting her eyelids. Our gazes locking, I flexed my ass, and she welcomed my entire length down her fucking throat. Leaning my forearms and hands on the wall above the headboard, I groaned, my own eyes closing.

"Your fucking mouth, Maci. Goddamn."

She hummed around my length, jerking my dick in her mouth. Her throat tightened around me as she swallowed.

Little witch could take me to the edge faster than my own fucking hand.

I pulled away after a few easy thrusts, her mouth popping off me, her ass grinding into my mattress.

Needing to cool the fuck down, I lowered onto my belly between her spread thighs, palming her squirming ass. "No coming until I say so," I murmured against her clit.

Maci whimpered, and I flicked my tongue over the tight bundle of nerves at the top of her soft folds.

"G-God." She gasped as I flicked again. Her limbs trembled hard enough the headboard shook, and inwardly, I grinned.

I shoved my tongue into her cunt as far as I could.

Back arching, she let out another gasp. "Fuck, Digger ... I'm going to come."

I backed off and blew over her soaked cunt while rubbing one thumb around her quivering hole and down to her puckered one. Plenty slickened with her juices, I pressed my thumb into her ass. She groaned.

"I'm going to fuck your ass," I murmured against her clit while working my thumb in deeper.

Little whimpers of need brushed past her lips as I pulled away to grab a condom and the lube off the bed stand.

She watched my every move, her lips parted, pupils dilated, that haze still in her eyes. Rather than watch me roll the rubber on, she stared into my eyes. Normally, such study unnerved me, but rather than the usual insecurity thoughts she studied me to find fault, my chest fluttered. Anticipation? Arousal? Whatever the feelings were, I fucking loved it.

A squirt of lube, and I palmed my dick, getting myself good and slick for her. Another on my other hand's fingers, and I readied her for me, using two in a scissor action to stretch her tight hole.

"You're going to be a good little girl and take every inch of my cock," I told her, replacing my fingers with my throbbing dick head.

Maci jerked her head up and down, lower lip between her teeth again.

I pushed in a few inches with the first thrust, enough to make her gasp and arch. She didn't tell me to stop or complain, so I pulled out and shoved back in again, gaining ground. I watched myself on the third, her rosebud stretched around my girth, pulling me in deeper.

My balls tightened, and I grasped her spread knees, thrusting in the final couple of inches. "Goddamn." I rolled my hips, pulled out to the head, and slowly slid back in, balls deep.

Brow furrowed, she watched my dick sink into her ass.

"Your ass is so damn tight." I thrust again. "So fucking hot. I could fuck you like this all day."

She whimpered again and closed her eyes, her back arching, pert, pebbled nipples begging for attention.

"You like my cock in your ass, don't you, little witch?" I asked, returning my attention to her face.

"Yes," she whispered, her frown deepening.

I held still. "Look at me." She whimpered and wiggled, but I didn't move. "Look at me," I said again, half-growling the words.

The skin between her eyebrows continued to pucker, but she listened. Hazel and hazed … her eyes snagged me, and I fought off the need to drown in her.

"You aren't FBI, are you?"

She blinked and stilled. "Wh-what?"

I wrapped a hand around her neck and squeezed until her eyes widened. "FBI. Law. Wires and bugs, that sort of shit."

"G-God, no!" Pain filled her gaze, but not the type that would result from my fingers wrapped around the tender skin of her neck. "I swear!"

I believed her—give the witch an Oscar if she lied.

Loosening my grip, I flexed my hips again. We both groaned. "I needed to ask," I grumbled, sliding out to the head. I pushed back into her tightness, and she nodded, lower lip between her teeth.

A few more thrusts set me on edge, and I clenched my jaw to keep from exploding. I tried to think about the damn Knucklehead I worked on at Hawk's garage. Tried to consider the sedan sitting outside.

Barely took the edge off.

Her muscle ring clamped down on my dick, and I growled in my chest. Couldn't last.

I rubbed a finger over her clit, and she bucked in her restraints. "Oh…"

"Like that?" I asked, repeating the movement.

"Mmm." Her body shook, skin pebbling.

"Come, Maci." I pinched her clit hard enough to hurt.

She shrieked and convulsed in my ropes. I fucked into her hard and fast as gasps flew from her lips, tremors through her body.

"Fucking hell." I groaned, my gaze on her passion-hazed eyes as my balls exploded, shooting jet after jet of cum into the condom. "So goddamn perfect. Fuck!" One last spurt, and I leaned against the wall to capture her lips.

Between gasps for breath, I tasted every inch of her mouth, breathing in her sweet exhales that hinted of maple syrup and bacon.

"So fucking good," I whispered and kissed her lips one last time.

"Mmm," she agreed, a small smile lifting her lips. "Better than good."

Maci

I winced as Digger pulled out. So damn big, he left me empty. Aching.

"Be right back," he said.

A shuddering inhale, and I relaxed completely, spent and smiling, my gaze on Digger's flexing ass as he walked across the bedroom toward the bathroom. I'd been in control of everything for so damn long, it was nice to give over to someone else. His sexy-ass body and grim demeanor cherried the top of that damn cupcake.

Holy fuck, I could totally fall for the guy. Badass or not, he got me going. Knew how to cook. *Knows how to care for a woman, too,* I thought as he returned with a hot, wet towel to wipe between my thighs and ass.

"You okay?" he asked, his dark eyes roaming over my face, reading me most likely. Couldn't blame him for questioning me like he had. In his shoes, I expect I'd have done the same.

"Yeah. I'm good."

Lips in a flat line, he retrieved a switchblade from his bed stand, and within a few flicks of his wrists, unbound my arms and legs. Calloused, yet gentle hands helped me scoot down on the bed, and I stretched, taking stock of my joints. The ache in my ass.

Digger sat beside my legs and picked up my foot, his fingers kneading into my muscles.

I moaned and smiled. "That feels so damn good."

His lips didn't twitch, but I recognized the smile in his eyes. Exactly how he took his coffee ... dark and sweet. I stretched my arms overhead while he massaged up my leg, kissed my bare mound, and worked down the other side.

One would think the silence between us would feel awkward. Uncomfortable, even after his questions, but I loved every second just being near him. Whatever connection linked us together, no longer flared or simmered with heat, but comforted like a warm blanket on a winter's day.

"What do you usually do on Saturdays?" I asked as he neared my foot and the end of my massage.

"I work out for a couple hours then head to my shop."

"Shop?"

"Tattoo place a few miles away. Don't have anyone scheduled for tonight, though."

I lifted up onto my elbows. "You're a tattoo artist?"

He nodded, glancing up at me.

"I've always wanted a tattoo. Mom doesn't—didn't—approve of them." My voice caught, but I smiled. "Would you ink me?"

"What do you want?"

"I..." I frowned while considering and laying down flat again. "If you're going to permanently mark your body, it ought to be something special, something important that defines you, shouldn't it?"

Digger shrugged and finally put my foot back on the mattress. He stretched out beside me, propped on an elbow. "Doesn't have to. Could just be something you like."

I ran my gaze across his chest and down one of his arms. Skulls, a badass bike with demon horns for handle bars, chopper engine parts—if I had to guess—the word "LOYAL" across his right hand's knuckles ... and don't forget the yin and yang, the knife. The "67" on his neck.

"I like all your ink," I said, trailing my fingertips along the barbed wire circling one of his biceps.

"You do?"

"It's sexy as fuck, same as the rest of you."

I ran my hand over his thick pecs, over his collarbone and defined shoulder with its bulging muscle.

"My scar doesn't bother you?" he asked, his voice quiet. Unsure.

My gaze followed my thumb as I swiped over his lower lip and up along the puckered skin leading to his ear. "Not even a little. It means you're a survivor. A fighter." I finally met his gaze.

Dark eyes, open and vulnerable peered at me.

"You don't believe me," I said.

"Hard to imagine someone can find this—" He grasped my hand and pulled it away from his face, "—something other than hideous."

I cupped the other side of his face and leaned up. "Maybe if I say it often enough…" I kissed him, hoping like hell he'd keep me around long enough to convince him of his hotness.

****

Too sore to fuck, I offered to make him lunch before heading into his tattoo shop. With cupboards and fridge almost bare except for protein powder and beer, we ended up going out for a roast beef and fries—with the sedan on our ass.

Whoever followed Digger, put him on edge. Wary eyes, pursed lips… God, how I wanted to make him smile.

Stuffed, and walking a little bow-legged, I followed him into his hole-in-the-wall shop. Dark walls covered in drawings and pictures of tattoos and people he'd inked met my appraisal while turning a three-sixty. He flicked on a few lights, better illuminating the small space. A couple chairs lined the wall, but only one made for a customer sat at the room's center.

"Isn't much," he muttered, coming to stand

beside me.

"You do great work." I meandered closer to an eight-by-ten of a man's back. Colored wings spread over his shoulders, the angel they attached to held his head in his hands, tears visible on his face. "Holy shit..."

"One of my best."

"I love it." I stepped back and breathed deep as Digger placed his hands on my hips. "Wings. Fly free." I turned into his arms and lifted my face. "That's what I want, but on a much smaller scale."

He palmed my ass and pulled me tight against his body. "Where?"

"Inside of my wrist?"

Lowering his head, he murmured his assent, and kissed me gently on the lips. The brush of his mouth, the soft whiskers, his sweet breath...

My knees grew weak even though he kept the kiss sweet, unhurried. I wound my arms around his neck and leaned fully against him, giving over to the connection, the crazy feelings he stirred throughout my entire body. Craving beyond lust. Desire beyond the mere need to experience a climax like only he could wring from me.

Pussy damp and throbbing, I stepped back and smiled up at him. "Kiss me like that, and you'll never get rid of me."

The heat in his eyes flipped my stomach in the best way possible. He rubbed his thumb over my parted lips.

I wanted him to say something. Anything. *Kiss me again.* He continued to caress my face and stare into my eyes. Reading me? Gaging the truth behind my words? The man was intuitive and observant beyond the norm of anyone I'd ever met. Even if I hid behind a façade, I felt sure he'd read me like an open book. Let him. I had nothing to hide, nothing to fear.

"Why 'fly free'?" he finally questioned.

"It's what I told my mom right before she passed."

"And she gave you freedom in return."

My throat tightened, and I nodded, guilt swarming in to squeeze my chest.

"What was her favorite color?"

"Blue," I whispered.

"And yours?"

"Green."

Digger dipped his head and stepped out of my personal space. He nodded to the chair and moved across the room—gathering supplies, I noticed while sitting down.

"Afraid of needles?" he asked without turning.

"Nope."

He settled onto the rolling stool beside me, and I sat back, closed my eyes, and remembered Mom while he marked me with her memory. We chatted pretty much non-stop while he worked. Conversation came so easily between us, a sharing of not just stories, but of hearts and minds. I'd never met such a self-aware man, one who knew his mind, his inner workings, and wanted to grow as a human being. Every moment, I fell harder, until my heart swelled, ready to break.

****

I cried when I finally opened my eyes and saw the art he'd created on my body. A blend of blue and green shaded the angel's wings, the scripted words in their center hitting me in the chest.

Freedom. A complete and utter lack of responsibilities other than caring for myself. I laughed through my tears, desperate to squash the lingering guilt.

"Tell me you like it," he said, his voice low.

Uncertain.

"I love it." I glanced up into his eyes, grabbed his whiskered cheeks, and kissed him. "It's perfect."

The corner of his lip twitched. Gaze lightened. His idea of a smile, perhaps, but I wanted more.

"Hungry?" he asked as I returned to study his work while he cleaned up.

"Starved."

"Want to hit the club? Grab some burgers?"

I glanced over at him. Back to me, broad shoulders hitched, he hinted at more insecurities. "As long as Capone is cooking and you *alone* take me upstairs afterwards."

He exhaled, his shoulders lowering. "I'd rather take you home, strip you naked, and stay that way the rest of the night."

I bit back my smirk as my pussy spasmed and nipples sprang to attention. "After burgers?"

"After burgers," he agreed with a nod.

Fifteen minutes later, we pulled into the darkened parking lot at the club. The sedan had disappeared sometime while we'd been in Digger's shop, erasing most of the palpable tension in his huge body. Tucked under his arm, I ambled alongside him toward the club.

Jam packed, music blaring... I grinned. So used to silence and sickness, the life and noise of the club filled me with excitement I hadn't felt for years. People. Alcohol. And don't forget the hottest man on the planet beside me. Definitely flying free, but good old guilt snuck into my brain like a wisp of smoke. Living—because Mom had passed.

I fought to keep my grin in place as Digger found us seats at the bar. Two of the club whores—ones I'd recognized from my dates with Capone—gave me the stink eye, but I ignored them. Probably jealous because

Digger's cock belonged to me for the night.

Hopefully, a hell of a lot longer. The thought made my smile easier to hold in place.

Digger flagged down the guy working the bar.

Piercings in his eyebrows, lip, and big-ass gauge earrings—definitely a younger punk than most of the other Gliders in the club. Vibrant green eyes and a killer smile, he turned his attention on me for a split second before giving Digger his full attention. "What can I get ya?"

"Maci, this is Rucker. Rucker, Maci."

Green-eyes turned toward me—as though he'd been given permission—and dipped his head. "Good to meet ya."

I smiled. "Same."

"My usual," Digger said, drawing Rucker's attention again. "For both of us."

"You got it." Another flash of his killer smile, and Rucker moved off.

"You okay?" Digger asked, his lips close to my ear so I would hear him over the ruckus of the club.

I nodded. We drank our beers as the club rocked around us. Capone escaped the kitchen with our burgers a short time later, a big grin showing off his pearly whites. He gave me a wink when setting my plate in front of me and dipped his head at Digger.

Zero discomfort, zero tension between the two. My smile came more readily, and we set to eating.

When we exited the club a good twenty minutes later, no car sat two blocks down where Digger had told me the sedan usually parked. Our breaths fogged in the cold air, and I crowded closer to him as we walked to his truck.

Tension stiffened Digger, but he continued onward. He peered at the entrance of a darkened alley one block down. The glow of a cigarette was the only indication someone stood in the shadows, but I swear the gaze of whoever puffed on the cancer stick watched us. Intently.

Without a word, Digger helped me into his truck, rounded the front, and climbed in, slamming the door shut.

"Who do you think it is?" I asked, sure the person in the alley had been what put him on edge.

"No fucking clue." He put the truck into gear and pulled out onto the road, his gaze on the rearview mirror. "No tail," he murmured a few minutes later after taking a couple random turns.

My brow furrowed as I considered who or what agency kept an eye on the club. As a motorcycle gang, I felt sure the Gliders had plenty of enemies—including the law they didn't pay off. Digger had admitted to being a bad man, so surely he had a few out to get him personally. A shiver rippled down my spine, lifting my hairs in its wake.

He reached across the console and untangled my clasped hands, wrapping one in his own. "Sorry."

"For what?"

"For being so damn suspicious of everyone and everything."

"Better to be that way than complacent, considering who you are."

He dipped his head, taking another turn. "Do you have any reason for the law—or anyone else—to be after you?"

I snorted a laugh. "Hardly. The worst I've done was drink and drive. Once."

Digger inhaled a deep breath. "Had to ask."

"Quite all right."

Digger

Maci stayed the weekend, but Monday morning when I went into Hawk's shop, she headed back to her apartment. The second she disappeared from my sight, my stomach twisted. Felt like a part of me had been ripped off without morphine to lessen the pain. How the fuck had I gotten so damn wrapped up in her in so short of a time?

The fuck was wrong with me?

I had opened up to Maci more than anyone in my life—brothers included. Never talked so much in my damn life. Same as with fucking, I couldn't get enough of learning about her. What made her tick, what turned her mind on. She in turn pulled stories out of me, one after the other, until I found myself confessing nearly every sin I'd committed.

Including how I got my nickname. I didn't name Nicky, but he was the brother I spoke of when telling her about the night I dug the first grave for someone who thought to cross the Gliders. Turns out, I was so damn good at the grunt job that I tagged along with Nicky whenever he got the go ahead to off someone, digging graves whenever needed. And none of the shallow shit ones, either, that a dog or coyote would unearth. We made sure no one would run across bones. Ever.

"'Sup?" Hawk called out as I arrived at the shop, two Dunks coffees in hand.

"Same shit, different day," I said, going with my usual. "Fuckers still trailing me."

Hawk's brow rose, and he moved to the garage window, flicked the toothpick from between his lips, and snagged his coffee from me on the way. "Same fuckers as before—driver's a blond, passenger a redhead." He swigged, and I strode over to peer their way.

I narrowed my gaze, but couldn't make out any features, only the mop of red hair and the hint of blond on the other. Both sported beards. "Far from clean-cut. Definitely not the FBI."

"Wouldn't think so, no."

We studied them for a few more minutes while I wracked my brain. "Who the fuck do you think it is?"

Hawk didn't answer long enough that I glanced over at him. He chewed on his lower lip.

"What?" I asked.

"Janie talked to her dad a couple weeks ago. Just caught up a bit, let him know how she was doing. I listened to their whole conversation—at her insistence."

Janie's dad, the president of our rivals, the Silent Demons. My brow furrowed. "If he wanted to keep an eye on her, he'd be on your place, not following me around."

Hawk heaved a heavy breath. "Who the fuck knows. What's Jonny have to say?"

"He thinks it's the FBI."

"Any news on the whole inside snitch front?"

"Nothing new. We'll see what happens with next week's shipment, though. He's got two cars headed north, one rumored to carry the goods, one *actually* carrying the goods."

We moved away from the window, but my mind refused to leave the sedan thing alone. Twice before noon, I texted Maci to check on her. She'd sent a sad emoji face as her second reply, so I gave her a call.

"What's wrong?" I asked when she answered.

Her sigh hinted at tears. "Just tough being here without her, you know? I've been caring for her so damn long…" She sniffed, and the desire to hold her, take her mind off her grief clenched my fist.

"What can I do?"

A huff of laughter eased the dent between my brows. "Just a process I have to go through," she said, and I imagined a smile on her lips even though tears probably wet her eyes. "I'm thinking I need to find a new place, though. Leave these memories behind and start over."

"You can crash at my place until you find something," I heard myself say. So much for not making myself vulnerable... I wanted her come hell or high water. If she tore my heart out, proving to not be as loyal as I wanted in an old lady, so be it.

"Seriously?"

"Wouldn't say it if I didn't mean it."

"I just might have to take you up on that offer," she said, her smile definitely widening, and my own lips twitched in response as I pushed my fears behind a steel door in my brain.

"It's supposed to be in the sixties this weekend," I said, needing to take my thoughts elsewhere. "Want to take a bike trip to the mountains? Get away for a couple days?"

"I'd love that."

My mouth tried to smile, but I forced a grimace knowing how ugly I'd appear even though Hawk worked on the other side of the shop.

"I thought maybe I could take you to the pond while we're up there."

Silence hit my ear, and I cursed inwardly at suggesting it. She'd want to wait for her sister, not have a near-stranger tagging along for sprinkling her mother's ashes.

"I—I'd like that," Maci finally responded, her voice quiet. Small.

"What about your sister?"

"She always hated the camp." Maci heaved a sigh

over the line. "I'll call her, but I'm sure she won't mind. She's said her goodbyes."

"We can go up Friday. Take the back roads and stay at a little B&B up near Pine River Pond."

"Sounds like a plan." The smile returned to her voice. "Can I cook dinner for you tonight?"

"I'd love that," I said, echoing her words, praying like fuck that she'd prove herself in the long run, or my heart would look like someone had taken a mallet to the fist-sized piece of flesh.

****

Hawk and I went to the club for lunch a little while later. We sat in Jonny's office while Capone grilled up our burgers. Yeah, I might fall over of a fucking heart attack from eating them so damn much, but the man cooked one hell of a good patty.

"Same men?" Jonny asked Hawk, his brow raised.

"Sure of it," Hawk replied.

Jonny stood and rounded his desk, grabbing a pair of binoculars from a small closet before making toward the door. "Upstairs."

Hawk and I followed on his heels, up to the third floor. He entered the door of the room overlooking the club's front without knocking.

"The fu—" Rucker said from the bed where two women worked him over, his curse cut off when landing on the three of us. Shelly and another skank started to back away, but Jonny ignored the trio and strode to the windows. We followed, and Rucker grabbed both women's hair, pulling them back toward his dick. "Back to it, girls."

Fucker didn't have a self-conscious bone in his body.

As Shelly wrapped her lips around one of his

balls, I turned away, pulling up beside Hawk.

Jonny held the binoculars to his eyes for a few seconds while the whores let out fake-ass moans alongside Rucker's real ones. Jonny handed off the binoculars to Hawk.

The sounds from the three on the bed distracted me while I waited my turn to check out the fuckers in the sedan. I imagined shoving my cock down Maci's throat, her swallows as I blew my load between her lips.

Hawk bumped my elbow, his brow raised, binoculars held toward me.

I cleared my throat and lifted them. My brow furrowed as I took in the two men. A redhead in the passenger seat, a bearded blond in the driver—same fuckers. Both sported tattoos and a couple face piercings.

"Anyone you know?" Jonny asked.

"Not your typical FBI, if that's what they are," Hawk muttered.

"Either they're going to attempt getting in under cover," I said while staring at the blond, who sent a tingle of unease down my spine, "or those motherfuckers are thinking about stirring up some shit."

I lowered the binoculars, the memory of the blond's face etched in my brain.

Jonny peered at me with his dark, assessing eyes—so like his father's who'd sat in the president's chair before him—but I didn't shift. No one had shit on me. I had nothing to fear.

Rucker let out a low groan behind us. "Fuck, yeah. Just like that..."

"What do you want to do?" Hawk asked.

"Go stir up some shit," Jonny and I both said at the same time as a shot of adrenaline spiked in my blood.

My lips actually pulled up into a grin.

"Blow your fucking load down Shelly's throat

already," Jonny said to Rucker while turning for the door. "Then get your ass downstairs."

The three of us trampled back down the stairs and downed a shot while waiting for Rucker. Only two other Gliders sat at the bar, and Jonny lowered the music to tell them it was time to confront the fuckers watching the club.

Once Rucker made an appearance, the six of us headed out the club's front door, Jonny in the lead. I imagined what we looked like, striding toward the sedan—badass motherfuckers, fists clenched, confident strides, and murder in their eyes. Must have scared the shit out of the two men, because they lit out when it became apparent we headed their way.

"You have a brother?" Rucker asked as the sedan sped past us.

I jerked my head his way to find him peering at me. "No. Why?"

"'Cuz that monster driving is an ugly brute, just like you."

One of the other brothers chuckled under his breath as we turned back toward the club, but I didn't take offense. My mind chewed on what Rucker had said, that tingle of unease rippling down my spine again.

We ate our burgers at the bar, the eighties music still lowered. While wiping his mouth on a napkin, Jonny glanced at the closed club door as though he could see through it clear to the street, two blocks down where the sedan had sat. "They'll be back, but probably not until after dark same as every night." He leaned on the bar to catch both Hawk's and my gaze. "Can you come back tonight at nine?" he asked, keeping his voice low.

I nodded without thought as Hawk also dipped his head in agreement. I'd have to reschedule the two tatts I had planned for that night, but it wouldn't be a problem.

"Have your ladies stay at home. Let's keep this as quiet as possible with no drama."

Again, we both nodded.

"I think if it's just the three of us and we act a little more nonchalant, maybe they won't jet before having a few words."

"Worth a try," Hawk said.

"I'm game for whatever." I met Jonny's serious gaze—he knew exactly what I meant.

Lips pursed, he nodded. "If it comes to that."

Hawk and I headed back to his shop, my mind on violence and the knowledge I had to protect Maci. She'd nabbed me with the first glance. Fucking owned me with the first kiss. Held my future in her hands whether I wanted her to or not.

Resigned to that fact, I prepared my heart and mind to be fucked over when she finally decided she'd had enough of my ugliness, enough of my lifestyle. But in the meantime, if knocking off a few assholes kept her and my brothers safe, I wouldn't hesitate to throw down.

Maci

Grinning and heart light, I poured a little more heavy cream into the alfredo sauce I had brought up to a simmer. A couple handfuls of shrimp, and I nodded. Ought to be perfect. I tested the linguini, deciding it needed another minute or two.

The rumble of Digger's truck pulled close, and my pussy tightened, nipples pebbled. It had been all of twelve hours since I'd seen him, and my body craved his nearness. I'd grabbed one of his shirts when I'd first arrived an hour earlier, and had decided to wear that to make him dinner—and nothing else. The navy-blue t-shirt hung to my knees, hiding my nakedness, but not my hardened nipples.

Digger hadn't even gotten all the way in the door before he groaned. "Fuck. Me."

"After," I said with a wink over my shoulder. "Don't want dinner to get cold."

He growled and swept me up into his arms, his hands on my ass. Nothing to do but wrap my legs around his waist, so I did. The attack he landed on my mouth spun my head. Accelerated my pulse until my heartbeat thumped in my ears. His disfigurement didn't hinder his ability to kiss me senseless.

My pussy clenched on nothing, desperate to be filled with all eleven point six inches of his huge cock.

"What's for dinner?" he asked while trailing kisses down my neck.

"Shrimp alfredo." I gasped and ground myself against his hard ridge as he bit me, my fingers tangling in the hair atop his head.

"Damn." He heaved a breath and tilted his forehead against mine. "I've only got a couple hours before I have to be back at the club, so let's hurry up and eat so I can devour you for dessert."

All kinds of yummy warmth flooded through me. "Gotta put me down first," I whispered with a smirk.

Another groan, and he reluctantly put me back on my feet.

I turned on weakened legs to dump the linguini in the alfredo pan, and Digger tugged on the back of the t-shirt covering my ass.

"Christ, what a witch you are."

Giggling, I sidestepped to put dinner on the table before he revealed my nakedness beneath. "Why do you have to be back at the club later tonight?"

"Jonny wants to have a little chat with whoever has been watching the club and following me."

I hesitated in setting the pasta on the table a couple heartbeats, my stomach in a vise as Digger sat. "Something like that could escalate."

He peered at me, sending a shiver down my spine—so not the kind I'd been looking forward to all day. "It could, yes, which is why I'm giving you this." A clink on the tabletop drew my attention to his hand. A sheathed knife rested beneath.

"I'm going, too?" I asked, my voice a squeak as I sat down hard.

"No." His gaze slid over my lips and along my collar bone before returning to my eyes. "But whoever the fuck is following me around … I don't have a good feeling about their intentions. I want you to have some sort of protection on you when you aren't with me. It's only a four-inch blade, but it will be enough to take a man out if he ever thinks to touch you."

I swallowed. Knowing he lived a dangerous lifestyle and possibly being threatened because of it were two totally different things. "You think *I'm* in danger?"

"If someone is after me, what's to stop them from

hurting you to get to me?"

Shit. "I—I'm a caretaker. Someone who set aside her life to keep another alive..."

Even through the whiskers on his jaw, I noted the tension. "Maybe you ought to get out while you can."

My throat thickened as the vise on my stomach tightened. "Is that what you'd prefer?" I whispered. Everything about Digger drew me in, and the thought he wanted me gone turned my stomach sour.

"No."

I chewed on his single word while gnawing the inside of my lower lip and the pasta grew cold.

He pushed the knife across the table.

Blinking up to meet his gaze, an overwhelming urge to accept the knife—character and life be damned— swept over me. "You want me to stay."

"I hardly know you, but the thought of being without you feels like that blade would if it was buried in my stomach."

Holy fucking shit. I stared. How was it possible to feel what I did, what he did, after a mere weekend together? Stuff like that only happened in romance novels and fairy tales, not real life, and especially not between two polar opposites.

"Say something, Maci."

I swallowed again, trying to work enough saliva into my mouth to get words out. "You want me to be your old lady?"

"Yes."

Grin, cry, or flee? I asked myself while studying his face. The softness in his gaze, the longing, loosened the clamp on my stomach.

My hand trembled, but I reached across the table and pulled the knife closer. Only a four-inch blade, I noted while pulling it out of its sheath.

"Capone forged it. It's a boot knife."

"Cooks *and* forges knives… Who'd have thought?" I murmured. Turning the blade in my hand had the overhead light glinting off the polished metal. The hilt fit my hand perfectly.

"You're killing me here…"

I lifted my head, a smile growing on my face. "I'm scared shitless over all this—" I motioned a hand between us and toward the front door, "—but I can't just walk away from you."

He expelled a breath, seeming to melt in his chair. A definite twitch lifted the scarred corner of his lips.

"You're smiling." Even I could hear the wonder in my voice.

"Ugly as shit, isn't it?" he asked, his eyes still betraying the insecurity wrapped around his self-consciousness.

"Not at all." I stood and leaned over the table, cupping his face in one hand. "You're hotter than hell. Every single part of you. Scar included." He leaned toward me, and I kissed the disfigured side of his mouth, sliding my lips up over the whiskers attempting to cover the scar running clear up to his ear. "Now, eat your dinner, so you can tie me up and fuck me until I forget my name."

He groaned, and I sat back, a saucy smirk tilting my lips.

"Witch," he muttered while reaching for the alfredo.

****

Digger didn't tie me up. Didn't wrap his huge hands around my neck to bring me to the edge of passing out before climaxing. No spanking. Nothing but tenderness, sending wave after wave of unnamed emotion rolling over me, sweeping me up in the undertow. Whatever it was, whatever the energy I felt between us, I craved it. Couldn't imagine life without it.

Had I lived before? Not really, I realized as I snuggled against his side, my cheek resting on one of his hard pecs. One of his arms lay beneath me, his palm resting on my lower back, keeping me close.

Eyes closed, I soaked in the warmth of his skin, listening to the steady thump of his heart beating in time with my own.

"What are you thinking?" he asked, his chest rumbling under my ear.

"That tonight could go terribly wrong," I whispered. "That the strong beat against my cheek..."

Digger smoothed my hair away from my face, tangled his fingers through my messy locks, and tilted my head back. "We're just going to go have a chat with them."

I could barely make out his face in the darkness. "And if they do more than chat?"

"Then I'll finish whatever they start."

His confidence twitched my lips even though my stomach twisted. "I'm not ready to be without you, so you damn well better."

"I will." He squeezed me tight against his side. "Promise." A few minutes later, he kissed the top of my head and slid out of the bed, leaving me alone and cold.

I hugged the comforter under my chin, breathing in the scent of his laundry detergent and lingering traces of his skin as he dressed in the darkness.

"I'll be back," he muttered from the doorway with an Arnold accent.

I should have laughed. Should have smiled, even, but I found my eyes filling with tears. "Hurry," I whispered, knowing I wouldn't fall asleep until he did.

Digger

Nine-ten, and Jonny headed for the door, Hawk and I on his heels. Just like he'd expected, the sedan had returned—but only because it had followed me from its spot outside my fucking house. The second I'd walked out and locked my front door behind me, I'd felt their stare. A quick glance down the street had confirmed my suspicion.

We ambled across the parking lot, and for a split second, I hesitated as realization of the stupidity of our actions sank into my head. What if they had guns and wanted us dead? A quick drive by, bullets flying, would easily drop just the three of us.

We all packed heat, but we were sitting ducks, our movements lit by the parking lot's lights while they sat in darkness, possibly readying their firearms. The hairs on my neck stood on end.

"Jonny."

My single word stopped him dead in his tracks. He glanced over his shoulder at me, brow raised. Hawk, too, stopped, turning to look at me.

I peered at the sedan, unable to see jack shit in the darkness beyond the parking lot as my breath fogged in front of my face. "I got a bad feeling about this."

"What's up, Digger?" he asked as I continued to stare at our watchers.

"They have the upper hand. If they think we're going to start shit, they might try to finish it. Finish us."

"Fuck." Hawk's word tore from his lips, and his hand twitched at his side.

"Don't do it," I said, my voice low, every muscle in my body tensed to grab my gun, same as Hawk. My legs flexed to spring into action if need be, but starting shit wasn't in our best interest. "I think we ought to go back inside. Rethink this."

"Jonny?" Hawk asked when he didn't respond right away.

"I trust your judgment, Digger." Jonny faced the sedan again, giving them his full attention for a few more seconds before turning back toward the club.

I gave my brothers a few paces' head-start to make sure the sedan stayed put before turning my back on them. My ears strained for the shifting of gears, for tires crunching on gravel from behind me.

Nothing happened, and by the time I walked back into the club, the adrenaline in my blood needed to be used up. Mighty fucking fast.

We decided against a confrontation, I texted Maci. **Be home in an hour or so.**

We sat in Jonny's office, my leg bouncing while we discussed what to do, how to approach the fuckers without them having the upper hand. Coming at them from all angles seemed our best option. If they went toward violence, at least they couldn't take all of us out before we put some bullets in them as well.

Last thing we needed, though, were gunshots around the club. Only so many cops turned their heads and falsified reports because of the cash we dangled under their noses.

"We have to do something," Jonny said, scrubbing a hand along the stubble on his jaw. "They're badass-looking motherfuckers, and they weren't sent here by Janie's dad to keep an eye on her."

Otherwise, they'd be on Hawk, not me. "The fuck they want with me?" I grumbled, my knee still trying to work out the adrenaline continuing to roll through my body.

"Don't know," Jonny said, "but we're going to find out. Tomorrow. Nine." He sat back in his chair. "I'll grab a dozen other brothers, and we'll set up a perimeter where the sedan usually parks. Coming at them calmly after you get here—hands empty—might keep things from getting carried away."

Hawk nodded. "Worth a try."

I heaved a breath. "Okay."

"Go home. Both of you." Jonny stood and moved toward the door. "Fuck the adrenaline out of your systems and get some sleep."

I shot out of my chair, my lips twisted in a grin. "And if the fuckers don't follow me here tomorrow night?"

"Then we shoot some pool and down a few shots of whiskey."

With a nod, I made for the front door, Hawk on my heels.

The sedan's spot sat empty.

****

Maci threw herself at me the second I walked in the front door, and our mouths collided as she wrapped her legs around my waist. One hand on her ass, I turned and flipped the deadbolt with my other. She grunted as I thrust against her, half-slamming her against the door.

"I fucking need you." I damn near growled the words while trying to yank down my leathers to free my straining cock.

"Hurry," she whispered against my mouth, her small hands finding their way beneath my jacket and over my flexing abs.

Maci didn't have on a damn stitch of clothing beneath my t-shirt. The back of my shaking hand slid against her soaked pussy as I tried to free myself. "Fuck!" I cursed again while fumbling with my leathers.

She pushed my hands away, and I grasped her ass, stepping back enough she could help me out. A whimper escaped her as she, too, fought the clasp.

"Thank *fuck*." I moaned as she finally freed my dick and stroked her hand down me.

I lifted her higher, and she squeaked as her back hit the door again. One thrust seated me halfway inside her soaked cunt. A second brushed the head of my cock against her womb.

"Oh, God!" She gasped, her head tipping back, and I pulled out again and slammed in a third time, drawn-up balls against her ass.

"Fuck!" We both cursed at the same time, and I captured her mouth, mimicking with my tongue what my cock did to her pussy—plunder and claim. Take what was needed. Burn off the need for action still singing in my blood.

"Goddamn you, little witch," I said against her neck, my hips pistoning, spurred on by her whimpers, her cries. "You're an addiction—" I thrust deep into her tight heat. "A fucking drug." She gasped as I pulled out and slammed into her again. "You make me want things…"

"Digger!" Her pussy contracted around me, pulling me deeper, as her nails scratched down the shoulders of my jacket. "Fuck! Yes!"

With a growl, I gave over to the throb in my balls—only too late realizing I'd never put on a condom. "Fuck, Maci … my little, beautiful witch." More words poured from my lips as I shot my cum deep inside her body, my legs threatening to buckle beneath me. "Goddamn you."

My hips finally stilled, and I leaned my forehead against hers, both of us sucking wind.

She squeezed me tight with her legs before contracting her pussy walls around me.

"Fuck." I growled, trying to thrust my semi in deeper. "The things you do to me."

"Mmm."

I leaned my head back to catch her smirk. "You okay?"

"Shit, yeah."

"I didn't wear a condom. Sorry ... I fucking needed to be inside of you so fucking bad. Couldn't think straight."

"It's okay. I'm clean and on the pill."

"Thank fuck." I heaved a breath and squeezed the plump flesh of her ass resting in my hands. "I get checked on a regular basis and haven't been with anyone since my last bill of health."

"Well." She full-on smiled, dimple and all, while cupping my cheek in her palm. "That's good, 'cuz I fucking *hate* condoms. I loved feeling your skin inside of me. Nothing between us."

I groaned and kissed her slowly, tasting the hint of hops on her breath. The emotion, the energy zinging between us, didn't let up, and I found myself swelling fully again inside of her.

"Too sore?" I asked, making my way back to the bedroom with her hanging on my body.

"No."

She'd left the bedroom light on, and I didn't bother flicking it off. Needed her too damn badly again. Cradling her to me, I laid her down on her back and captured her lips, our combined cum easing out of her body making for one easy, messy fuck. The second she started to climax, I pulled out and flipped her onto her belly, lifting her hips high. Her cum pulsed from her swollen lips.

"Fuck me!" she shrieked while writhing in my hold.

I lined up, slammed in a dozen times, sending her over once more before allowing my balls their release. A deep growl rumbled my chest as I leaned over her, fucking into her hard and deep, milking my cock dry in her body. So fucking hot, so fucking wet.

My head spun like I'd downed one too many shots. Ears fucking rang like I'd spent a day on the shooting range without earplugs. Muscles quaked as if I'd gone at the gym hard for hours on end. My heart slammed in my chest, and I closed my eyes, propped on my elbows beside her head, trying to catch my breath.

Everything about Maci…

A shudder rippled over me, and I kissed the back of her head before climbing off of the bed to finally take my damn clothes off.

She lay like a dead body in the middle of my bed, limbs askew, hair a mess, my t-shirt pushed up beneath her armpits. My cum leaked from between her legs, dripping onto my comforter.

I grinned and turned toward the bathroom for a wet towel to clean her up. Fucking heaven, and no one on the earth would take her away from me.

Maci

Still on family leave from my job as a PA to a local psychiatrist, I enjoyed three days of sheer bliss. Three days of sleeping in while Digger went to the gym and Hawk's bike shop. Three days of watching him ink skin at his hole-in-the-wall place near the club. Three days of too many burgers and eighties music, never mind my attempts to beat him at pool.

In those three days, the sedan didn't make an appearance at its usual haunts. Digger and his brothers didn't have to attempt a dangerous confrontation—thank fuck.

I met Hawk's girl, Janie, a sweetheart who looked worn out and sad. Digger explained her manic and low episodes to me later, and I decided she'd be my new best friend. Guess it was that caretaker part of me that needed someone to help. We agreed to meet up the following week after Digger and I returned home from sprinkling Mom's ashes on the pond.

My sister didn't mind our going without her. She'd never returned to the pond after our dad had died—too many memories to induce tears, she'd said. Having to face those along with saying a final goodbye to Mom ... she couldn't handle it. I promised to send her a pic of the sunset reflecting off the pond, Mom's favorite time of day.

Unseasonably warm, Mother Nature shone the sun down on us as we headed north on one of Digger's bikes that had a passenger seat behind him. Big-ass saddlebags cradled my seat, holding our clothes and the bare necessities for our three-night getaway in the sticks.

Once we checked into the bed and breakfast, we headed north for another half-hour before pulling into the dirt parking lot of a back-woods bar and grill.

"Mel's, huh?" I asked as Digger cut the engine and I climbed off his bike.

He dipped his head, gaze taking in the two-story building, its door propped open, windows wide to let in the warm air.

"Nicky's girl," he said, putting his hand on my lower back and ushering me forward.

"Oh." He'd told me about the Glider who'd handed in his colors the spring before, and how the man had completely cut ties with his brothers. "I thought he didn't want to keep in touch," I said quietly, glancing up at the mountain of a man beside me. "What if he's here?"

"Then he'll answer for *not* keeping in touch." The scowl on Digger's face deepened. "I just want to make sure he's all right in his new life. Bastard could at least let us know that much."

I fought off my smile. Digger cared about his lost brother, that much was certain. *Big old sweetie.*

We walked into the dim interior and paused for our eyesight to adjust, the quiet country music a nice change from eighties music to my ears. A long bar ran the length of the room, stretching away on our left, while a few tables lined across the opposite side of the room beneath the many windows spanning the wall. Exposed overhead beams gave the place a warm, homey feel.

Two people sat at the bar. One was an older gentleman with watery eyes, the other a man at the far end, his vivid blue eyes sparking recognition as his gaze landed on Digger. The man stood and made his way toward us. A tight, white t-shirt hugged his upper body, leathers his lower. Gray hair spattered throughout the dark atop his head and the beard lining his jaw.

"Digger." He stuck his hand out, and my man stepped forward and grabbed who had to be Nicky in a half-hug, slapping his hand on the older man's back.

"Nicky," Digger said, slapping him a second time. "Good to see you, brother."

Nicky didn't return Digger's greeting, but the warmth in his eyes spoke of how he felt. "What are you doing up this way?" he asked as Digger released his hold.

"This is my girl, Maci," he said, grabbing my hand and pulling me close. "Her mom recently passed, and we're heading up to Pine River Pond to sprinkle her ashes."

Nicky shook my hand, his grasp firm, one that let me know all I needed to about the man with the "67" tattooed on his neck. His brow furrowed as grief flitted through his eyes. "Sorry for your loss."

I tried for a smile, remembering Digger had told me about his sister's death a year earlier. "Thanks."

I bet my life he was the man who Digger had learned from, the man who had given him the nickname. Badass or no, Nicky, too, seemed like a big teddy bear, I thought while peering into his eyes, feeling somehow connected in our grief.

Most would consider me crazy, but when a dark-haired woman closer to my age joined us, her smile lighting her brown eyes, Nicky's gaze softened, the love in his gaze the type that inspired timeless love songs and fairy tales.

"My Mel," Nicky said, tucking her against his side.

"So you're the reason Nicky here won't return our calls," Digger said, grasping her outstretched hand but peering at Nicky.

"I'm trying to move on, Digger, and that means cutting ties." Nicky's voice stayed low—with just enough tension to raise the hairs on my neck.

"You could at least let us know you're okay. Brothers worry."

Nicky's face didn't twitch. "I handed in my colors."

"Doesn't matter to *me*." Digger rubbed a hand along his beard. "You'll always be my brother."

I glanced at Mel to find her focus on me. "Hungry?" she asked with a smile, probably feeling the same tension I did.

"Couple of burgers would be great," I replied, tugging on Digger's arm toward the bar. We sat, and Nicky settled onto the stool beside me while Mel disappeared behind swinging doors behind the bar.

The watery-eyed man at the other end of the bar stared us down.

"Old Toothless is harmless," Nicky said.

Unlike the men book-ending me, I thought glancing between the bikers. Nicky leaned on the bar, a mass of muscle under his short sleeves, tattoos to rival Digger's on most of his exposed skin. "Did Digger do some of your tattoos?" I asked, eyeing the black, two-digit number on his neck.

"All my newer ink." Nicky twisted his forearms around, revealing a myriad of color and shape, most blending into the next. A seamless tapestry, telling the Fallen Glider's story that he couldn't leave behind after handing in his colors.

"We miss you," Digger said, his voice quiet.

Nicky nodded, but kept his lips tight.

"Sorry about your sister. Wish like fuck it hadn't been our doing," Digger continued when Nicky held his silence. "Wish like fuck we could find some other way of bringing in money. Rumor has it the Demons are into sex trafficking."

"Jonny even thinks of going that route, I'll do him in myself." Nicky's promise—for that's exactly what his tone indicated—merely got a nod from Digger.

The two men downed a shot of whiskey while I shifted on my seat, my stomach in knots. No longer brothers by bond, but still... My heart ached for Digger. The stories he'd told me, even while not naming Nicky, revealed how much he cared for the older biker. If having to name his feelings, I'd go toward the way a young boy looked up to his father. Idolized the figure who ended up playing that role in his life.

Mel brought out our lunch a short while later, and while we ate, Nicky and Digger chatted about mostly meaningless stuff. Hardly the closure I expected Digger had hoped for.

We left a short while later, and the slump of Digger's shoulders on the bike in front of me thickened my throat. I knew grief all too well. Guilt, too, and Digger obviously dealt with both emotions over his friend.

I leaned my cheek on the Gliders' logo on his back, eyes closed while we rumbled up the road, wishing like hell I could send positive energy to him. Help carry his burden as he'd held me that first night and I released the tears over Mom.

A subtle shift of his body tightened the muscle beneath my cheek and hands around his waist. Muscles taut.

I sat up, but unable to ask because of the rush of wind and the loud motor beneath us.

Digger turned off the main highway, taking a back road I knew well from my younger years of heading to the pond. He remained tense as we pulled into a Mom-and-Pop gas station at a small intersection. Pulled up alongside the pump, Digger cut the engine, and I climbed off.

He stood, a mountain of a man, shoulders bunched as his gaze followed after a sedan slowly driving by. A tattooed, bearded blond stared at us through the driver's window, the hatred in his eyes sending a shiver over me, pebbling my skin.

"Digger?" I whispered, laying my hand on his forearm as the car passed from sight.

"The same guys," he said, pulling out his cell and swiping. "Jonny," he said into the phone a second later as I processed what he'd meant. "They followed me up here. Yeah." His gaze swung toward the empty road leading into the woods where the blond had driven. "I've had enough." Another pause as he dug through one of the saddlebags and quickly slipped a handgun behind his belt. "Will do. I'll give you a call soon as I can."

Digger pocketed his cell and turned to face me, lowering his head a bit to peer into my eyes. "Jonny gave me the go-ahead to confront those two fuckers."

I nodded. "You want me to stay here, don't you?"

"Yes."

"Well, I'm not going to. I'm not going to sit here on the side of the road twiddling my thumbs wondering what the hell is going on, wondering if you're okay."

I expected him to argue, but he climbed back onto the bike and tipped his head, silently telling me to get on. Finally getting the whole heart-in-the-throat saying, I did as he ordered, adrenaline rushing through my body.

The engine roared to life, and Digger pulled back onto the road. A few bends, and the sedan appeared in the distance, heading toward us. I clung to Digger and closed my eyes as they drove past. Digger continued down the road, taking a few turns until I lost track. He turned into a hiking trail head parking area, one overgrown with weeds, its sign faded and falling apart.

Out in the middle of nowhere, my mind whispered... What the hell had I gotten myself into?

Digger

The fucker hadn't even bothered with pretending while driving by the gas station, and the look in his eyes was something I'd seen a thousand times. Violence. A hellbent yearning to lay something out.

Jonny had given me the okay, so I was going to let the blond fucker give it a shot.

A secluded, back-woods dirt road and small parking area off the beaten path offered exactly what I wanted, what we needed to finish whatever the fuck needed to go down.

I cut the engine, and the sedan rolled to a stop at the parking lot's entrance, cutting off any escape route. Climbing off my bike, I kept myself between Maci and the car, my hand itching for the gun I'd tucked at my back.

Their engine quieted, and silence fell. A warm breeze rustled through the leafless trees, and a lone bird chirped. My shoulders tensed as a rush I usually enjoyed, one I lived for, infused my blood with the need for action as Maci stood behind me.

Both the driver and passenger doors opened at the same time. The redhead I'd seen through Jonny's binoculars joined the blond, and they took a few steps toward us before stopping.

I slowed my breathing. Forced my mind to quiet. Kept my eyes glued to the two men, waiting…

"Raymond Hearst?" the blond said.

"Who's asking?"

Maci touched the back of my left arm, but I remained focused.

"Someone who's been looking for you for a long, fucking time," the blond replied, not taking his hateful stare from my face.

I merely raised an eyebrow in question.

"Who gave you that scar?" he asked rather than answer me.

"The bastard who raped my mother, knocked her up, and left her for dead."

"That bastard was my father."

My ears rang as my breath left in a rush. Unease rippled down my spine as Rucker's voice about my having a brother whispered through my head. "The fuck?"

"Took a lot of digging, a lot of payoffs, but I finally found you, didn't I?" the blond asked, but nothing about his low, threatening voice indicated our meeting would end well. He hadn't come looking for a long-lost brother. He'd come after the man who'd killed his father.

"Guess you did," I said, with the same intent in my own voice. Suddenly, I wished I'd fought Maci, made her stay back at the little store. Safe. Away from the fucker who wanted to watch me bleed out. She shuffled a step and grabbed my left hand, and for a split second—one fucking breath—I became distracted.

The redheaded fucker drew his gun like Billy the Kid before I could pull mine from my back with my right hand.

Fuck... The only thought I had as pain ripped through my side, spinning me sideways.

Maci shrieked, and I hit the ground, losing my breath. My sight. Blackness swept over me, and I thought sure as shit I was about to see the bastard who'd sired me again. Another shriek kept me grounded, and I fought off the darkness at the edge of my mind.

"You took him," a voice sounded on the edge of my conscious, "so I'm going to take her."

"Digger!" Maci screamed again, and I groaned, trying to roll over. Move. Breathe.

"Motherfucker," a voice overhead growled. A blow landed in my kidney, pulling a grunt from my chest, but also bringing clarity back with a motherfucking force enough to match a freight train. Pain in my right side. Pain in my left from the boot of the redhead looming over me.

"Digger!" Maci sobbed.

"Bitch!" The blond hollered. "I'll put a fucking bullet through your fucking brain!"

My body wanted to curl into a fetal position, but the screams from a few feet away, drew me up onto all fours.

Another kick laid me flat on my stomach, and I blinked the parking lot into focus.

Fucking hell. Maci... The blond, my fucking brother, held her down on the rocky ground. She fought like a feral cat, scratching and screaming. I struggled to find my voice, remind her of the knife in her boot...

Red-headed fucker kicked me again.

The blond held Maci's arms overhead in one of his meaty palms, his other hand ripping at her jeans. "Don't kill him!" he hollered at his friend as my attacker landed another kick, pulling a grunt from my lungs. "He's all mine—after I finish with his bitch."

"No! D-don't!" Maci writhed beneath him, bucking and biting.

I pushed up onto my elbows, shaking and weak.

"Motherfucking whore!" he hollered as she sank her teeth into his forearm. He clobbered her across the face.

Maci stilled beneath him, and he released his hold on her wrists to rip the crotch of her jeans.

I'd lost my last fight—gaining a scar for life—and I wasn't about to fuck up again. I growled, red hazing my vision, giving me strength when I wanted to roll over and die. I pushed onto all fours again as Maci's head lolled to the side, her eyes blinking, gaze meeting mine.

Knife, I screamed in my head, tapping my boot with a finger, praying like fuck her caretaker nature could be overridden. *Knife!*

She blinked as the fucker kicked me again. Teeth gritted against the pain, I started crawling toward them. The blond sat back to yank his dick from his leathers, filling me with the need to bash in faces. Knife the shit out of both of the fuckers.

"I'm going to fuck you so damn hard, you'll forget all about that piece of shit," the blond said with a sneer while palming himself.

Gaze on me, Maci lifted her legs as if to wrap her legs around the would-be-rapist's hips. He lined his dick up, and my sweet, little witch pulled her knife.

"Motherfuck—" The blond's voice cut off as I lunged at the redhead's legs, tackling him to the ground. Rage overcame me, took my humanity on vacation, and I smashed my fist into his face. He went limp from one fucking hit, the pansy ass, but I didn't waste another thought on him.

Pulling my gun, I scrambled in the dirt toward the blond grappling with Maci for her knife. Blood poured from his side as he gripped her wrist, the blade clutched in her fingers dripping red.

He'd thought to put his cock in my woman... A bullet wouldn't give me the satisfaction I needed.

His head whipped toward me, and he tried to scramble away. Maci locked her legs around his hips, keeping him from the gun he'd put on the ground beyond the struggling pair.

Rising onto my knees, I pulled back my arm and smashed the fucker in the temple with my gun stock. He collapsed onto Maci.

Rage buzzed in my ears. Sent tremors through my muscles. I fisted the fucker's t-shirt and yanked him off my woman, tossing him to the ground like a ragdoll. Growling like a feral animal, I climbed atop him, landing the butt of my gun against his face again and again. Curses spewed from my lips as I rearranged his fucking face, sending splatters of blood over my torso.

"Digger!" Maci's yelp whipped my head around. Breathing heavily, I blinked, trying like hell to focus past the rage clouding my vision.

"Back the fuck off." Red-headed fucker had Maci pulled up against his chest. Gun to her temple.

Every muscle in my body trembled. Yearned to kill. I tightened my grip on my gun while glancing at Maci's hand. No knife.

She whimpered, and I pushed off the limp blond, settling back onto my haunches.

He glanced at his friend, his eyes wild. "Drop the gun, or I swear to *fucking* God—"

Maci bashed her head against his nose.

I whipped my gun up, and she leaned forward as her attacker hollered and loosed his hold on her.

My gun barked in my hand, and a spray of gore shot out the back of his head. His body slumped to the ground, and Maci scrambled to my side, whining keens pouring from her lips.

She clasped her hands to my side. "Oh, fuck! Fuck... Goddamnit!"

"I'm okay," I pulled her against me with one arm, my gun still in hand. Adrenaline crashed through my system, keeping me alert.

Maci trembled against me, and with a grimace, I made myself stand, pulling her up into my arms. "We have to move, Maci." A quick glance at both men assured me neither would ever twitch another muscle voluntarily. I tucked my gun back in my waistband and pulled my cell from my back pocket.

Praying like *fuck* he would answer, I dialed Nicky.

Maci

I clutched Digger's hand in mine, my mind flooded with images from the previous four hours, but I couldn't form words. Couldn't form coherent thoughts. He lay on Mel's bed, eyes closed. Finally bandaged by some old guy covered in tattoos and wrinkles.

Four hours of numbness.

Four hours of anxiety wrecking my insides.

We'd killed two men.

I swallowed rising bile as images flashed in my head, over and over.

Digger struggled to toss the two men's bodies into the car's trunk, but he refused my help. He scraped up bits of brain matter and the blood-soaked dirt while I sat on a large rock, arms wrapped around my waist, shaking. My ears waiting for the sound of sirens.

Nicky pulled into the lot, Mel on the back of his bike.

The two men chatted while Mel's voice buzzed in my ears. She grasped my elbow. Pulled me toward Nicky's bike.

I stared down at Digger while fighting off the memories, his face as pale as the pillowcase beneath his head. A flesh wound, he'd said. The hole in his side hadn't looked like a damn scratch to me as I had bound his waist with his bloodied t-shirt while waiting for Nicky.

Heavy boots sounded on the stairs leading up the back of Mel's place. Her apartment sat over the bar she owned, its back steps nestled against the wooded lot behind.

It had taken a dozen assurances from both Nicky and Digger before I'd allowed myself to sit behind Mel on her man's bike and let her drive us back to her place while the two of them "took care of things".

I'd climbed those narrow, steep stairs on deadened legs, uncaring of the ruined jeans exposing me to the world.

A hot shower.

Borrowed clothes.

Two shots of whiskey.

I clenched my eyes shut and leaned my head down on Digger's shoulder. Solid. Warm. Breathing in, I counted to ten. Exhaled on five.

"How's he doing?" Mel's soft voice sounded from behind me.

Forcing my head up again, I glanced her way. She studied the drugged-up mountain of a man sprawled on her bed. "Good, I guess," I managed to rasp past my lips.

Her own lips pursed and hands on her hips, Mel dipped her head and turned her attention on me. "How are *you*?"

I shrugged and swallowed.

"Nicky just got back. He said everything has been taken care of."

I didn't want to know.

"Jonny is on his way up here to get you two."

I nodded.

"You know," she said, speaking quieter, "for all Nicky's talk about leaving the Gliders behind, he didn't hesitate to answer when Digger called. Didn't hesitate to agree to help clean up the situation."

Tears pricked my eyes. "I'll never be able to thank him—you both—for everything you've done for us tonight."

"Seeing Digger today brought a sparkle to Nicky's eye I've never seen before. Like he'd found his long-lost family or some shit. Not that I want him to go back, or anything."

The corner of my mouth quirked even though my throat stayed tight.

"He should be out for a while," Mel said, motioning toward the bed with her chin. "Why don't you come out to the kitchen and have something to eat?"

"I'm not hungry," I managed to whisper, "but thanks."

She nodded and offered a small smile.

I turned back to Digger. Even passed out, he still scowled. I kissed the corner of his disfigured lips and laid my head on his shoulder again, keeping my eyes open so the memories in my head wouldn't be as vivid.

The press of my attacker's dick against my dry pussy had made stabbing him with a knife easy. I'd never been one for violence, would rather cut myself than someone else, but being a hair away from having some stranger's cock shoved inside of me had snapped something in my brain.

He'd backed off pretty fucking quickly when I'd buried the knife in his side.

I heaved a breath as exhaustion swept over me.

Digger wasn't awake, but I still took comfort in him. His presence filled the small bedroom, soothing the tension in my shoulders and neck. I nuzzled my cheek against his warm shoulder, breathing in the scent of him.

It's going to be okay, I told myself. He'd killed before. Hidden bodies. Covered plenty of asses.

He must have learned from Nicky like I'd suspected. The brother who Digger had said wrote them off. Turned his back against everything the Gliders stood for.

That man had come when called, though. Without hesitation. If not for Nicky, we both probably would have ended up in jail.

I finally gave over to my bottled emotions.

Release came in a torrent of tears.

Digger stirred, and I crawled onto the bed beside him, careful to avoid his right side, tears dripping onto his bare skin.

"Shh," he whispered against my hair while pulling his hand free from mine and working his arm beneath me. "'S'all right." His slurred words accompanied his one-armed hug, and I snuggled against his side, somehow knowing he spoke the truth.

****

A mere hour before sunrise, we finally got back to Digger's house. Jonny and Capone got him into his bed with only a dozen or so curses from the three of them.

Nicky had only spoken a few words to the two men when they'd arrived. He merely dipped his head as both thanked him—at least twice—and he'd offered no reply when Jonny told him to reach out if he ever needed anything.

Jonny sent me to the kitchen with Capone while he had a little chat with Digger. Again, I didn't want to know.

I slumped at the kitchen table, my head in my hands.

"You okay?" Capone asked as the legs of the chair beside me scraped against the floor.

Unsure how to answer, I sighed.

"Maybe you ought to think about getting out while you can," he said, his words eerily similar to Digger's from the weekend before. "This lifestyle doesn't really suit you."

I lifted my head and met his gaze. Blue eyes filled with pity studied my face, lingering on the bruise across my cheekbone. "That fucker had his dick pressed against me, Capone. One thrust, and I'd have been raped.

Raped." My brow furrowed as tears filled my eyes. "I enjoyed sinking that knife into him. Never felt such satisfaction as when he grunted and warmth slid over my hand. I'd do it again without a heartbeat's hesitation."

"Maci—"

"It was self-defense. He shot Digger."

"It was."

"I mean—" A half-laugh, half-sob spilled from my lips, "—what woman wouldn't try to kill a man who was about to take her dignity? Right?"

Capone continued to study me. "Right."

"You know what bothers me even more than the fact I stabbed the man?" I asked, blinking a few times to stop more tears from flowing. "That Digger ended his life before I could."

He shook his head, but not in a judgmental way. "So damn perfect for him."

"Am I sick?" I asked, too focused on my own thoughts to give his words consideration.

"Not at all." He grabbed my hand and squeezed. "Digger's one lucky bastard."

I sucked my lower lip between my teeth and glanced back the hallway toward the bedroom. "I've never been so caught up in someone before. It's kind of terrifying. Do you think I'm crazy? Being with him?" I waved my free hand around the kitchen. "This lifestyle?"

"You lit up when he put his hands on you that first night."

"I did?"

His slow, lazy smirk also twinkled in his eyes. "First time in my life I felt incompetent."

"Oh please." I actually smiled. "You're hot. Got a great body, and that tongue..."

Capone's smile widened. "Better not let Digger hear you say things like that. He's one jealous prick."

My smile faded. "I like that about him."

"I think you're making the right choice, Maci, even though I hate to see you caught up in this shit."

"You're a good man," I whispered while squeezing his hand.

He snorted a sarcastic laugh. "I'm no badass like Digger, but you can't be good and be a Glider."

"Our definitions of good must differ," I said, thinking of Nicky as well.

The bedroom door opened, and I squeezed Capone's hand again as footsteps sounded in the hallway.

"He's asking for you, Maci," Jonny said, his presence filling the kitchen entrance.

I glanced up at him and released my hold on Capone. "I'll take this to my grave," I said, my voice low.

Jonny studied me, his dark eyes peering into mine for enough seconds to make me shift on my chair. He dipped his head, lips in a tight line, before nodding Capone toward the door. "Call if you need anything," Capone said, standing to follow his brother.

"Will do."

The door clicked shut behind them, and I locked up before making my way to the bedroom.

Still pale, Digger lay on his back, eyes half-mast. "Come here."

Needing to feel his warmth, I slipped out of my borrowed clothes and crawled under the sheet beside him, careful of the bandage on his far side.

He grunted his displeasure, snaked an arm beneath me, and pulled me snug against his good side. "Better." He half-sighed the word. "Sorry you didn't get to spread your mom's ashes."

"That's okay," I whispered. "We can do it later." I rested my cheek against his chest, my hand lying above his heart, one leg draped over his. "How are you feeling?"

"Been worse."

"The pain meds that old man gave you working?"

"Too well." He exhaled deeply, his hand splayed over one of my ass cheeks. The sheet over his hips stirred as he squeezed. "So plump and juicy. I feel like I could fuck this ass—"

"You'll do no such thing until that hole in your side is healed."

"Take off your panties."

"Digger…"

"Take them off."

Shaking my head, I tugged them down my legs.

He pulled me back up against him. "So soft," he murmured, his fingertips sliding over my hip, around my ass cheek and between.

Warmth stirred in me.

"Did that fucker put his cock in you?"

My breath caught as his fingertip brushed over my pussy. "No."

"Thank fuck." He rimmed my hole, drawing moisture from my body. With his other hand, he slid the tented sheet off his thickening cock. "I need to be inside you." The low, rumbled words flooded me with heat, and when he took himself in hand and slowly pumped down his length, my pussy spasmed with need.

I shook my head. "You need to take it easy."

"I will." He pulled me on top of him as though I weighed nothing, and my legs settled on either side of his hips on their own. "Ride me, Maci," he murmured. "My fierce, beautiful witch. Gotta have you." He flexed his hips, rubbing the back of his cock up through the wetness coating my pussy.

I'd heard that near-death experiences can cause

the need to fuck to consume a person. I needed Digger so damn much—to fill me up, take away the memory of the bastard who almost took from me without permission. "Put your right arm down," I whispered, sliding my hand from his shoulder to his wrist while he did as told. "Keep it there."

Lust burned in his dark eyes, his permanent scowl drawing me down until I breathed over his lips. A shift of my hips notched the head of his cock inside of me. He groaned. I flicked my tongue over his bottom lip. "Hold still," I reminded him, pushing back and slowly filling myself with his massive cock.

Stretched. Full. So damn perfect a fit, I wanted to cry.

"Fuck me, baby," he said, that rumble enticing me to gyrate my hips. Another groan passed his lips, and I brushed mine over his, a gentle taste while clenching his length with my pussy.

Digger grabbed my hip with his left hand, his fingers digging into my flesh, showing me how he wanted me to move. Glide forward, dragging his cock out of me, sliding back until he bottomed out against my womb.

"God." I whined the word while sitting up to better move with his guidance. "You feel so damn good inside of me."

Digger grunted his agreement, and released my hip once I set the rhythm he seemed to desire, his hand closing around my breast. He rolled my pebbled nipple between his fingers while flexing his hips every time I backed down onto his cock again. "Fuck, baby ... just like that."

I grabbed his hand and moved it between my thighs, taking over playing with my breasts while his thumb slid along my clit.

"You're fucking gorgeous," he said. "Pinch your nipples. Pull on them."

Doing as he said brought a gasp from me, and I fought to keep my rhythm.

"Faster." His rumbled word moved my hips, the sweet, wet friction between our bodies raising my climax to the surface.

"I'm going to come," I said, grinding my pussy against him and pinching both of my nipples.

"Yes." He pressed his thumb against my clit, and I bucked beneath him. "Milk me, baby. Squeeze my cock, yeah—fuck!"

I pitched over the edge, my pussy clamping around his girth, my back arching. "Oh Digger!" A wave of emotion and arousal swept through me, tingling through to my toes, pebbling every inch of my skin in exquisite awareness. Satiated bliss.

Two deep thrusts, and Digger grunted, his fingers once more digging into my hip as he shot hot cum deep inside of me. "Goddamn." He groaned and went boneless beneath me.

I fought for breath, and leaning forward, cradled his cheeks in my hands. "You okay?"

"Mmm." His eyes closed, and I brushed my lips against his. "Never knew…"

"What?" I murmured against his mouth, nipping his bottom lip.

"Love would feel like this."

I stilled and lifted enough to focus on his face, my heart thumping. "Are you still high on those meds?"

His lashes lifted, those dark orbs seeing down into the deepest part of me. "No."

My throat tightened as I offered a wobbly smile. "The 'L' word, huh?"

"Yes."

A simple word said without hesitation. With confidence. I caressed his scar, my fingertips coming to rest against the soft pillow of his lips.

"You're mine."

I nodded, unable to find my voice.

"No man will ever touch you again." He peered up at me, serious as hell, the scowl marring his lips and brow. "Tell me you want that, too, Maci."

I swallowed against the tightness in my throat. "Yes."

The scowl dissolved on Digger's face as light twinkled in his eyes.

"My God." I breathed the word. "You're smiling."

"You make me happy, beautiful witch," he said, the unmarred side of his lips curling upward. "And once these stitches come out, I'm going to show you just how much you mean to me. How much I want to please you in every way."

"You already do, you sexy slab of man-beef."

He choked out a barked laugh, and I rested against his chest, smiling like an idiot. "God, you are hot."

"You're blind."

"Love *is* blind, isn't it?"

The twinkle remained in his eye as he fisted his hand in my hair and pulled my face down a breath from his. "Thank fuck."

The End

FALLEN GLIDERS MC: VOLUME TWO

DEDICATION

For my marshmallow man

FALLEN GLIDERS MC: VOLUME TWO

CAPONE

Fallen Gliders, 4

Lynn Burke

Copyright © 2018

Capone

Mom reached over the pew and grabbed my hand as I slid onto the cushioned bench behind her and Dad. She offered a small, tight smile, and in return, earned a glare from the narcissistic prick beside her. He didn't acknowledge me as Mom's smile faded and she turned away.

Even after five years of staying away from my parents, I still managed to get my feelings hurt like the pansy Dad had always said I was. Jaw clenched, I stared at the back of his head, reminding myself of what I was—who I really was since I'd left that toxic relationship behind.

A Fallen Glider. A badass biker who hung with brothers ten times worse than I had ever managed in my twenty-six years. A player who took what he wanted from any woman willing to drop to her knees or spread her legs. 'Course, I always made sure they enjoyed the experience, too. Call me a gentleman, but I preferred to walk away knowing the lady had been satisfied as well.

My brother and his groomsmen entered the church from a door to the right and took up positions beside the priest. A spitting image of Dad in his black-on-black tux and every bit a prick like him, too, my brother caught my eye, his face deadpan. At least he dipped his head in return when I offered a nod of greeting.

Three men stood beside him, all assholes, all of his friends who had loved to gang up on me when we were younger. They were more his brothers than the one he hadn't asked to be a groomsman, the one who wasn't welcome to sit with their shared parents in the front pew.

Why had I even bothered coming to my brother's wedding? The invitation had come as a surprise—the invite, not the fact he would marry his long-time submissive girlfriend who'd put up with his shit since high school.

She was just like Mom … subservient like a doormat, giving up all sense of self and dreams to the man who ruled her.

Fucking made me sick.

Muscles ticking in my jaw again, I returned my attention to the balding head in front of me. I tried to squash down the resentment I'd dealt with since middle school when I had realized what my father was—and finally had a label to put on the person who was supposed to love me unconditionally and teach me how to be a good man.

Instead, I'd gotten "pussy" and "pansy" thrown in my face, all because I preferred being in the kitchen with Mom instead of hanging with my brother and his obnoxious friends—"real men" as Dad had called them even back then while frowning at my blackened eyes and tears.

Things had only gotten worse when my dad's

sister died and left her farm a couple hours north to me—
the only nephew who'd spent time with her whenever my
family went to visit. I'd slaved in her garden, and in
return learned how to be somewhat self-sufficient. Not
that I put that knowledge to good use, but her land—
mine, much to the disappointment of my father—was the
perfect place to grow a couple marijuana plants.

The organ whined, drawing me back to the
Catholic church I'd grown up attending. Two women
walked down the aisle, turned to the left and took up
their spots, smiles bright and eyes shining.

Why the fuck did women enjoy weddings so
damn much? Who in their right fucking mind wanted to
tie themselves down to a ball and chain, someone who
would never give them the adoration they expected?
Marriage equaled bullshit in my opinion. Better off
fucking when you felt the need and leaving not long
after.

Pussy had pretty much become my favorite
pastime after cooking once I realized my cock found
more pleasure in a wet, clenching hole than in my damn
fist. I'd been fourteen at the time, a fumbling moron, but
she'd been older. Experienced. She taught me what a
woman needed, how to keep her on edge long enough
that her cries while coming would wreck her voice.

I shifted on the church pew, pushing at the good
old Catholic guilt that pricked me when sitting in a
church. I hadn't stepped foot in one in over five years,
but that didn't keep the past from rushing over me—
especially when I glanced at the crucifix again looming
over us.

As a Fallen Glider, I'd seen more than my fair
share of blood. Torture and gore. Hell, less than twenty-
four hours earlier, I'd sped north with Jonny, our
president, to pick up one of my Fallen brothers who'd

been shot. The bodies of the two men who had thought to take Digger out had been dealt with before I'd arrived, but the damage they'd inflicted on him had me wishing I'd been around to help do those two fuckers in.

My Fallen brothers might not be blood, but they treated me better than the men in my family ever had.

The third bridesmaid drifted past in a waft of feminine spice, the slope of smooth skin from the edge of her up-do of dark hair to the top of her strapless maroon dress drawing my gaze. My cock thickened without thought, and when she turned at the church's front to face the witnesses, I nearly groaned.

Mila Kunis has a fucking twin. Fuck. Me.

It took me a few seconds to find my feet as the bride's march spilled from the pipes, drawing everyone to stand. I stared at the maid-of-honor rather than turn to watch my brother's bride-to-be as she walked down the aisle.

Catlike eyes with arched brows. A square jaw, pouty, pursed lips—unsmiling. I held in a satisfied snort. At least one woman in the damn church wasn't - disillusioned by thoughts of happily-ever-after, rainbows, and white picket fences.

Her gaze flitted my way and past, but jerked back to my face in less than a heartbeat. A slow, lazy smile lifted my lips as pink highlighted her prominent cheekbones.

She was fucking gorgeous. Sexy as fuck, too, in the sheath dress that hugged the type of curves a man could get lost in. The scent of her perfume lingered in my nose, thickening my cock to the point of pain.

Dad cleared his throat, and I tore my attention from the woman I planned on fucking before night's end. Dark eyes narrowed and lips in a thin line, Dad glared at me. I wanted to flip him off, but I turned slightly to watch Sarah's march toward her doom.

Fresh-faced innocence, big brown eyes filled with hope and expectation like every bride, she clutched her flowers and offered my asshole brother a dazzling smile. Sarah had always been too good for him. Too sweet. Too kind, just like Mom.

Poor girl should have known better after so many years with my brother, but I couldn't be bothered with her impending broken heart and tears that would soak into a thousand tissues in the coming years. I sent up a quick prayer to Mother Mary they wouldn't have kids to witness her heartache.

Narcissistic assholes didn't change. Selfish pricks who always had to one-up in every conversation. Know-it-all, arrogant dicks who only thought of themselves, laying waste to those closest to them.

We sat, and I turned my attention back on the maid-of-honor. Head high, back straight ... tits enough to overflow my palms, and an ass that promised to swallow every inch of my cock with plenty of cushion for the pounding.

Fuck.

I shifted again, and the priest started droning on about marriage, vows, and the shit that brought stars to most women's eyes.

Not my beauty. Pouty lips still unsmiling, she stood in witness, holding the bride's bouquet in a white-knuckled grip, offering Sarah the ring she'd kept on her thumb of her left hand... No band on her own fourth, I noted. Not that one would have stopped me from getting my hands up under her dress.

No panty lines showed beneath the tight dress hugging her hips and ass. Bare? Shaved smooth? Was she the type who spritzed perfume down the length of her body, coating her curves in the spicy scent still lingering in my nose?

My mouth watered. Would she taste sweet? Tangy? My balls fucking ached, and I fought off the need to adjust the hard length pressed tight against my right thigh by black slacks I'd actually bought for a goddamn wedding.

I'd planned on offering my congrats in the receiving line and getting the fuck away from my toxic family for a joint and some sleep, but the temptation of those curves, those greenish catlike eyes that glanced my way twice during the ceremony ... yeah. I could handle being up a few extra hours if it meant I'd get to bury my cock inside of her.

Because, have her I would. Come hell or high water, I'd have my face buried in her pussy, her thighs holding tight to my head, and fingers pulling at my hair as she came, coating my tongue with her cum.

Fuck, that damn ceremony lasted longer than any Sunday Mass, and until I stood in front of her in the receiving line, my brother and Sarah's necessary greeting over, I was ready to steal her away and bring a smile to her lips.

"You're David's brother," she said before I could utter a word.

I flashed the smile that usually made women swoon and stuck out my hand. "Capone."

Her brow rose at the nickname, and she slipped her palm against mine. "Helina."

Soft and warm, her hand fit in mine better than my broken-in, winter riding gloves. Tingles spread up my arm, stiffening my cock again to the point of pain. Her lips parted as pink once more tinged her cheeks.

I'd definitely be tasting her before long. With a wink, I released her hand and made quick work of the rest of the line before heading out into the cool air to climb on my Harley and fire it to life, drawing a few dozen heads my way from the guests lingering outside of the church.

I'd taken the metal out of my face for the wedding, but there was no hiding the tattoos on my neck—especially the "67" on the right I'd had inked to prove to my dad that I was no fucking pansy. Outwardly, I appeared the badass I strove to embrace.

Muffler rumbling, my bike took me away from the prim and proper for a joyride before the reception began. While I'd have loved to crash my head on my pillow from having been up for over thirty-six hours straight, I had a woman to bed.

****

"Who is she?" I asked the second my brother finally found his way to me. The DJ's music thumped, I had my good friend Jack Daniels in my hand ... and the bridal party shaking their asses to some dumbass pop song kept my eyes occupied.

"Hello to you, too," my brother said, leaning against the bar beside me. "Couldn't even bother buying a nice suit for my wedding."

I noted the scowl in his voice, but didn't give him my attention he wanted. "At least I ditched the leathers," I said, lifting my drink to my lips.

"And took that damn metal out of your face."

"Fuck you."

"I don't do family."

I sipped, gaze plastered to the dark-haired beauty who had my cock hard as a rock. "So, who is she?"

"It's always about the pussy for you." My brother snorted—his jealousy over my easy time getting laid too apparent, same as it'd always been until he hooked Sarah. "And Mom wonders why I didn't ask you to stand beside me today while I vowed to be *faithful* to Sarah."

I ignored him, knowing full well why he hadn't—his friends meant more to him than his own blood. Always had, always would. Hell, he didn't even have the decency to seat me at the family table. Not that I'd have sat near Dad anyway. I hadn't spoken to him for years and had no plans to speak to him for whatever years I had left.

"So," I said, "are you going to be a prick, or are you going to answer the fucking question?"

"Helina Bodnar. Sarah's best friend, and you're not man enough for her."

She glanced my way, and I smiled, undeterred by my brother's declaration.

"She needs someone with a firm hand," the asshole continued, his voice carrying the haughtiness that usually made me sneer. "An alpha man to put her in her place, bring her to heel. She thinks she's too good for anyone now that she's opened up her own law firm."

"Lawyer?" I asked.

"Damn woman doing a man's job...."

Fuck, did he sound like Dad. Poor Sarah. I glanced at his new wife, who shimmied beside Helina, the woman I planned on sinking into balls deep before the clock struck midnight. So my beauty was an independent. From the lack of joy on her face during the ceremony, I expected jaded as well. She moved like she knew how to fuck ... and not looking for a knight in shining armor to fulfill her.

My type of woman.

Helina glanced over her shoulder at me, catlike eyes giving off that "come and get it" shimmer as her lips lifted in a small smirk. She held a glass of champagne in her hand, the fourth from what I'd seen, while swaying that ass.

I downed the rest of my drink, turned to plunk the

empty glass on the bar, and clasped my brother's shoulder. "Congrats, and best of luck in trying to make Sarah happy." Not waiting for a reply, I strode toward my soon-to-be conquest, my cock leading the way.

Helina

God, those eyes... Crystal blue and intense, they sent awareness through my body I hadn't experienced in a long time. Every second of the damn ceremony, his gaze had sent tingles down my spine to settle between my thighs. Every second of the too-damn-long reception while I guzzled bubbly rather than eat filet mignon. Toasts. Cutting the cake. When Sarah's tossed bouquet had landed at my feet because I stepped back out of its way, I felt his stare and my pussy responded.

It'd been too long since I had given into my baser instincts. Too long since I'd allowed a man in my bed. Too long since someone other than myself and my trusty vibrator had given me an orgasm.

I wanted Jeremiah Caldwell—or Capone as he called himself—wherever the hell that nickname had come from. Sarah's brother-in-law. Pretty boy with mussed black hair, strong jawline, wide shoulders, and tattoos peeking from the button-down shirt tucked into black slacks ... slacks that did nothing to hide the hard ridge along his right thigh as he leaned against the bar. I wanted him, so I would have him—just like every other goal I'd ever set for myself, the man would be conquered.

His throat bobbed as he downed his drink, and my breath caught when his attention once more riveted on my face. Our gazes locked. Sexual energy rippled across the room between us as music blared and dance lights flickered.

Mouth watering, I wiggled my hips again and waited for his steady gait to bring him to me. Still staring, he continued with that killer smile while pushing his way through the dancing crowd, lips unmoving with apologies he should have offered to those he jostled against. The distance between us lessened, and heat rushed over my skin, settling in my cheeks.

When had I last blushed over a guy? High school? It was probably the shots we'd done in the limo ... and the champagne I couldn't seem to get enough of.

I hadn't been able to celebrate the opening of my firm downtown earlier that week because of Sarah's wedding details, so I decided to silently toast myself a few times in between her family's congratulations. Went straight to my head, but I didn't give a shit. Years of college, loans out the ass, but I'd done what I'd set out to do, something my stepfather told me I'd never accomplish. I deserved a night of drunken debauchery, and *Capone* would be the cherry on top.

I managed one last shake of my ass before his palm settled on my hip. Firm and confident, his touch burned through the thin material of my dress, and I cursed myself for going without panties. A subtle, yet mouthwatering, aroma of man and cologne clouded the air, weakening my knees as moisture smeared between my thighs.

The rest of his body pressed against my back, and I bit back a groan as his breath caressed my ear. No words of how hot he thought I was, no cheesy pick-up lines poured from his lips. No womanizing bullshit, just pure electricity igniting between two bodies.

Goddamn, could he *move*.

I closed my eyes and gave over to the buzz tingling through my blood and spinning my head. Gave over to the arousing heat building inside of me and allowed him to lead, something I rarely did. His other hand slid around my waist to rest on my stomach, and I leaned back against his hard chest when he tugged me close.

Good God. I moaned, uncaring if anyone heard—

not that anyone would over the thump of the bass. Capone held me tight, his slow, erotic grind against my lower back thrumming my pulse—and pulsing my pussy. If we had been in a club rather than my best friend's wedding, I'd have dragged him home without a backward glance and fucked him until I couldn't move.

I forced my eyes open and found Sarah frowning at me. Well on my way to drunk, I smiled and lifted my glass. She rolled her eyes and turned away, not that I gave a shit whether she approved or not.

Capone, or Jeremiah as she called him, was the black sheep of his family, going so far as to join a motorcycle gang and all but disown his family for a bunch of thieves and rapists. A badass, one who would take what he wanted and disappear without a trace. The type of man a woman should guard her heart against, the type of guy who would soothe the ache between my legs and never call afterward.

So damn fine, but so not the type I should be messing with even if it was just to fuck. Last thing I wanted was to end up beneath an alpha biker, for Christ's sake. All too familiar with old ladies and their men, I should have shied away the second I noticed that "67" tattooed on his neck when he had taken my hand in the receiving line.

But he was so damn fine.

Perfection, just like the muscle, heat, and heady scent of pure male wrapped around me. We could both have what we wanted with no emotions involved, no expectations—just like I preferred. And if he *did* want more, I'd simply tell him to take a fucking hike.

Ride him, then be rid of him. God.

I tipped my head back against his chest and guzzled the rest of my champagne. The cool bubbles raced down my throat as his breath skittered down my neck and back up again to heat my ear. His hand on my belly lowered until his pinky rested close enough to my pubic bone I moaned again.

Sarah scowled.

I grinned and pressed harder against Capone's cock digging into my lower back.

His low groan in my ear pulsed my pussy again. I'd never been so damn turned on in my entire life.

Fuck this.

I wanted him, so I would have him—end of story.

"Want to get out of here?" I asked loud against the music, my head turned enough my lips brushed his chin as I slurred the question.

Without a word, he grasped my hand and led me away from the crowd, our fingers entwined, my entire body thrumming. Out the double doors into the hotel lobby … a few steps toward our left and through another set of doors.

Naughty boy…

I didn't have much time for thought over the fact he'd led me into a coat closet, because he crowded me against the few hanging coats until my back hit the wall. My drunken giggle cut off as his lips caught mine.

Electrical charges simmered along my skin as lightning exploded behind my eyelids. Talk about fireworks … I blamed the champagne for the way my body went limp against his. My moan sounded loud in the silence of wool and darkness surrounding us. His subtle cologne swarmed my senses as his lips and tongue swept me up into a world of pure lust. Pure need.

He tangled his hands in my up-do, tilted my head, and devoured every inch of my mouth. He kissed me like he owned me, like he could lay the world at my feet.

Wetness beyond what I had ever experienced welled, and I whimpered as he slid a knee between my knees and lifted, taking my skirt high enough his thigh rubbed against my pussy.

I grabbed at his shoulders. His back. His ass. Couldn't keep my hands from mapping every hard inch of his body, and when he tore his mouth from mine and sank to his knees, my fingers found hold in his hair.

Our heavy breaths filled the muffled silence. My gasp broke it as he wrapped his hands around my knees and slid them to my waist, taking my skirt all the way up.

He nudged my pubic bone and trimmed patch with his nose, his deep inhale loud in the quietness. "Divine," he whispered and licked through my soaked folds.

My head thumped against the wall behind me, the darkness behind my eyelids spinning. "*Fuck…*"

"Mmm," he agreed, his lathing tongue finding my throbbing clit.

I ground my pussy against his face, so damn ready to combust from a man's touch for the first time in ages, I bit my lip, knowing I would scream.

Capone had a tongue to match the rest of his perfection. He tasted every inch of me, licking and nibbling with enough sting to make me gasp. Enough pressure to take me to the edge over and over. Enough intuition to leave me dangling on the cliff I teetered upon … so ready to tumble headfirst into the waiting rush of euphoria I damn well deserved.

He fucking stopped. Backed off, the prick.

"The fuck? Give me what I want." I yanked on his hair, trying to pull him back to me, but he rocked on his heels and stood.

"*I* want you spread out on a bed, naked and crying for release."

I rubbed against him like a cat in heat, imagining what he said in my buzzed head, but not wanting to wait.

"Give it to me now."

"No, darlin'." He cut off my responding growl with his luscious mouth, once more melting me against the wall.

I wrapped one leg around his waist, grinding against his hardness, chasing the orgasm I wanted.

"Tell me you need a ride home," he whispered against my lips, my tangy scent clinging to his breath, his hands sliding down over my breasts, beneath the dress, pulling at the beaded nipples that ached for his kiss.

"I need a ride home," I agreed without thought, my drunken need to fuck already owning every inch of my brain.

Maybe too much alcohol, I realized as he grasped my hand once more and led me out into the hallway. My feet didn't want to cooperate. Neither did my focus as we walked out into the cool, spring night.

I didn't give a shit about the purse I'd left in the wedding party's private room. Didn't give a second thought to the fact I'd left without letting anyone know.

Capone climbed onto his Harley, and I slid on behind him, my dress riding up.

"Where to?" he asked as I pressed against his back.

I murmured my rental's address in his ear, adding a flick of my tongue along his lobe.

He groaned. "Hold on."

The engine roared to life, and seconds later, wind whipped into the night the pins Capone hadn't already dislodged from my hair. My head spinning and dark hair flying behind us, I fought to cling to his trim waist. The heat of his skin, the dips of his six-pack kept me somewhat focused—and turned on as fuck.

The short ride across town seemed an eternity. My stumble up the steps of my rental house brought giggles to my lips, the type that hadn't escaped me for years. I fumbled to get the spare key from atop the doorjamb as Capone palmed my ass and grumbled about the lousy hiding spot.

We fell into my entryway, but before he could utter a word, my stomach turned.

"Oh God..." I pushed his hands off me and rushed back the hall, my shoulders banging me around like a pinball on the walls as I tried to focus on the bathroom door.

Somehow, I ended up on my knees, crawling over the cool tile.

I managed to hold off heaving until I bent my head over the toilet.

"Shit." Capone's murmured curse accompanied his hands gathering up my hair.

He fucking held me while I puked my guts up into the porcelain throne.

Thoughts of my being a moron for drinking so much rang with each gagging heave that hunched me over the toilet. A sexy-ass man ready to blow my mind, and I end up blowing chunks in front of him.

My eyes watered with every heave, and although I expected my makeup smeared in rivulets down my cheeks, I couldn't find it in myself to give two fucks. I spit a few times, and swallowing against the burning sting of bile in my throat, I sat back, eyes closed.

"Damnit all to hell," I rasped out, hands still clenching the toilet seat.

"You okay?" Capone murmured, one hand holding my hair, the other smoothing down my back.

"Ugh." I struggled to stand on shaking legs, and he held my arm as I attempted to move toward the sink. "Toothbrush," I managed, needing to rid my mouth of the puke taste.

Blinking repeatedly didn't bring the toothbrush in my hand into focus. Didn't clear up the fuzzy image of the wrecked face in the wavering mirror above the sink.

"I've got you, darlin'." Capone's arms wrapped around me from behind, and I sighed back into him, allowing my eyelids to rest.

****

My head fucking pounded. I groaned and rolled, burying my face in my pillow against the bright light streaming around my closed blinds.

Had I closed them before going to bed?

Is it fucking Monday already? I forced an eye open and blinked into focus the red numbers on my clock.

Eight.

Wait.

I rolled faster than I should have, noting my complete lack of clothing and the empty bed beside me. Sitting made my head scream, and I scowled.

My bridesmaid dress sat at the foot of the bed, folded neatly.

Blinds closed...

I slid off the bed and walked toward the bathroom on weak legs. No mess near or around the toilet. Toothbrush put back in its holder. No condom wrapper in the trashcan.

No sign of Capone in either room—or evidence of him between my legs. No leftover cum dripping from my pussy, no sweet ache or sting of welcomed invasion.

My scowl deepened.

Naked as a jay, I stalked into the kitchen, hands on hips. Door locked. Key on the island, and fucking Keurig ready to roll with my favorite mug beside it... *How the fuck did he know?*

"Fuck." I slumped on a stool. A glance around the

kitchen didn't reveal the purse I normally wouldn't go anywhere without. Had I left it at the hotel?

Yes, goddamnit. That meant no cell phone.

No phone, but I wasn't about to let Capone off the hook. Failing to attain one of my goals didn't sit well. Never had, never would. I got what I wanted, when I wanted, unlike my weak mother who gave up her dreams for whatever my stepdad had wanted.

Not this woman, I told myself, rising once more to my feet and heading to the bathroom. Jeremiah Capone Caldwell owed me a fucking orgasm, and I was going to claim it. Two-fold.

Capone

I hadn't slept worth a shit. Thoughts of Helina sent shots of cum into my fist as I'd jerked off in my own bed an hour after tucking her into hers, but my dick still ached to be buried inside of her. I'd stripped her down, stared at her gorgeous body while folding the bridesmaid dress with shaking hands, and covered her limp form without taking advantage of her drunkenness.

My fingers had itched to trail down over her skin, my mouth watering to taste every inch of her, but motorcycle gang member or no, I was no rapist.

I scowled as I cursed my decency for at least the tenth time since pulling myself out of bed at the ass-crack of dawn and climbing onto my bike.

Jonny had called a meeting, and I headed to the club with only one cup of coffee sloshing in my empty stomach. Cool air licked at my face as my Harley rumbled beneath me, but the absolute sense of freedom my bike brought didn't even wipe away my frown.

I had missed out because I couldn't take advantage of a woman. *You're a damn motorcycle gang member,* I grumbled at myself in my head while parking my bike in front of the club. A badass who was supposed to take what he wants, fuck the consequences.

Pussy... Dad's voice chimed in my head along with my brother's, *Pansy-assed little bitch.*

Still scowling, I pushed through the front door. For once, eighties music didn't blare through the overhead speakers. Instead, voices of my brothers gathered in the bar area rumbled. A few called out greetings, but I didn't offer my usual grin in return.

Hawk, our Sergeant at Arms, flagged me over toward the end of the bar where he sat beside Jonny. The two lacked their usual monster of a bodyguard Digger, who, I noted while glancing around the room, must have stayed in bed where his shot-up ass belonged.

"How's he doing?" I asked while sliding onto the stool beside Hawk.

My brother moved the toothpick in his mouth from one side to the other with his tongue, hazel eyes hard and unsmiling as always—unless Janie hung on his side. "Better than this whole fucked up situation is about to get."

"That bad?" I whispered as Jonny stood.

Lips pursed, Hawk nodded and turned his attention on Jonny.

Dark eyes assessing the group before him, our president straightened, tilting his chin out the slightest bit. "We had an incident Friday afternoon."

A fucking pin could have dropped, the sound echoing through the club.

"Digger and his woman were attacked by two men while riding north," Jonny continued. "Digger took a bullet to the side, but he'll be fine. Can't say the same for the two assholes who thought to take him out."

A few muttered curses sounded, and Jonny waited for silence to settle before continuing. "Nicky answered Digger's call—"

More than one of the Gliders shouted their approval, grins sprouting up over the fact our former Sergeant at Arms who'd left us the spring before still responded to a brother in need.

Jonny's mouth twitched as though he, too, wanted to grin.

We all missed the old man, the last original Glider from the old days, but he'd left us when his only sister OD'ed on the drugs our club dealt throughout New Hampshire. Couldn't blame the man. I'd have done the same.

"Nicky and Digger didn't leave any loose ends," Jonny continued once the men quieted down again.

As if either would. Between the two of them, nothing had ever come back to bite the Gliders in the ass over the years. I'd only gone up north after finding out Digger's woman had been involved, the woman I'd had first, shared with Digger, then willingly stepped back to allow my brother to stake his claim once I realized she belonged to him.

Perfect for each other—just sucked ass Digger wouldn't be my partner in crime anymore. We'd shared dozens of women, including the handful of club whores who always had a hole willing for a brother or two at the same time.

Ball and chain, I told myself, trying to push away the longing in my gut for something similar to what both Hawk and Digger had found.

"So now what?" one of my brothers called out once Jonny finished up telling them about the two men's demise.

Jonny scanned the room. "The two taken out were the same keeping watch on the club—and Digger last week."

"They FBI?" someone from the back of the room asked.

"Sure as shit didn't look like it," Hawk said around his toothpick.

"We're going to ride this out," Jonny said. "See what happens. You're the only men who know what happened, and if I hear whispers about this from anyone outside of this room—including the club whores who have no business outside of our pants—"

Laughter filled the place.

"—I'll find out who squealed, and I'll bury you so fucking deep even the devil himself won't be able to find your dismembered body."

Silence settled so fucking thick, I shifted on my stool. Jonny always followed through with his threats. Hell, I'd seen a man's tongue sliced out by Nicky's blade the first year I'd joined the Gliders because the guy wouldn't shut up like Jonny had told him to.

Someone pounded on the locked club door, and everyone froze, silence once more descending.

Jonny nodded to one of the Gliders in the back. "See who it is."

He stood and peered through the peep hole. "Some dark-haired bitch. Looks pissed off at the world."

She pounded on the door again. "Open the fuck up!" Her muffled scream accompanied by one last fist to the metal door.

Jonny nodded when my brother turned from the peephole, brow raised.

The door squeaked, and men shifted to catch a glimpse of the woman who dared to show up uninvited at the Fallen Gliders' private club.

Green eyes blazing, Helina stepped into the doorway, hands on hips, and my cock sprang to attention.

"Fuck." I hadn't realized I'd cursed out loud.

"Know her?" Jonny asked as she scanned the room.

"Yep."

Her gaze landed on me, and her brow furrowed. "Jeremiah Caldwell, get your ass over here!" She stomped her booted foot.

Laughter rang out, and face heating, I stood and pushed my way through the club. A few backslaps and wishes of good luck followed along behind me.

"Put that bitch in her place," one of my brothers hollered, earning a few chuckles.

"I'll set her straight," I said, grinning and

swaggering, but inside wanting to wiggle like a fucking worm on a hook. Even my damn palms sweated.

I grabbed Helina by the arm and dragged her back outside into the morning air with mocked confidence even my dad would have been proud of.

"Don't you fucking manhandle me!"

The door slammed shut behind us, and I dropped my hold on her arm, stepped back, and shoved my hands into my pockets to keep from pressing her up against the wall and devouring her pouty lips.

She hauled off and slapped me across the face. Hard. "Don't you *ever* touch me like that again." She seethed like a hissing cat, fire glinting in her eyes, hair a wild mess of dark tresses hanging over her shoulder.

Sexy. As. Fuck.

I told myself I had to be tough just in case anyone watched through the peephole or listened through the door "Don't *you* ever show up here uninvited and make demands like you own the place—and me."

Helina lifted a hand to slap me again, and I grabbed her forearm, gritted my teeth, scowling while meeting her gaze. "Do *not* hit me again." Sexual tension strung between us like a livewire. Fuck, did I want her...

"I didn't fuck you while you were out cold, if that's what you're worried about," I said, keeping my voice low and releasing my hold on her.

"I know." She fisted her hands at her side and tilted her chin up.

"So what's the fucking problem?"

"You ... you ... fuck." She heaved a heavy breath, drawing my attention to the cleavage and pebbled nipples her bra and t-shirt didn't hide.

I met her gaze, brow lifted. "I what?"

"Didn't give me what I wanted."

The corner of my lip quirked at her petulant pout.

"Which was?"

Her gaze narrowed again. "Don't play coy with me, Jeremiah."

"Capone."

"What*ever*."

A car buzzed past on the road, but I didn't take my gaze off her gorgeous face. "You've got balls, woman, showing up at the club like this all because I left you hanging last night."

"I always get what I want."

"Spoiled brat."

"You have *no* idea," she ground out between her teeth, hands clenched at her sides

I stepped into her personal space, crowding her up against the club's brick wall. "Frustrated, Helina?" Her breath caught as I pressed my hard cock into her soft belly and twined my fingers in her hair, but I didn't give her time to respond. I took her lips in a bruising kiss, tongue lashing and teeth nipping.

Helina pulled at my hair. Punched my shoulders and tried to knee me in the balls, but she kissed me back, taking more than I'd hoped. She bit my lower lip, tilting her head back to pull the flesh taut.

"Goddamn," I growled against her mouth and slid a leg between her jean-clad thighs. She rubbed against me like a cat in heat, hot-as-fuck mewling noises rising from her throat as I leaned in to lick every inch of her delicious mouth.

My cock leaked inside my leathers, creating a sticky mess, and Helina's hands shoving up under my tight shirt and mapping my abs didn't help. The heat of her pussy pressed against my thigh seeped through the clothing separating us, drawing another growl from my chest.

I forced myself to step back. Either that or fuck

her right there in broad daylight for the world's enjoyment. God knows I would stop to check out the show. Watching turned me on.

She slapped me. Again.

"The fuck?" A feminine voice gasped, whipping my head toward the right. Shelly, one of the club whores I'd had dozens of times, strode toward us, hands on hips, purse dangling from one wrist. "The fuck you do that for?" she asked again, her ruby-red lips scowling while her gaze slid down and back up Helina's body. She stopped a few feet away from us. "You need to tell that bitch to back the fuck off," Shelly spouted at me, unable to keep her goddamn trap shut.

"Shut up, Shelly."

She glared at me. "You going to let that cunt touch you like that?"

I fisted my hands to keep from clobbering the whore.

"Any other brother would give that bitch a good slap in return!" she continued, eyes glinting like a knife.

Arguing her wrong assumption wouldn't do anything but piss her off. "How about you back the fuck off?" I glared at her, wondering how the fuck I'd ever found her pretty enough to stick my dick into. "I can *handle* this woman on my own."

Shelly snorted. "Handle it, my ass." She turned away, and I swear to fucking God I heard her mutter something about me being a pussy while passing through the club's front door.

Jaw clenched, I turned back to Helina, surprised as fuck she hadn't gotten involved in my little discussion with Shelly.

Eyes narrowed, she once more spit fire from her gaze at Shelly's back. "How many times have you had *that* club whore bitch?" she asked, settling her glare on me.

"None of your fucking business."

"Let me guess ... you're the club pretty boy who loves pussy no matter the age or shape. The player who takes whoever he can, whenever he can. I'll bet your dick has sampled half of this town's—"

"You've got me pegged," I said, holding my arms wide, but not backing out of her personal space.

Pink tinged her cheeks, her green eyes sparkling with a wrath like Kahn's. *"Handle it...* You're just like all the other alpha assholes hoping for a chance to take down an independent woman and show her who's boss."

"You have *no* idea, darlin'," I shot back her own words with the same emphasis. Close enough to ravish ... we both heaved for breath. More pre-cum leaked from my straining dick as I tried like hell to fight off my need to fuck the little spitfire.

She shoved at my chest. "Leave me alone!"

"Gladly!" I stepped back even though her dilated pupils and hard nipples disagreed with her words. I had enough of a headache with my brother's issues...

Helina stormed off, her swaying ass snagging my attention.

I sure as shit didn't need woman problems. Even if said woman got under my skin like a fucking tick intent on sucking me dry.

Groaning at the thought of her mouth on my cock, I shoved the club's door in, adding the swagger to my walk that made me appear like the badass I'd always wanted to be. Fucking woman had me by the balls whether I wanted her to or not, but I couldn't let my brothers know—if loudmouth Shelly hadn't already told them.

Helina

Fucking player. Asshole.

I slammed my car door and tore out of the Fallen Glider club's parking lot, so frustrated I couldn't see straight. The damn man had my head fucking spinning—and not in a good way. My pussy ached. Clit throbbed. And all I had was a damn vibrator that just wouldn't cut it.

"Asshole," I mumbled out loud, pulling up in front of the old brick building I'd signed a lease on earlier in the week. My firm. My fucking life.

He didn't know the first thing about me. How dare he call me a spoiled brat as though my daddy had handed me everything? I worked my ass off for everything I owned. No help—zero spoiling from anyone.

Self-made, I didn't *need* anyone else.

The anger biting at me eased off a bit as I used the key to open the front door. Boxes sat in disarray along with the still-wrapped chairs I'd bought for the reception area I stood in. Hands on hips, I glanced around the small space. My old desk sat near the far wall, beside the door that led to my office. Another room sat on the other side, leading to a room I would use for conferences. A bathroom beyond that, and then stairs leading to the second floor, a wide-open space outfitted as a studio apartment.

I planned on leaving my current rental, but one damn thing at a time. Needed to hire a secretary. Needed to advertise my services as a kick-ass lawyer. Needed to send out a nice letter to my old clients from the firm in the neighboring town I'd slaved in for the previous five years, letting them know I'd relocated. Screw the old firm—they'd used me like a slave and didn't deserve my loyalty in any form whatsoever.

Heaving a breath, I tossed my keys aside and grabbed a box off the top of the stack, before heading to my office. A little organizing and hard work would take my mind off everything I had to do ... along with Capone and those crystal-blue eyes. Those lips ... that tongue.

"Focus, Helina."

I grumbled at myself for a few more minutes, unable to get the damn man off my mind. Hatred for the type of man he must be and need for his sexy ass warred in my head. Panties soaked and clit still throbbing, I locked myself in the tiny bathroom and took care of my needs. Sucked ass that I wasn't satisfied afterward.

Far from it.

****

By Thursday morning, I'd gotten the office organized, sent out that letter, interviewed a couple women, and given my landlord a thirty day notice I was moving out of my rental house. I sat drinking my coffee, still in my robe, the news from the living room TV filtering through the wall of the kitchen. At the mention of the Fallen Gliders, I hopped up and hurried into the neighboring room.

A car sat on the side of Route 95, surrounded by police vehicles, lights flashing. Drug bust ... a car loaded with narcotics ... suspected local motorcycle gang... Turned out someone had ratted on the Gliders, anonymously giving the police the information they needed to track down the north-bound car.

"Damn." Shaking my head, I reminded myself of the type of man Capone was. That "67" on his neck made him off limits in so many ways. Even though the memory of him had kept me up tossing and turning every night since Sunday, I needed to get my head and body moving in a different direction.

I muted the TV and picked up my phone. The week before, I'd gone to a singles' dating event at a local dig downtown and met someone decent enough for a one-night stand. He wouldn't sleep with me. Wouldn't even fucking touch me beneath my clothing. *Respect*, he'd said before asking me out a second time.

I wasn't interested in a budding relationship where a man assumed he had the right to tell me what to do—I only wanted to fuck and move on, take care of needs and remain my independent self.

Time to go hunting and, I hoped, find someone to distract me from the blue eyes and easy smile haunting me every hour of the day.

****

A flirty skirt for easy access, no panties, tight tank with a built-in bra, hair in waves down my back, and smoky makeup … yeah, I was so ready to get laid. The newest restaurant downtown had done up their second floor for local events—and cooking classes every Friday night that doubled as a singles' meetup.

Unnaturally warm spring air licked at my tingling skin as I locked up my ancient Audi and made my way through the town's parking area. Old brick buildings lined the main road, the restaurant I walked toward only a few doors down from my firm. They served lunch and dinner seven days a week, and I had already sampled most of their menu with takeout.

Knowing I needed to get on a stricter budget, I decided I needed to learn how to cook for myself. Why not combine work and pleasure? Best way to make the time pass since I couldn't care less about roasting versus steaming.

Diane, the restaurant's owner, met me at the top of the stairs. "Welcome back, Helina!" *How the hell she remembers my name after a single event...*

Good business mind, right there. I handed her my card, letting her know about my new firm, and made my way into the open space. The small bar to the left held court, the other patrons mingling, drinks in hand.

I made my way toward the group, smiling and dropping pleasantries when needed. Glass of red in hand, I turned, taking in the five men in attendance. Double the number of women clustered like clucking chickens fighting for a nibble of grain to fall from the poor guys. None of the men's looks did jack for me, and with a sigh, I headed toward the table closest to the door in case I decided to split early.

"Let's get started!" Diane called out from across the room a few seconds later, and I settled onto the stool in front of a stainless-steel table set up for the evening's meal we would be preparing. The stool beside me remained empty as others took their seats, those lucky enough to nab a male partner for the night smiling like they'd found the fattest worm on the farm.

My phone dinged, and I grabbed my purse from beneath the table.

The door opened while I read a text reminder of my dentist appointment the following day. A waft of familiar male slid past my nose, tingling me between the thighs as I stuffed my purse beneath the table once more.

Jean-clad legs appeared beside me, and I glanced up.

Jeremiah Caldwell.

Oh, fuck it all to hell and back again.

Capone

Helina ... goddamn. My cock twitched as I slid onto the stool beside her, grinning like a fucking fool at my luck.

Lips parted, she stared at me for a good three seconds before snapping her jaw shut, eyes narrowing. "Stalking me?" she whispered as Diane chatted from the front of the room.

"I could ask you the same," I shot back, keeping my voice low as my gaze settled on her plump lower lip. Her spicy perfume, like a subtle cloud, shifted around me, wrapping me up in a cocoon of lust. I'd had my fair share of women, but I'd never experienced sexual tension like the electrical currents zapping the short distance between us.

Jaw clenched, she turned away, focusing on our teacher for the night.

I'd been friends with Diane since high school. We had attended cooking school together until I dropped out from catching too much shit from my dad and joined the Gliders. She often asked me to fill in for her Friday night singles' cooking classes, and on the occasion I found someone to cover the club's kitchen, I jumped at the chance.

Food and available women ... yes, fucking *please*, the whole reason I'd shown up that night. Rucker, one of the Gliders who'd earned his colors two years earlier, covered the club's grill—'cuz I needed to fuck Helina out of my system and knew I could find an easy lay at Diane's.

It figured Helina would be there, keeping me from hooking up. Fuck knew I wouldn't be able to look at another woman with her in the same damn room.

Not the type of woman I needed. I doubted

Helina had a submissive bone in her body. She would rule whatever household she lived in, and I'd catch nothing but shit from my family.

What the fuck...

Shaking my head at the stupid-as-shit thoughts in my head of a future with the woman I didn't even know, let alone what my family would think of her, I tried to focus on Diane as she shared information we'd learned in the first semester at school. My attention span with Helina beside me was short as shit.

Heaving a heavy breath, I next turned my thoughts to the issues we'd been having at the club. The police had intercepted the shipment Jonny had sent north on Wednesday. Only a handful of Gliders had known about the two cars carrying the shit our club supplied to the northern New Hampshire dealers. The ploy had arrived at its destination, without being detained. The other? Pulled over on 95, the driver, not a Glider thank fuck, knew not to say jack shit and sat in jail for possession.

Until we figured out who the fuck had snitched, Jonny decided to lock down all outside business. The income properties his father had invested the club's money into years earlier more than took care of the club's overhead.

Personally, I hoped the Gliders found a way to turn completely from their lawless ways.

Dad would call me a pussy, and while my blood brother would agree, I expected more than half of my Fallen brothers wanted the same. Nicky had lost his only sister to the shit the club dealt, and he'd almost lost his niece as well. And, there were others known to my brothers who had unintentionally overdosed.

We fed the fucking plague...

The guilt ate at my stomach, same as it always

did whenever I thought too long on the club's main source of income. Better to give into the lust for the woman beside me.

Every chance I got, I brushed my fingers against hers. Leaned close while offering encouragement on how she sliced and diced. Repositioned the knife in her hand for chopping garlic.

"I'll bet you're one hell of a lawyer," I murmured near her ear as Diane made her way from table to table, checking on everyone's skills.

"What makes you say that?" she asked as the hairs on the nape of her sloping neck stood on end.

Grinning, I shifted her wrist once more, my other hand settling on her lower back.

She shied away.

"David said you just opened your own firm. At what? Twenty-five?"

A soft snort escaped her nose. "Hardly. I just know what I want, and nothing stops me from getting it."

"And how's business?"

"Not good."

"It will be."

Helina glanced up at me, the knife poised. "What makes you think that?"

I studied her face, noting the golden flecks in her green eyes and trying not to drown. "You're the most determined woman I've ever met. Hell." I chuckled, glancing at Diane as she neared our table. "You showed up at the fucking club and demanded to speak to a Glider without an ounce of fear."

"How's it going?" Diane asked, smiling and looking over the progress we'd made.

"Helina's a natural," I said, settling back onto my stool.

"Hardly," Helina said with another soft snort on

the word's heels.

"She took charge," I said. "Attacked tonight's tasks with tenacity." I didn't add said tenacity turned me the fuck on.

"Good," Diane murmured with another smile. "Good." She moved off, and Helina glanced at me.

"What?" I asked.

"Does your bullshit get you into every pair of panties you set your mind on?"

"Isn't bullshit. You've got spunk. Resolve. And—" I grinned, my gaze dropping to her lips, "it's sexy as fuck."

At least no snort left her lips. She turned back to her task, a slight frown denting the skin between her arched brows.

We worked well together over the next half-hour, even if every subtle shift of her body made my cock leak with the need to slicken her pussy for fucking. The pulse in her neck, the way she crossed her thighs when I spoke near her ear had me wondering if she'd even need help getting wet.

The fuck was I thinking about sex without a condom?

She dropped one of the cherry tomatoes, and I bent to retrieve it, breathing in deeply as my nose passed a mere foot from her skirt.

Musky and sweet, her scent teased at my memory, and clenching my jaw to keep my groan trapped inside, I stood, my mouth watering.

Our gazes collided as I held the small tomato in my hand, palm up.

Helina stared up at me, and my stomach bottomed out at the desire in her eyes. My heartbeat thumped in my ears, fading the noises of the people cooking around us.

"What I wouldn't give to taste you again," I said,

unable to help myself.

She fucking licked her lips, her gaze dropping to mine as she plucked the tomato from my hand, but she turned away without a word.

Fuck it. I want her.

I shifted closer and leaned down, my breath teasing the hair beside her ear as she sliced through the fruit with a serrated knife. "That skirt can't hide the sweetness of your wet pussy," I whispered. "Tell me you don't want my tongue on you. In you."

She shuddered.

"Tell me to leave you alone again—if that's what you *really* want—and I'll walk away right now." I stepped back, giving her a few extra inches to consider my words.

Licking her lower lip again, she put the knife down. "Goddamn you ... infuriating man." She murmured the words as though to herself, without any trace of anger. Grabbing a towel, she glanced over at me.

The war in her eyes made my inner child want to grin, but I held back, keeping my gaze serious as shit.

"Let's go." She grabbed her purse and made for the door.

I left the table without a backward glance, following after her like the dog I was, wanting to shove my nose up her ass and breathe her in.

Down the stairs. Out into the night. Up the sidewalk for a couple blocks, the click of her heels in front of me and the sway of her ass luring me along.

She unlocked the door of an office, but I didn't pay attention beyond anything but getting her alone, somewhere I could give her what I'd denied her before she'd passed out in my arms the weekend before. Through a reception area that smelled like new furniture, through an inner office door, and Helina tossed her purse aside. She turned, but I stepped close, spun her around again, pulling her back against my chest.

I bent enough to slide my hand up beneath her skirt, my face buried in her neck.

No fucking panties.

I groaned in her ear while her pussy coated my hand with wetness as I cupped her. "Christ..."

"You had better deliver," she said, pulling away.

The dimness of the office barely allowed me to see two large windows with heavy wooden blinds—closed to outside foot traffic—and a very large desk, half-covered with papers and boxes.

Helina hopped onto the edge and leaned back.

I didn't need a verbal invitation, but dropped to my knees and lifted hers, placing her high heels on the edge of the desk. Her scent swarmed over me, and I leaned in for a deep breath.

"So fucking sweet."

The first slow lick from her ass to her clit had her cursing. The second, she grabbed at my hair, nails digging into my scalp. "Holy shit." She gasped as I latched my teeth onto her clit and nibbled. "Oh..."

Smiling, I slid lower again, licking every crease, every indent of her body, lapping up the arousal slipping from her swollen pussy lips. Puffy and quivering, she was slickened enough two of my fingers slid into her tight sheath with ease. I curled my fingers and gently rubbed, finding the roughened spot that lifted her back off the desk.

"God, yes, right there." She moaned and lifted her hips higher.

"You like my fingers in you, darlin'?"

"Fuck, yes."

I pumped in and out a few times, soaking up the whimpers panting past her lips. She complained when I replaced my fingers with my mouth, but uttered another lust-laced curse as I shoved my tongue inside of her body.

"Oh, fuck. Don't stop!"

Lazily, I meandered up through her folds again until my lips brushed over her clit.

"Fuck me with your fingers," she said, holding my head tight to her.

Only too happy to oblige, I did as told, pressing in deep and rubbing that elusive spot.

"God." A few curses spilled from her lips as I thrust and rubbed, my teeth nibbling away at the swollen nub, my nose buried in the trimmed hair atop her pubis. Tangy, soft, and sweet, her pussy was better than any candy or liquor.

"I'm going to come." She moaned the words, her hips rocking up with every thrust of my fingers, her thighs tightening against my ears. Holding me still as if she could stop me from denying her again.

As fucking if.

Helina gasped once … twice, and her back arched off the desk. With a whining cry, she came, her pussy grasping at my fingers in pulsing waves, cum drenching my knuckles. "Don't. Stop." She swallowed between the words, a half-gasped, half-moaned intake of air on its heels as I pulled her clit taunt with my teeth. A flick of my tongue over the hardened flesh sent another spasm through her body. *"Fuck!"*

Cum gushed from her pussy, sliding down my fingers to coat my knuckles and drip to the floor.

I slid my tongue up atop her clit a few more times, coaxing every last whimper from her lips. Her body released my fingers with a wet, sucking sound, and I licked both clean, inhaling until my lungs hurt. A kiss on the inside of each thigh, and I stood, my straining dick pressed between her lax thighs.

Helina sighed, and I cursed the darkness of the office. I wanted to see her face, her eyes. See the satisfaction, the bliss of a sated woman.

I placed my hands on her knees and slid them along the insides of her thighs, pressing between her skin and my jeans to rub my thumbs along my hard length. "You taste even better than I remembered."

"And that was better than I expected."

Grinning, I moved back, but she grasped my wrist before I could step away.

"You're not done yet."

My brow shot up at her tone, but fuck if her bossiness didn't twitch my already pain-hardened cock. "That a fact?"

"Mmm." She sat and grabbed hold of me through my jeans, her grip bringing more pre-cum to my dick's throbbing head. "There's no way in hell you didn't stash a few condoms in your jeans somewhere."

"I might have one or two."

Helina released me and sat back, propped up on her elbows. "Get one out. I want your cock in me."

I bit back my brain's "yes, ma'am" and offered a cocky grin even though she wouldn't be able to see me clearly. "Ask nicely," I said instead, fighting at the discomfort of the alpha male skin I'd been trying to live in for over five years.

I couldn't see her glare, but sure as fuck could feel it singeing my face. "Sheathe that hard cock and fuck me."

Goddamn... The words on her lips. The command in her voice. I bit my lip to keep that "yes, ma'am" inside and pulled a foil packet from my back pocket. My fingers shook while undoing my jeans and fumbling to put the damn condom on.

Thank fuck for the dark.

When was the last time I acted like an innocent teen, so damn excited to finally fuck that I had trouble rolling on a rubber?

A pre-ejaculate mess, hard and throbbing with the need to ram into a woman so damn fully I would see stars...

She grabbed my shirt and pulled me close. "Now, Capone."

I had no fucking words for the torture of her soaked, tight pussy pulling me in. Wanting to savor every second, I eased into her, inch by inch until bottoming out, my drawn-up balls resting against her ass as her thighs wrapped around my waist and tightened.

Slow and steady, I told myself—reminded myself—while pulling back out to the tip. Drive her insane until she's writhing on that big-ass desk. Begging.

"Fuck me like you mean it," she demanded, her nails digging into my forearms as I leaned over her body. Using her heels, she yanked me close, burying me balls deep again. "Hard. Fast."

I wrapped my hands in the hair spread over her desk to hold her in place, gave into her bossiness, and let go of my restraint. She wanted me to lose my fucking mind and rut into her like an animal, she could have it. Her back arched as I pounded into her over and over again, my fists tight in her hair, hips bruising against the inside of her thighs.

"Yes ... fuck, yes!" She cursed, moaned, and groaned, every noise on her lips like a fucking drug. I couldn't get enough. My balls tightened. Sweat beaded on my brow.

"Come for me, 'Lina," I managed past the burning lust licking my entire body with flames.

"Harder." She gasped the word.

Fucking her harder meant she *would* have bruises, but I aimed to please. A low growl escaped from my chest, my hips pistoning, thrusting my cock into her body over and over, jostling the desk beneath her.

"O-oh..."

That little intake of air ... the second ... and she came, arching up and shrieking.

"Goddamn!" A deep groan emptied my lungs as I buried deep and erupted. "Fuck..." A few more thrusts emptied me into the condom, and I sucked wind, trying to calm my racing heart as she went lax beneath me.

Fucking Helina was like running a fucking 5k. I needed to kneel over and catch my breath, walk the shakiness out of my limbs.

I stayed buried inside of her instead, released my hold on her hair, and rested my forehead on hers. *Wholly sated,* I thought, in a way I'd never been before. An image of my alpha skin cracking and peeling flitted through my mind, like I was on the brink of recognizing some cosmic moment in my life—

"You okay?" she whispered a few second later when I still hadn't moved.

I groaned, but couldn't move. "Damn near killed me, woman."

"Would it make it worth it if I admitted to being completely satisfied?"

"Fuck, yes," I said with a chuckle, lifting my head and cradling hers in my hands. That close, I could make out her eyes in the darkness. A million words flitted through my brain, mixing with the thoughts of a dreamy-eyed teenage girl rather than that alpha male I wanted to be.

"You are so fucking gorgeous. Fierce. So damn sexy, and the way you speak to me—" I bit my tongue. Letting onto the emotions racing through my fucked-up head probably wasn't the best idea. Too soon. Too much.

She pressed her lips against mine, softly, completely the opposite of how we'd fucked on the desk. Once more allowing myself to be led, I responded to her initiations of a slow, sensual dance of tongues and lips. Her pussy tasted delicious, but her mouth? Divine.

Helina Bodnar fucking wrecked me, and being the pansy I was, I ignored the alarm bells ringing in my head. The sudden realization that my thickening cock wasn't as restricted as it should have been brought reality back with vivid clarity, and I backed the fuck out quicker than a rattler strike.

Helina

Capone pulled back abruptly from the most lush, mind-blowing kiss I'd ever experienced. I blinked in the darkness, trying to gather my bearings as he pulled out and stepped back.

Cum gushed from my body.

"Fuck!" His low curse hit my ears like a train at the same time I sat up, mind focused like a laser.

"The condom fucking broke!" I whispered harshly, scrambling off the desk. Cum leaked down my legs as I scrambled across the room to flick on the lights.

"Fuck!" Capone had had a forearm thrown over his eyes, his cock in his other hand.

I blinked, cursing the slowness of my eyes to adjust to the sudden light.

Sure enough, the tip of the condom had ripped.

Fuck, fuck, fuck... The word continued to ring in my head as I stared at the semi gripped in his palm—with cum remnants all over the uncovered head. I was on the pill, but so had my mom been when she'd gotten knocked up, too.

"Goddamn it all to fucking hell and back again!" I stalked across my office into the private half-bath and slammed the door behind me. "Fucking hell," I muttered while gathering my skirt up around my waist to sit on the toilet.

When was the last time he got off? I wondered, trying not to focus too much on the amount of cum dripping from my body. A hot biker ... women had to be lined up for a taste of his cock. *Fuck.* Eyes clenched shut, I cleaned up and blew a huge breath between my lips while gripping the sink.

I would get through this, just like everything else in life. A blip, nothing more.

"Hey." Capone gently rapped on the door.

"Be right out," I snapped, all trace of euphoria gone from my body and mind. *Goddamnit.* One last deep breath, and I pulled open the door to find Capone all up in my face. Concern furrowed his brow, his blue-eyed gaze flitting over my face, searching for who the hell knew what.

"Don't worry," I said, lifting my chin. "I'll get a morning after pill, and we can forget this little accident ever happened."

"The fuck you will." His frown deepened as his shoulders hitched. "If you're pregnant, that child is half mine, and I have the right to help you decide what to do. If you think I'm going to just stand aside and let you—"

"That's exactly what you're going to do," I shot back, my raised voice cutting him off. "You may or may have not set something in motion inside of me, but regardless, you have no say in what I do. It's not your choice. It's my body—*mine.*"

"But I helped to make it. I'm entitled—"

"Just because you put your penis in me and donated some unwanted sperm doesn't entitle you to jack *shit*, Jeremiah Caldwell. You do not own me, my body, my pain, or time because we fucked and the goddamn condom broke!"

He stared down at me as my nostrils flared. Somehow, my hands had ended on my hips, and holy shit, did I glare right back at him.

It didn't take long for him to back down, and thank fuck, because I sure as shit wasn't going to. The furrow in his brow eased until his shoulders slumped. "If that's what you want," he murmured, the hurt in his eyes almost making me feel bad.

"That is what's going to *be.*"

He hesitated another handful of heartbeats, the

quietness of my office broken by a muted horn from a car driving by outside.

"I think you should go," I said, my voice deadpan.

"Can I clean up first?"

I glanced down to find he still held his softened dick with its ripped condom in his hand. Stepping out of the bathroom door, I waved him in.

The click of the latch behind me rang in the silence as I grabbed my purse off the floor. A quick text to my doctor—who happened to be a close friend—and I rested easy. She would call in a prescription without questions, and like I'd said, I could forget all about the little accident. Get him out, get him gone, and wash my hands of the whole damn mess.

Capone exited the bathroom and shoved his hands in his pockets.

"I'm going to stay and get some work done," I said without meeting his gaze while straightening my desk.

He hesitated for a few heartbeats before striding out into the reception area without a word, and the second I heard the front door close, I hurried out of my office to lock myself in.

Falling into the closest chair, I buried my head in my hands and bit my lip to keep the tears of self-pity at bay. Giving into the one guy I knew I shouldn't...

"Stupid. Plain stupid," I muttered in anger. I'd known better. Hell, I'd told myself he wasn't the type I needed to get involved with.

But his tongue. His lips. Fuck, did that boy know how to use both. Warmth sprang to life between my thighs again, and I cursed the fact he'd responded to my every demand, that he found my bossiness sexy.

A good reminder of what he felt he was *entitled*

to cooled my arousal quicker than a dousing of ice water. *Fucking alpha asshole.*

Capone

Jonny fucking laughed when I told him what had happened.

"Shut up," I grumbled, slouching in the chair across from his desk in the club's office. "What if she's pregnant with my kid right now?"

"She said it isn't your problem."

I glared at the man who had replaced my big brother even though Jonny had a dozen or so years on the asshole who owned the real title. "It *is* my problem." I sat up and leaned my elbows on my knees. "I helped to make the fucking kid, so I've got rights!"

"Her body, her choice. That's the law."

"Fuck." I slid back into the seat as quickly as I'd sat up. "Are you fucking serious right now?"

Jonny shrugged. "Far as I know, yeah. But who the fuck knows with how this whole country is fucked up the ass. Everyone having rights, everyone bitching about what's right or wrong." He shrugged again. "You could always ask a lawyer."

"*Helina's* a fucking lawyer."

A smirk toyed with his lips. "Then I'd say you're fucked."

"Fuck." I tipped my head back and stared unseeing at the ceiling. "I want to do the right thing. Support her like a man should after knocking a woman up."

"Support her choice if that's the only option you have."

I closed my eyes, the memory of fire in Helina's eyes as she'd stared me down knifing me in the gut. "She's hard as nails. Strong as steel. Damn woman doesn't need anyone's help." The words rang true as I said them. Spoiled? I highly doubted it. I'd probably misjudged her, same as she'd done with me.

Jonny got up and walked around his desk to clasp my shoulder. "Let's go get a drink or two."

Heaving a breath, I followed him into the bar, glad to see Rucker had the bar in hand with the lunch rush over. We sat, the eighties music too damn loud, and downed a couple just like he'd suggested.

Right. Wrong. Morals ... all the shit swirled in my head, around and around again.

"What are you going to do about the club's problem?" I asked, desperate to get my head off Helina.

Jonny's lifting hand with the shot of whiskey paused half-way to his mouth. "Don't know." He tipped his head back, and I followed suit, the burn a welcome distraction.

"Any news on Digger?" I asked, twirling my empty shot glass between my fingers.

"Talked to Maci earlier today. He's up and moving, and she's having one hell of a time trying to keep him at home."

"Fucker's lucky he didn't need surgery, but he needs to relax for a change and heal."

"You know him."

I nodded, pouring us both another round. We tipped back at the same time.

Jonny's cousin, and the Gliders' adopted mother, pushed through the door. Graying curls a riot atop her head, she flashed us a smile.

"How are ya, darlin'?" I shouted across the room with a grin.

Sweetie Jane—no lie on the name—the woman cleaned up after us, made dozens of cookies every week, and patted cheeks where and when allowed. "Are you behaving, Capone?" she asked as she drew near.

"Never, Sweetie."

My grin held as she pecked Jonny's cheek.

"Hey, cousin," Jonny said, still unsmiling. "How are you feeling tonight?"

She'd had a bad epileptic seizure a few days earlier, leaving us to fend for ourselves. "Better."

She and Jonny chatted, and I considered the two joints I kept stashed on my bike. Marijuana wasn't yet legal in New Hampshire for every Tom, Dick, and Harry to grow, but...

"Ever consider registering for medical marijuana, Sweetie?" I asked a few seconds later as she turned to go.

"My doctor was just talking about that when I went in for my checkup."

"When the bill to legalize passes in a couple weeks—"

"Ha!" Jonny snorted. "As if."

"—I'm going to get a few dozen *legal* plants," I said with a smirk. "Thinking about opening a retail store and selling edibles."

"Edibles?"

I poured myself another shot. "Brownies. Gummies. Infused oils. The possibilities are endless." I felt Jonny's stare, but kept mine on Sweetie as she blinked a few times. "'Course, you'll be able to grow your own at that point."

"I've never been one for drugs." She cast a hard glare at Jonny. "But the doctor really thinks it would help."

Jonny ignored her, his gaze on his shot glass.

"Give it some thought," I said. "I'll gladly help you out if you decide you want to give it a try."

Sweetie Jane patted my cheeks. "You're a good boy."

"Anything for my Sweetie." I offered my panty-melting smile—even though I didn't want in *hers*—and with a soft chuckle, she headed toward the stairs and the third-floor hotel-like rooms where the Gliders took women for a little hanky-panky.

Without a word, Jonny and I tilted back at the same time, downing our shots.

"You serious about growing more pot and opening a retail store?" he asked while wiping a thumb across his lower lip.

I nodded, glancing at the door as it squeaked open.

Shelly.

I turned back to my empty shot glass, the mere sight of her turning my stomach. "I don't want to slave in the club's kitchen for the rest of my days, and seeing as how I always wanted to be a chef where I'll actually make some money..." I lifted a shoulder and let it drop. "Legalizing marijuana will open a lot of doors. I plan on applying for a retail license the hour they become available."

"I'd think being a Glider would raise a red flag."

"I've got a squeaky-clean record. Figured if I ran into trouble that you might know of a string or two that could be pulled."

He stared at me with his dark eyes, probably assessing and probing into my soul, but I couldn't tell what the fuck he thought. The man's face was unreadable as always.

"Looks like you boys could use some company." Shelly sidled up to me, pressing her tits against my shoulder, her lanky blonde hair tickling my bicep. "Need some help forgetting whatever's on your mind?"

"Nope." I shifted away from her overpowering, flowery perfume, filled my glass, and motioned toward Jonny's shot glass with the bottle.

He dipped his head, his intent study of my face

broken. I poured as Shelly moved into his personal space and ran her fingertips down over the tight t-shirt covering his chest. "How about you, Jonny? Need help relieving some tension?"

"Your mouth couldn't get me off yesterday," he grumbled. "What makes you think today will be any different?"

"How about we go into your office and I ride you until you come?" she asked, her painted lips sending a shiver over me.

So fucking gross.

"The thought of your pussy isn't even making my dick twitch," Jonny said, his voice still low.

"You haven't taken me in the ass for a while," Shelly continued, trailing her finger down over his chest again. "And you know how much I love having your cock in my tight hole."

"How 'bout you go bother someone else, Shelly?"

She stalked off with a huff and muttering under her breath about being dismissed. A club whores since before I'd earned my colors, she knew better than to lash out at a brother if one pissed her off. She knew better than to cross the president, too. She's lucky he didn't hear—or just didn't seem to care—about her bitching. He'd toss her out on her ass faster than she could blink, to hell what other brothers might think of the readily available pussy, ass, or experienced mouth on her.

"Fucking whore," Jonny muttered.

I glanced at him from the corner of my eye. He downed his shot, a scowl on his lips. Rumor had it, no one had gotten Jonny off for one hell of a long time.

"Need to get some new blood in here," I said, repeating what I'd heard Hawk and Digger say a handful of times before their old ladies swept into their lives and turned them into faithful bastards. *Ball and chain*, I reminded myself.

"Got that right," Jonny grumbled.

I swallowed down another shot, relieved to find a buzz growing in my brain.

"One more," Jonny agreed as I motioned with the bottle again. "Whores, snitches, drug busts…"

"To figuring all this shit out," I said, lifting my glass toward him.

"I'll fucking drink to that." He clinked his shot glass against mine, and we slammed the drinks back.

****

Digger finally showed back up at the club, cheers welcoming him home. Maci stayed glued to his side, the bruise on her cheek from the dead asshole who had hit her almost faded, and she only moved away from him when I held out my arms. Smiling, she hugged me tight, Digger lifting his brow my way but not punching my lights out. Shelly glared enough for the both of them, her gaze on Maci rather than me.

Ignoring the whore, I hugged Maci tighter and grinned at Digger. I still hadn't found a brother I could share women with. Most were too possessive, too insecure. Digger, though, was intimidating as fuck and didn't have an insecure bone in his body. He towered over my six-foot height, had shoulders the width of a bull, and a cock that widened women's eyes.

I released my hold on Maci and stuck out my hand. "Good to have you back," I said with a grin, clasping Digger's hand, but taking care to not bro-hug him too tight. "All healed up?"

"Good enough," he said, his low tone serious.

I glanced at Maci, who leaned against his good side. "Taking good care of my brother?"

Pink tinged her cheeks as her lips curled up in a

satisfied smile. "Always."

"He's one lucky bastard," I said, still grinning.

"I'm one lucky bitch."

We laughed together, and even Digger cracked a rare smile.

A few rounds of celebration ended with Digger, Hawk, Jonny, and me in the office, the door shut with Maci and Janie all cozy-like at the bar together, Shelly giving the two of them the stink eye as usual.

Jealous bitch needed to get over her shit or get the fuck out in my opinion.

Jonny asked for the full story—every detail Digger could remember—nothing left out, pulling my mind off the cattiness of the club whore.

The blond guy who had confronted and shot Digger—then attempted to rape Maci—turned out to be the son of one of the men who had gang-raped Digger's mother thirty-seven years earlier. Silent Demons, all three, and one had unknowingly fathered my Fallen brother.

Fucking mess ended with Digger bashing his attacker's head in with the butt end of a gun before using a bullet to end the other fucker's life.

Two men dead, one his fucking blood brother. According to Digger, neither had sported tatts that named them Silent Demons, but it was highly possible considering the blond fucker's father had ridden with our rivals, and the two had definitely looked the part.

"Janie talk to her dad since the attack?" Jonny asked, turning toward Hawk.

She'd latched onto Hawk while out in Sturgis the summer before, and Hawk claimed her as his old lady before finding out her father was the president of the Demons.

Talk about another fucked up situation. It had

ended well enough, though, without bloodshed, Janie choosing to stay with Hawk and threatening her dad with spilling Demon secrets if he didn't allow her the freedom to choose.

"She's called him twice." Our Sergeant at Arms sat, palms resting on his knees, toothpick between his teeth. "She called the first time on her own, hoping he'd drop some sort of hint, and again yesterday at my insistence. Speaker phone both times, and nothing."

"No fishing whatsoever?"

Hawk shook his head, lips in a tight line around his toothpick, hazel eyes hard as always. Stoic fucker was lucky to have Janie light up his life.

Lucky ... what the fuck is with that word tonight?

Grumbling to myself, I turned my attention back to Jonny, who took up thrumming his fingers on his desktop.

"Taylor isn't going to just let this slip away under a fucking rug if those bastards were Demons," Digger said about our arch rival's president, his lips twisting in a grimace as he shifted on his chair.

"Think we ought to face this situation head on?"

"Fuck, no." Digger scowled. "If they were Demons and he wants to start something, he can come up here where the cops will look the other way. Down there? Who the fuck knows what would happen with the law in his back pocket?"

"Fucking cops haven't been looking the other way up here lately, though," Hawk said, finally sitting back in his chair.

"New blood in their ranks," Jonny said with a dip of his head, "with pockets that refuse to be greased."

"What's up with Chief Rosedale?" I asked, leaning forward, elbows on my knees.

"Talking about retiring," Jonny said of the cop he

considered a close friend—and paid nicely to look the other way.

"Shit," Digger muttered.

"It's the new recruits who have sticks up their asses, and Deputy Jenko leads the fuckers." The cop who refused to be bought, the man who would undoubtedly be appointed by the mayor—his cousin—to the position of Chief once Rosedale decided he'd had enough... Jonny continued to thrum his fingertips on the desk. "Fucking trouble on the horizon, that's for sure."

A few curses and not-so-well wishes spilled from all three of my brothers as I glanced between them.

"We ought to open a couple retail marijuana stores instead of dealing opioids," I said, the words spewing from my mouth without thought.

All three heads swung my way. Jonny's brow raised, Hawk deadpan, Digger scowling. All hard-eyed bad-asses unlike my pansy-ass.

"Or maybe open a social club or two at one of the buildings you own," I continued to babble at Jonny to fill the tense silence as all three continued to stare at me like I'd lost my fucking marbles. "They're real popular in Maine. You know ... we could go legit and not have to worry about the damn cops and Feds anymore."

They continued to stare, unmoving and tight-lipped.

Palms damp, I shrugged and grinned. "Lighten up, guys. Can't a brother joke?"

Digger snorted and turned away. Hawk shifted his attention without a crack in his facade.

Jonny, however, lingered in, studying my face until I shifted on my chair. "I'm not going to confront Taylor," he finally said, changing the topic, thank *fuck*.

Digger nodded.

"And the drug raid on Wednesday?" Hawk

questioned.

"The driver has his lawyer—and knows better than to talk—but other than that?" He chewed on the corner of his lip and shook his head once. "We have to find the fucking rat."

"Give me the word," Digger said.

"Sweep the club for bugs again," Hawk said, "and we can poke around enough to stir up shit that needs to let off enough stink we find the fucker spilling secrets."

"We're going to have to handle the other brothers with care." Jonny rubbed a hand down his stubbled cheek. "We start interrogating, and colors will be dropping on the floor. The brotherhood isn't what it used to be." He glanced at Digger. "Use tact when poking."

Digger dipped his head in agreement, but the hint of a smile pulled at the scar on the left corner of his mouth. "Tact is my middle name."

Hawk snorted, the closest to a laugh I'd ever heard pass his lips.

The ridiculousness I'd tossed out seemed to be forgotten, and we left the office not long after to down a couple shots together.

Helina

Turned out, I didn't need that morning-after pill. My monthly friend came calling a mere two hours after I'd kicked Capone out of my office while I'd stalked around my office, wide awake and pissy as hell. I realized that explained my mood, my need to treat him so shitty.

It's best that way, though, I told myself—for the tenth time—a few days later while sipping my coffee and leaning on the kitchen counter, the local news filling my ears with the lack of an update on the whole opioids bust and not having anyone to blame except the dealer they'd cuffed.

The guy was screwed. Getting caught with that kind of stash in a car, with obvious intent to sell...

Snorting under my breath, I flicked the TV off and strode back the hallway to the bathroom. I so didn't need that kind of shit in my life. Didn't want it.

But.

I couldn't stop thinking about the kiss that set my life off its axis. The gentleness, the tender emotion, never mind the soft fullness of his lips, his sweet breath I inhaled as deeply as possible, trying to pull him inside of me.

"Fuck." I whispered the curse with more anger than I truly felt. Trying to force my mind on my one client—my one source of income at the moment—and how to build my firm, I climbed into the shower.

Whether I wanted to admit it or not, Capone's "bullshit" while at the cooking class had given my self-confidence a boost. The man didn't know me that well, but his assurance, his certainty of what I would accomplish... A near-stranger, and his encouragement had given me the boost I needed to get my backbone straight again.

Two hours later, I sat in my office, staring at my computer screen, still pissy, still torn—trying like hell to work rather than daydream. Capone haunted my mind, the memory of him like the most stubborn witness who refused to be broken.

Needing to get my thoughts off Mr. Hottie Pants and his tongue, I picked up my phone and dialed Sarah since she'd gotten home from their short honeymoon the day before.

"Helina!" she answered, breathless, with a smile in her voice.

"Hey." I found myself smiling in return. "How was Nova Scotia?"

"Even better than I expected. Cold—don't ask me *why* David wanted to go there." Her light laughter faded my smile so damn quick, I frowned in a heartbeat. Her asshole husband had insisted on heading north after their spring wedding. Who the fuck wanted to go to Canada in April?

"There's still snow clinging to the ground in spots. And the winding Cabot Trail … just gorgeous."

"I'll bet it's even nicer in the summer when you can keep the windows down for the drive."

Sarah sighed. "A sandy resort in the Bahamas definitely would have been better."

I bit my tongue.

"We had a good time, though," Sarah continued, "and David really wanted to go there. His bucket list, you know." Her smiley voice sounded forced to my practiced ear. God knew, I'd heard enough of her excuses for her asshole man over the years.

I'd tried countless times to talk her out of marrying her high school sweetheart. A narcissistic prick who treated her like shit, like a doormat, a servant to cater to his every whim. Exactly the type of man who had donated sperm to my mom. I hadn't called him "Dad" since I was little. I never would ever again.

My teeth found the inside of my lip at the thought I might be falling into the same cycle my mom had. Beyond those eyes and hot body, was I attracted to Capone's badass reputation? His dominant nature? Just like Mom—twice over—she fell for men who controlled her, manipulated her into doing what they wanted rather than chase her own dreams.

I closed my eyes. *I can't get involved with a man like him… I need to stay strong.*

"Still there?" Sarah asked, drawing me back to the present.

"Yeah."

"So, how's your firm doing? All moved in?"

I blew a breath between my lips, slumping back in my office chair. "It's been one hell of a tough, bumpy ride, but I'm here now. Moving into the apartment upstairs in a couple weeks."

"Any new clients?"

"Just my cousin's divorce."

"Damn," she whispered. "What can I do to help?"

The sincerity in her voice eased the dent between my eyebrows. "You're the most giving person I know, Sarah."

"I'm serious."

"Okay." I found myself smiling. "I could really use a cheap secretary for a couple weeks—months."

"Oh. Well." Sarah cleared her throat. "David doesn't want me to go back to work."

I sat up. "What?"

"We're trying for a baby, and—"

"Already?"

"Yes, and he thinks we'll have a better chance of

conceiving if I'm at home keeping house. Less stress, and all that."

My frown reappeared. "Is that what *you* want?"

"It's not what I'd prefer, but if we're going to start a family, I want to do it right. David's mom was a stay-at-home mom, and he wants the same for me."

Yeah, I'll bet he does. "And what makes David happy makes you happy," I repeated what she'd told me a thousand times.

"Yes," she breathed the word as though relieved I understood her reasoning.

Again, I bit my tongue.

"So ... after the wedding ... you and Jeremiah?"

My eyes fluttered shut on their own as I once more slumped in my chair. I tapped my fingernails on the desk a few times before finding words. "Not really."

"I hear a 'but' in there…"

I heaved a sigh. "We made out. Met up again a week later, had sex, and I kicked him out."

My short but sweet confession must have rendered her speechless.

"You're not going to preach at me?" I asked when she didn't give her opinion on the matter.

"At least you got rid of him."

"And that's the problem." The words flitted through my brain and escaped before I gave them proper thought.

"What?"

I shrugged even though Sarah couldn't see me. "I can't get him out of my brain."

"He's no good, Helina."

Oh, but he is... I cleared my throat. "I know that, but my body hasn't figured that out yet."

"He's that good in the sack?" Sarah's whisper tugged on my lips.

"I'm *not* going to discuss David's brother with you."

"You know," Sarah's voice dropped even further, "I always thought David was jealous of him. He always treated Jeremiah like shit."

Too bad she couldn't see David's treatment of *her*. "Is David any good in the sack?"

"Best I ever had."

"He's the *only* one you've ever had."

Sarah giggled, but I failed to see the humor. One man, with nothing to compare him to... I couldn't imagine. It was no wonder she stayed with David. I should have gotten her drunk enough to sample some of the other fish in the sea, helped her realize how a woman should be treated.

"So what are you going to do?" Sarah asked.

"You said it yourself, he's no good. Just like the bastard who fathered me. Bad boy biker, deals in drugs, probably enjoys beating the shit out of people—"

Sarah's snort cut me off.

"What?"

"Jeremiah wouldn't hurt a fly."

"Explain." My voice took on a litigious tone.

"He's a softie. Always has been. David and his friends always used to make fun of him. Call him names, just like their dad did—does. That's why Jeremiah wrote off his family, I'm sure."

He held my hair back while I was throwing up. Respected my body when I'd passed out. Hell, I topped him from the bottom pretty damn easily—

"It's probably why he joined that motorcycle gang," Sarah continued as thoughts clouded my mind.

"To prove he was a *man*," I added as the picture of Jeremiah Caldwell became clearer in my brain.

"Probably."

"Is your father-in-law anything like David?"

Sarah laughed. "Looking at David's dad is like seeing my husband thirty years from now."

"And personality-wise?"

"Oh, they're cut from the same cloth, all right."

My frown deepened. "And I'll bet you're a lot like David's mother."

"Funny you should say that. She tells me that exact thing all the time."

Narcissistic assholes always went for the same type.

We chatted for a few more minutes before hanging up, and I stared at my black computer screen for a full five minutes.

I'd misjudged Capone's character, but that didn't change the fact he *was* a Fallen Glider. He ran with the wrong crowd, one known for its lawless ways, and therefore, a man I should avoid.

The mail slot on the front door clanked, drawing me to my feet. I'd already received that day's mail a few hours earlier—nothing but bills.

A small envelope with my name written on it lay on the mat.

I ripped it open, read the dozen lines, and was quickly swayed into going with what my body desired, rather than what I needed.

****

I chewed through an entire pack of gum while waiting in my car, the open windows allowing a spring breeze to ruffle my hair. It had been seven days since I'd kicked Capone out of my office, and a few hours since he'd slipped a note into my mailbox.

He apologized for coming off like an asshole—his words—and assured me that he supported whatever decision I made.

Realizing that I *had* misjudged the man thoroughly, I chewed every single one of my fucking fingernails clean off after breezing through my pack of gum.

Crisis averted, and I felt guilty as hell after realizing what sort of man Jeremiah Caldwell truly was.

I'd decided to talk to him again, but wasn't about to call Sarah back and ask for her new brother-in-law's phone number. The club it was, but I also wasn't about to force my way into the place demanding to speak to him like I'd done the first time. He had a reputation to uphold, after all. Patience wasn't one of my virtues, but seeing how he obviously wanted to change how he appeared, I could deal.

This time.

Parked a block away, I kept an eye on Capone's bike by the front door. Bikes and trucks packed the parking lot. A party from the looks of it.

The blonde bimbo bitch who had given us a hard time the first time I'd shown up at the club exited by herself around one in the morning. A minivan pulled up alongside the curb, and she glanced around real quick before climbing in. I yawned while staring at the broken taillight as they drove away.

My need for sleep tugged at my eyelids, but being the stubborn mule that I was, I shifted a few times, scanning the radio to keep myself awake.

It wasn't until after three in the morning that the final two Fallen Gliders left the club, locking it up behind them.

A burst of adrenaline shot thought me, setting my hand to shaking as I started up the car and eased into the club's parking lot.

Both men turned my way, the one beside Capone placing his hand inside his leather jacket. His not knowing my car, and my approaching in the dead of night, I expected he thought a gun would be necessary.

The second the streetlight hit my face, Capone's brother dropped his hand.

I turned the wheel to put the car sideways a good way away from where they stood, driver side facing them, and cut the engine. "Can I talk to you, Capone?" I called out, keeping my hands on the steering wheel where they could see them.

The two exchanged a couple words, and the second man straddled his bike, brought it to life, and left. The sound of his rumbling muffler faded in the distance before Capone walked over to my car.

"You okay?" he asked, leaning down to put his hands on the bottom of the window's frame, his face and blue eyes hidden in shadow.

"Yeah. Get in?"

He walked around the front of the car, head swiveling as though checking every dark corner—but not in the shifty way the blonde bitch had done. I unlocked the doors, and the second he slid into the passenger seat, his presence sucked all the air from my lungs.

Piercing blue eyes ate up my face until the interior's automatic light flicked back off, leaving us to play peekaboo in the streetlight's illumination.

"I got your note."

He nodded, but didn't speak.

"I appreciate your apology and your offer of support."

Again, he didn't utter a word.

"I'm not pregnant."

"You took the pill?"

"I didn't need to."

Capone heaved a sigh and relaxed back in the seat. "The idea of ending a pregnancy didn't sit well with me. I'm sorry for lashing out at you."

"A man telling me what I can or can't do doesn't sit well with *me*."

"I got that memo loud and clear," he said, the hint of a smile in his voice.

I studied his face in the semi-darkness, trying to figure out what the fuck to do.

"Come home with me and I'll make you an early breakfast," he said, sounding too much like a dominant alpha for my liking.

Raising my brow, I cocked my head. "Care to rephrase that?"

He chuckled. "Can you come over to my place so I can make you breakfast?"

"I *can…*"

His turn to cock his head, his smile growing. "*Would* you? Please?"

Even though I'd been determined to set us straight, not leave a string for guilt to hang onto, the man intrigued me to the point I told my inner voice all up in arms about being strong and independent to go pound sand. "I'd like that."

"Follow me," he said while climbing back out the passenger door.

Heart thumping, I started the car and eased out of the parking lot, realizing that I'd allowed a man to toss a command at me without a rebuttal.

Capone

Helina Bodnar sat at the island of my kitchen, cup of coffee in her hands. I turned my back to her as I cracked eggs into the iron skillet I'd fried up bacon in while the coffee had perked. I'd wanted to make some French toast, but she said she needed to watch her carb intake.

Whatever.

The woman's body rocked—made me hard every time I thought about the curve of her hips and round ass, but I kept the thoughts to myself.

Three-thirty in the morning, and I was acting the chef while sporting a hard-on rather than devouring every inch of her body. I'd considered slamming her against the wall and taking what my aching balls wanted, but she hadn't put out the vibes she'd agreed to come over for sex.

Breakfast, it was—unless she tossed an order my way to please her, which I'd be pleased as fuck to obey.

The toast popped, and I shifted sideways to pull the two slices from the toaster, grimacing at the press of my dick against my leathers. Why the fuck did her bossiness turn me on so much?

"You're way more comfortable in a kitchen than I am," Helina said, breaking the tense silence that had lingered over us for the previous twenty or so minutes.

Inwardly, I snorted at her word comfortable—I was far from it. "I went to school with Diane."

"So how did you end up a gang member rather than a chef with your own restaurant like her?"

My stomach twisted as I turned and set our plates on the island. "Long story."

She studied me with those damn cat eyes. "I don't have to be in the office for a few hours," she said, her lips twitching.

"Yeah, but you'll want to catch some zzz's before then."

Helina shrugged and picked up her fork. "Food looks good. Smells even better," she added after an inhale over the plate.

I sat with another grimace, adjusted the bulge between my legs, and dug in, hunger, tiredness, and lust all battling for dominance in my body. If Helina noted my discomfort or the hard ridge alongside my right thigh, she didn't say a word.

"Sarah told me about your father."

My head jerked up, and I forced myself to finish chewing the bacon in my mouth. "What about him?" I asked once I swallowed, a frown denting my brow as my dick lost all fucking interest.

"He's where David got his narcissistic asshole-ish-ness, isn't it?" She continued to peer into my eyes as though trying to reach into my soul and yank on all the unpleasant strings knotting up the memories of my life.

"What do you know about narcissistic assholes?"

"Mom finally grew the balls to leave my father, but she'd waited until he'd passed out drunk on the couch when I was five. He used to run with a biker gang like yours. Her second choice didn't run with a brotherhood, but he isn't much better than the first in my opinion."

"Shit." My heart sank as a million questions flitted through my damn head. "How much do you remember about your dad?"

"More than I care to."

I nodded slowly, my gaze flitting over the frown on her brow, the slight downturned lips. "You're lucky you got out early."

"You didn't."

"Nope." My fork clanked on the plate as I stabbed at a pile of scrambled eggs.

"Should I be afraid for Sarah?"

I chewed, considering. "David's an asshole, all right, but I don't think he'd ever lay a hand on her."

"What if she finally realizes he treats her like shit and decides to leave him?"

"Then she'll have me in her corner."

Helina continued to study me. "That's why you joined the Gliders, isn't it? Because no one was in *your* corner."

"I feel like I'm on trial here," I said, putting a twinkle of my hidden grin in my eyes. Fuck, did her intensity turn me on—even if we were discussing my shitty family.

She shrugged and finally looked away while picking up a piece of bacon. "It's what I do best... If only some more people in this damn town realized that."

"They will," I said, with confidence in my voice. "Might take patience and time, but your firm will grow. Just keep being you."

"Well?" she asked, glancing my way again with a small smile.

"Well, what?"

She lifted a brow and waited me out.

Damn woman.

Heaving a breath, I pushed my plate away and sat forward, propping my forearms on the island. "I joined the Gliders to prove to my dad that I'm not a pansy-ass or pussy like he always claimed I was. That I'm a manly man, just like my brother and his asshole friends."

Helina snorted and bit into her bacon.

"What's so funny?" Gaze glued to her pouty lips, I watched as she chewed, my dick getting harder again by the second.

"A real man is one who is emotionally mature," she said once she swallowed, raising her fork into the air and rotating the prongs in a circle. "Not an asshole who think the world revolves around him."

I lifted an eyebrow.

She forked up her last bite of eggs. "He knows his mind and heart, and has no issue with communicating what's in both."

"No such man exists."

She shrugged again while chewing. "I'm prone to agree."

"Should I feel offended right now?" I asked with a grin even though I'd said it first.

Light laughter puffed past her lips, and she placed her fork and knife upside down on her plate. "I don't know you well enough, but I'll admit to lumping you in with the rest of the men I've run across in my life."

"Because of what I chose to do with mine." It wasn't a question, merely a statement of what anyone in her situation would have done.

"Yes."

"I forgive you."

One of her eyebrows arched. "For?"

"Misjudging me." I held her gaze, a slow, lazy grin tilting my lips as hers twitched.

"So you're not an asshole?"

"Some might think so," I said, shifting on my stool, "but my insides are gooey as marshmallows melted in butter."

"Add a little snap, crackle, and pop, and you'd be one of my favorite downfalls." Her eyes twinkled, and I leaned into her personal space, holding her gaze.

"*You're* full of snap, crackle, and pop..." I let my voice trail off, hoping she understood exactly what I tried to *communicate*.

She tried to bite back her smile, but failed. "What exactly are you trying to say, Capone?"

She knows, but fine. I'll play her game. As if I could help myself.

I slid to the edge of my stool and leaned all the way in, pressing my lips against hers.

A quick inhale through her nose, and she responded, angling her head and opening as I licked across the seam of her mouth.

Coffee, bacon, and pure sweetness…

I groaned and slid an arm around her back, tugging her closer. Every swipe of her tongue, every nip of my teeth on her lush lips sent an ache through my cock. Again trapped between my thigh and leathers as I leaned forward, my damn dick fought for freedom.

Needing some space in my leathers, I pulled away, running a thumb over her swollen, lower lip. Eyes a bit hazed, she stared at my mouth.

"Want to sit on the couch and communicate more about our feelings?" I asked with another lazy grin.

Helina blinked and lifted her attention to my eyes. "Trying to prove you're a real man?" Her voice, all breathless and hitched, betrayed exactly what she felt.

"If that's what it's going to take for you to go out with me tonight and tomorrow, and the day after that, then yes."

Helina

Holy fuck, did his lips and tongue rock my world. My body honed in on the heat radiating off his as my focus narrowed in on getting what I wanted rather than staying strong.

"How about you put this to good use," I said, sliding my hand down along the hard ridge inside his leather pants while standing between his legs, "and then we'll talk about next time."

"Condoms are in my bedroom." His brow rose, those sleepy, blue bedroom eyes twinkling as he palmed my ass.

I smiled, feathering my fingertips over the swollen head of his imprisoned cock. "They had better be a different brand and newer than the last one you used while fucking me."

He groaned. "Same damn box."

His admission widened my eyes a bit. "Honesty. I like that."

"Am I still going to be able to put this to good use?" The lust in his eyes made me damn near cream my panties as he closed a hand over mine and squeezed his hard length.

I leaned in and tugged on his lower lip with my teeth, slowly pulling back until the plump flesh popped free. "Which way to the bedroom?" I whispered.

"Goddamn, woman…" He stood and lifted me, both of his hands palming my ass as I wrapped my legs around his waist.

He strode, and I sucked on his neck. He moaned, and I tangled my fingers in the longer hair atop his head. He dug his fingers into my ass, and I gyrated in his hold, pressing my pussy against his cock.

We fell on the bed, Capone planked over me, his

mouth devouring mine, blowing every thought out of my head. But, God … the *feels* he woke inside of me.

"Your mouth is sinful," he whispered against my lips. "Delicious. And the skin on the slope of your neck…" He skimmed his nose down to my collarbone as I clutched at his hair again, and lifted my hips to press my aching pussy against his hard length. "Your perfume drives me fucking insane." Flicks of his tongue along my neck sent shivers clear to my toes.

I panted beneath him as he shifted slightly off to my side, propped on one elbow, his free hand sliding across my stomach.

Flutters rippled through me as he skimmed first one finger then another beneath my t-shirt.

"I want to see every inch of you," he murmured, nuzzling my ear. "I want to taste you. Feel your tight pussy clench my cock as you come. I want to hear my name on your lips."

He sure as hell knows how to communicate what he desires… The thought curved my lips.

"What?" he asked, his fingers trailing up over my rib cage.

"I thought we were going to talk about feelings, not wants."

"What I feel for you is an unquenchable thirst. Silly butterflies in my stomach. It's like an eighth-grade crush all over again," he replied without hesitation.

I actually giggled, but it cut off as he rubbed a thumb over my aching nipple, a mere scrap of lace between us.

"You're all I've thought about since you walked down that aisle, a spicy cloud of that damn perfume filling my nose, your mere presence filling every space in my head. I can't sleep." He tugged on my nipple through my bra while tracing my ear with his tongue. "Can't even be bothered to consider one of the club whores no matter how much they offer."

"As a badass motorcycle gang member, I think you'd tap any willing ass."

"Not when Helina Bodnar is the only one I want."

My breath caught as he lifted his head. He peered down at me, his blue eyes nearly dominated by black pupils in the shadowed bedroom.

"Because I'm a challenge?" I asked.

"Because everything about you—all that damn snap, crackle, and pop—turns me the fuck on." The openness in his eyes—like a direct window to his soft soul—dragged me in deep. I found myself sinking and couldn't find a single fuck to give. "You're strong and independent. One hell of a fierce opponent."

"You aren't intimidated by that part of me?"

He shrugged. "A bit, but I find it sexy as fuck, too."

"What? The fact that's who I am or that you're a little intimidated by me?"

"Both," he replied with a small grin.

I tugged on the back of his neck, but he didn't need much persuasion to end the chit chat. Holy shit, had I misjudged him—thoroughly. He gave in to me, gave in to what I wanted without a second's hesitation, without needing to put on an alpha-like show.

Dangerous...

Capone peeled off my clothing one piece at a time, kissing and licking every inch, sweeping responsible thoughts I might have into the wind. Still trapped in his leathers, he settled between my spread thighs and ate me out like a starving man, tongue, teeth, lips … every lick and nibble stirring the caldron of need boiling through my entire body.

My skin flushed, heated through. I clung to his

hair, my thighs to the side of his head as he showed me how a woman ought to be treated. The second he slid two fingers deep inside of me, I combusted, my back arching and limbs trembling as I cried out his name.

I'm so damn screwed... The thought rang in my head as I lay catching my breath, my gaze on Capone as he yanked off his clothes. Dips and planes, muscles and sinew... I licked my lips, the aftershocks in my pussy clenching at emptiness.

"Hurry," I whispered.

Capone

One command from her lips, a mere whisper, and my body obeyed. I sheathed myself in record time and climbed atop her once more. Her legs wrapped around me as I slid in, fully-seated with one flex of my ass cheeks.

"Fuck." I groaned the word in her neck as she gasped against my ear.

"Yes."

An agreement with my thought or another command, I couldn't tell, but I went with the latter. Satisfying Helina lay at the forefront of my mind, driving me on with every slow roll and thrust of my hips. Keeping me in check from blowing my load too damn early.

Her pussy clenched around me, her whimpers and orders to go faster, harder, buzzing my brain.

Too fucking good.

Too fucking much.

I held her face in my hands and kissed her while sliding in and out of her soaked pussy. I devoured her mouth, tried to breathe in the exhales from her lungs in the hopes of trapping her inside of me.

She fucking owns me...

Strangely, the thought warmed my chest rather than knifing my gut. Groaning, I tilted my head back, lower lip between my teeth, eyes clenched shut as I thrust in and out of her, harder and faster, exactly as she wanted. Every muscle in my body trembled. Sweat dampened my skin. Helina whined beneath me, her thighs tight against my hips, her fingernails ripping at my back.

"Come, 'Lina. Please, fucking come." I slammed in deep and captured her mouth again, grinding my pelvis against her clit.

She let go, giving over to me. Back arching, she pressed her tits against me and clung fiercely to my shoulder blades, keeping our mouths fused as groans mixed between our lips.

My balls detonated, and with each thrust of my hips, I filled the condom with jets of my cum. "Goddamn," I half-croaked, fighting for breath as my cock continued to jerk deep inside of her. "Fuck, are you divine."

Drained and shaking, I propped on my elbows, our heavy breathing caressing the other's face as our foreheads met.

I wanted to cuddle, our heads sharing a pillow as we shared our thoughts. Our feelings.

Fucking teenaged pansy-ass...

Jaw clenched, I backed off, her legs and arms falling to the bed as though boneless as my semi slipped from her hold. What a fucking sight... Dark hair spread everywhere, chest still heaving with those plump, dark nipples. A shudder rippled down over her body.

"So good," she murmured before heaving a sigh.

"Does that mean you'll go out with me tonight?" I asked, a grin working at my lips as I studied her gorgeous body.

"Maybe."

Chuckling, I turned for the bathroom. A quick clean up, and I returned to find her unmoved. She reached for the warm, wet towel I had in my hand, but I pulled it back from her hand. "Let me."

Helina settled back once more, and I took my time wiping the slickness of her cum from her thighs. From between the swollen folds of her pussy. One last swipe over her clit caught her breath, and my cock twitched in response.

"You're like the worst drug," I said, tossing the washcloth aside.

She stiffened and shifted away as I stretched out beside her. "I have to go."

The fuck...

"Need to catch some of those zzz's," she said, grabbing her clothes up off the floor where I'd thrown them as though unfazed by what had rocked my world—the realization she owned me. Did she not feel it? Didn't she see what she did to me?

Frowning, I watched her tug up her panties, hiding heaven from me. "You're welcome to stay here—"

"I can't." She shook her head and continued to dress without looking at me, her movements jerky.

I found myself swallowing against sudden nausea. "What did I say?"

"Nothing." A quick, fake smile tossed my way, and she started toward the open bedroom door.

Nothing. "I thought lawyers needed to be good liars."

She pulled up short, hesitated for a few seconds—just long enough to send a rush of adrenaline through my blood—and turned. Eyes hard, she peered across the room at me, and I fought not to shrink against the mattress. "You might be a real man," she deadpanned, "but that doesn't dismiss what you've chosen to *be.*"

I stared, mute, as she turned and walked away. A minute later, my front door shut, the finality of that damn barrier between us knifing my fucking heart.

A drug... That's what I'd compared her to, that's what reminded her of what I'd chosen to be—a lawless dealer who profited from weak addicts.

I'm a fucking loser, I thought, pressing the heels of my palms against my eyes.

Digger had warned me a woman would someday break my heart, but never in my years had I expected a woman to wreck me in the way that Helina had done.

I fucking cried. An actual tear slid down my cheek, and both Dad and David's voices rang in my ears, calling me all kinds of names.

****

"Don't come in," Jonny whispered harshly over the line.

I blinked in the bright sunlight streaming through my open curtains, failing to process what he'd said. "The fuck time is it?"

"Don't come in," he repeated.

"What?"

"Chief Rosedale had a heart attack last night." Jonny's voice remained low. "Cops are here." He hung up.

Goddamnit. I glanced at the clock. *Ten.*

"Fuck." I clenched my eyes shut, my mind waking fully as realization of what Jonny had said rushed through my brain.

Chief Rosedale had a heart attack, which meant the asshole Deputy had probably stepped in to do what he'd been bent on doing for a couple years—take down the Gliders.

"Fuck!" I climbed out of bed with a groan and tossed my cell onto the rumpled comforter while glancing around the room. Helina should have still been in my bed, her head on my pillow, my sheets and blankets tucked up beneath her chin.

Jaw clenched, I grabbed a pair of jeans and a long-sleeve t-shirt from my bureau. Still bleary-eyed, I left my colors on the back of a kitchen chair, jumped into my truck, and pulled out of the driveway.

The fuck happened? While there'd been a hell of

a lot of tension in Jonny's voice, the club had sounded quiet behind him. Why the fuck had he told me to stay home?

I saw the flashing lights from three blocks away and pulled over when a shiver slid down my spine. Six cop cars parked askew in the club's lot. The three brothers who had apartments on the second floor stood in cuffs outside.

Shelly and another of the club whores stood by one car, arms wrapped around themselves, staring at the club's entrance.

Deputy Jenko himself strode out the front door, leading a cuffed Jonny.

"Shit," I muttered under my breath, my hands clenched on the steering wheel. While the alpha skin I struggled with demanded I go find out what the fuck had happened, Jonny's command rang in my ears, keeping my ass on the seat, and the truck in park.

If Jenko wanted to take down the Gliders, he wouldn't hesitate to cuff every single one of us for some reason or another.

Staying out of their clutches and figuring out how to help became my priority number one.

I pulled my cell from my back pocket and rang Digger.

He didn't answer.

I tried Maci.

"Capone!" She sobbed. "They must have found out. Oh fuck..." Another sob ripped from her throat.

"Calm down, Maci." I slunk down in my seat as two cop cars with my brothers in the back pulled from the parking lot and started toward me. "What the fuck happened?"

"Cops showed up at the door. They took Digger. Janie just called and said they hauled Hawk off in cuffs—didn't even give him a chance to put a shirt on!"

"They hit the club, too," I said while pinching the bridge of my nose and closing my eyes.

"You think they know about those two men? They must. Why else would they arrest Digger?"

"They took three Gliders from the club. Jonny, too. It's not because of *that*."

Jonny had warned us the law might be listening in—we knew better than to discuss details of the night Digger had taken two lives.

"Where are you?" she asked, hysteria still lacing her voice.

"I'm a few blocks from the club." I peeked up to find only two cop cars left in the lot. "They must have a warrant, so I'm sure they're pulling the place apart."

"They won't find anything, will they?"

"Of course not." Jonny didn't allow anything but alcohol in the club. Any brother found with illegal drugs—or caught high from them—found their asses thrown out. Twice, he'd demanded a brother's colors after a second offense. We might deal the drugs, but the using of said narcotics wasn't tolerated.

Talk about a fucking double standard. Twisted my stomach.

"Stay put, Maci. Let me make a call, and I'll get back to you."

My nerves remained strangely calm while thumbing through my phone for a number I'd never had to call but Jonny insisted I keep.

"Mr. Stanton's office." A polite, feminine voice answered after two rings.

"Morning," I said. "I ... uh ... need to talk to Mr. Stanton immediately."

"And you are?"

"Jeremiah Caldwell."

"Are you a client of Mr. Stanton's?"

"No. Well, yeah. Sorta. I'm a friend of Jonny Hayes."

"Jonny Hayes…" The secretary paused for a few seconds. "Oh. Yes." She didn't sound pleased. "Can you hold one moment."

It wasn't a question—she put me on hold where classical music flitted through the cell.

"Come on," I grumbled and ran a hand through my hair.

The line clicked. "Mr. Stanton."

"Sir." I sat up straighter at the commanding, low voice. "Jonny Hayes and a few other Gliders were just picked up out front of the club."

"Yes, I know."

"Jonny called already?"

"No." Mr. Stanton cleared his throat. "Mr. Caldwell, is it?"

"Yes, sir."

"I'll be honest with you, son. There's been a lot of trouble lately, personal stuff I'm unable to share, but at this time, I'm unable to be of assistance to the Fallen Gliders."

The fuck? "What?"

"Please inform Mr. Hayes that he'll need to seek representation elsewhere."

The line went dead, and I stared at my cell, fucking baffled. Jonny paid the Gliders' attorney well— too damn well even though the club hadn't had the heat down our necks for over twenty years.

"The *fuck*?" Cell clenched in my fist, I turned my attention back on the club.

Shelly still huddled beside one of the cruisers, unmoved from the last time I'd seen her, but a cop stood beside her, a tablet and pen in hand.

Frowning, I turned my focus on the front door. Cops came and went, empty-handed, thank fuck.

I chewed on the inside of my cheek. They wouldn't find any drugs, but we needed a lawyer in case they did find something that warranted bringing charges against us.

Another slew of curses flew from my lips. Couldn't go home in case they had a probable cause warrant out for my arrest, too. Sure as fuck couldn't go to the club.

The state would appoint an attorney, but I wouldn't trust anyone outside of our circle. Knowing Jenko, he'd be fattening someone's pockets to get what he wanted—the Gliders disbanded and out of town. My brothers needed a lawyer. Fuck knew I needed her, too.

Butterflies taking flight over the twist in my stomach, I started up my truck and pulled away from the curb.

Helina

A million "I never should haves" flitted through my brain, but the two then weighing heavy were sleeping with Capone and thinking I had what it took to open my own damn firm.

I sat behind my desk, staring at my black computer screen—again. Seemed that's all I did while in the office. Trying to think up ways of getting clients before I ran out of money. *Won't be long,* I reminded myself while moving the mouse enough to bring my screen back to life showing my online banking statement.

While I'd figured it would be a struggle for a while, I had really hoped a few of the clients I'd worked with at the firm in the neighboring town liked me enough to remain loyal to *me* rather than the bastards I'd slaved for. No such fucking luck.

I blew a breath between my lips.

Two months, tops. That's all I had funds for—if I ate ramen noodles rather than visit Diane's restaurant. If I ate toast and made my own coffee rather than hit the Dunks drive-through every morning. If I became vigilant about turning lights off when leaving a room.

Less than sixty days.

For the first time since setting my life on the course of becoming an independent attorney, a strong woman who wouldn't bow to any man, I faltered in my confidence. My stepfather had told me I would fail. God knew my real dad would have said the same thing—if he'd even been in my life to begin with.

My throat tightened, and for the first time in years, my eyes stung bad enough I couldn't keep the tears from welling.

Goddamnit. I swiped at my cheek as one broke free.

Failed...

I wanted to tell myself that I hadn't yet. I wanted to cling to those sixty days like a needy woman, but that, too, would make me like my mom.

Opening my eyes wide to help my eyes dry, I tipped my head back and peered at the high ceiling. A few slow inhales while counting to eight both in and out, calmed my emotions, but didn't ease the vise squeezing my heart.

Without help, I would fail, plain and simple. There was no way in hell I would succeed on my own. I swallowed back my disappointment, sending up a silent Hail Mary even though I'd left my mother's faith far behind. *Can't hurt,* I told myself, adding a second for good measure.

A knock sounded on the front door.

Seeing as how I couldn't even afford a secretary, I made my way into the reception area. The glass door allowed me an eyeful of the one person I didn't want to see again. The one man I needed to stay away from.

Every muscle in my body trembled as his stare liquefied my bones.

Goddamn him...

I unlocked the door but didn't step back to let him in. "What do you want?"

"I need a lawyer."

I snorted even though his eyes didn't twinkle, nor did his flat-lined lips suggest a joke. "You're not getting in my pants, Capone."

"No. I need a *lawyer*." The intensity of his gaze, and not the *I want to fuck you* kind, tightened my stomach.

I stepped back and motioned him in. "What happened?"

He strode into my office without answering.

"*Okay...*" I dragged the word out while shutting and locking the door again.

Capone collapsed into one of the chairs across from my desk and slouched down, running a hand through his hair. "Cops hit the club. They took Digger and Hawk from their homes."

I shouldn't have felt bad for him, but I realized I did while sitting down across from him. "Tell me what you know."

Took less than five minutes for him to fill me in on what he'd seen. "Can't let Jenko have a hand in getting the state-appointed attorney. I need someone I can trust."

Trust. I bit my lip as he studied my face, waiting for my answer.

"You've made it clear you don't approve of my lifestyle," he continued when I didn't reply, "but you're an incredibly strong woman, one who won't shirk her responsibilities as an attorney." Capone leaned forward, elbows on his knees, his blue-eyed gaze unwavering from my face. "I need that fire, Helina. That snap, crackle, and pop that has helped you win every single case you've argued."

I opened my mouth and shut it again.

"Google has lots of great stuff to say about you." A smirk crossed his lips, but dissolved within seconds. "I'll do whatever you need me to. Help in any way I can. Hell, I'll get on my knees and beg, Helina. Please."

My Hail Mary? I heaved a breath between my lips. "Here's what we're going to do..."

****

Twenty minutes later, I waltzed into the police station as though I owned the place, briefcase in hand. Capone's words of encouragement, his support, had boosted my flagging confidence. I'd ordered him to stay at the office in case there was a warrant out for his arrest, too.

I handed the secretary my business card and straightened my shoulders. "I represent the Fallen Gliders," I said by way of a greeting.

The woman eyed me from my messy bun to the black pumps I'd thrown on earlier that morning after dragging myself out of bed. I hadn't dressed for court, but slacks and a nice blouse at least made me appear professional.

"I'll let Deputy Jenko know you're here." She turned away, but I stayed put and kept my attention on her as she made a quick call. "A Ms. Bodnar is here claiming to be the Gliders' attorney, sir."

Claiming. I held in my snort.

She listened a few seconds before hanging up without a goodbye.

"He'll be right with you," she said. "Please have a seat."

"Thank you." Rather than sit, I moved back a few feet and remained standing. It took Deputy Jenko a full fifteen minutes to make it to the reception area, but I didn't fidget a single time.

"Ms. Bodnar?"

"Yes." I held out my hand.

He ignored the greeting, the skin between his eyebrows furrowed. Anger glinted in his brown eyes. "You're here for Jonny Hayes and the rest of his gang members?"

"I represent the Fallen Gliders, a social club that has given thousands to local charities here in town over the past forty years."

Lips pursed, he tipped his head toward the door he'd come though. "This way."

Chin lifted, I followed. "What are my clients

being charged with?" I asked once the door to the reception area clicked shut behind us.

"We have witness statements that gave us probable cause of illegal drugs to request warrants."

"Have formal charges been brought against any of my clients?"

"Not yet." He cut his words off, but he implied they would be.

Statements, as in more than one. Capone had informed me about the possible rat, but had the driver of that north-bound car filled with narcotics spilled the beans?

We stepped into a room, its one-way mirror revealing Jonny cuffed and sitting in front of a metal table. "Considering what these men *are*," Jenko said, his disgust all too apparent in his eyes and the downturn of his lips, "we're holding them here until the search is completed."

Twenty-four hours until they had to either let the Gliders go or bring charges against them...

I hoped like hell the cops wouldn't find anything in the club—exactly as Capone had said, but from what he'd told me, I wouldn't put it past Jenko to plant evidence, either.

Jonny's dark gaze landed on me as I passed through the door. He glanced behind me, and I straightened my shoulders, ignoring that he probably thought a second attorney—probably male—would be needed.

"Capone sent me," I said quietly. "I'm assuming you spoke with Mr. Stanton?"

Jonny dipped his head, his face unreadable, a mask of calm.

"Are you willing to let me represent you, or would you prefer a court-appointed attorney?"

"If Capone trusts you, I trust you."

I sat across from him. "I'm assuming they showed you a copy of the search warrant?"

"Yes."

"You haven't been charged with anything, but Deputy Jenko seems to think they'll find illegal drugs inside the club, and with them having hauled quite a few of the Gliders' asses in, they must believe there's enough evidence to convict you all for intent to distribute."

"They won't find any drugs inside the club."

He seemed so sure, so confident, that I rested easier in my chair. "He said there were witness statements that gave them probable cause."

"Lies. They won't find a damn thing."

"Have you told the deputy that?"

"I haven't said a single word other than to say I wouldn't speak without my lawyer being present," he said, "and the other Gliders know to do the same."

"Good. Deputy Jenko will be in shortly," I said while pulling a legal pad and pen from my briefcase, "so let me do the talking."

"Thank you."

I glanced up to meet his gaze. "Of course."

Capone

Helina texted me a few times in the next couple of hours, keeping me updated while I sat and stewed in her office. I called Maci then Janie, letting them know what was happening.

Every single Glider had a warrant out for their arrest because of two witnesses, one stating illegal drugs were in the club—a complete lie—and that our intent was to distribute.

The rat and the north-bound driver? Who else other than brothers knew about club business? Like Jonny had said, the club whores didn't know jack shit.

My cell rang, and when I glanced at the screen, I actually grinned. "Sweetie!"

"Capone." She half-choked on my name, sitting me upright in Helina's office chair. "Thank God! Why isn't Jonny or Hawk answering their phones?"

"Long-ass story, but a handful of the Gliders were arrested and are currently sitting at the police station downtown."

Her breath caught. "Oh."

"They showed up late morning with a search warrant."

"Good Lordy almighty," she whispered before landing a couple choice curse words—something I'd never heard pass her lips. "That's why my boys haven't been answering all day."

"You okay, Sweetie Jane?"

"N-no." I frowned, but she continued before I could ask why not. "I think I may have found what those police were after while cleaning early this morning. Jonny didn't make it in before I had to leave, so I took the box with me. Not about to let my boys get their hands on this stuff."

"Shit." I sat back real damn quick. "What's in the box?"

"Pills. Lots of them. Way more than a single man would be prescribed."

I cursed a few more times, realizing that someone must have planted the shit, because I'd bet my life none of the Gliders used. "Where'd you find it?"

"Under the sink in one of the third-floor rooms."

One of the hotel-like rooms outfitted for a quick suck or fuck. I scrubbed a hand down over my face. "Can you do me a favor, Sweetie, and hang on to it until I get in touch with you?"

"I'd rather flush it all down the toilet and torch the bottles and bags in my burn barrel out back."

"Even better idea."

She huffed. "Good thing I found it first."

"You're not kidding. I'll give you a call as soon as I know more, Sweetie. Thank you for saving the Gliders' asses."

I tossed my phone back onto Helina's desk after Sweetie hung up, sat back, and pinched the bridge of my nose for at least the tenth time in the previous two hours. Cluster fucked-up bullshit. Digger's poking around for the rat hadn't stirred up anything to the surface that I'd heard, and we had no other way of figuring out who spilled club secrets. What we needed to do was set a trap—once the whole warrant bullshit faded.

An incoming text chimed my phone.

Helina: **I'm going to be here a while. Since there's still a warrant out for your arrest, why don't you head to my place and crash. I'll be there when I can.**

I grinned, my fingers flying over the screen. **You're hiding a man from the law.**

Helina: **Don't give a shit since I know you're**

never going to be charged.

A chuckle rumbled my chest. **Awfully confident.**

Helina: **That's my job. Now do what you're told.**

I couldn't help but reply, **Yes, ma'am.**

I needed to tell her about Sweetie's news, but wasn't about to spill secrets over the line—just in case.

****

Four hours later, the squeak of Helina's bedroom door woke me up. I'd slept like a dead man, burrowed in pillows and blankets that smelled like her spicy perfume. Talk about fucking arousing ... surrounded by everything Helilna—except the woman herself. Not jerking off had been one of the toughest temptations I'd dealt with. Ever.

Exhaustion had eventually won out around one.

The overhead light flicked on, and I blinked against the light, trying to focus on the beauty approaching the bed. She kicked off her shoes and collapsed beside me, face down.

"You okay?" I asked, rolling and sliding an arm beneath my pillow.

"So damn tired."

"Why don't you get out of those clothes and burrow under here with me? I give one mean backrub."

Helina made a grunted noise of agreement and tugged off her clothes without standing. White lace bra. Thong panties. A flick of her fingers freed her lush breasts, but she collapsed onto the mattress before I thought to reach for them.

My cock swelled to attention with my groan, and I sat up, my fingertips trailing over the tanned, smooth skin of her back.

"Jenko's men still haven't found anything," she murmured, her cheeks smooshed on the pillow.

I pressed my thumbs into the muscles of her

lower back and rubbed in a circle. "They won't because Sweetie found it this morning."

Helina stiffened beneath me. "What?"

"Sweetie Jane—our cleaning lady. She found a box of narcotics in one of the rooms above the club."

"Does she still have it?"

"She told me she was going to flush them down the toilet and burn the containers."

A heavy breath blew between her lips as Helina sank back onto the mattress. "Who'd they belong to?"

"None of my brothers, I'd bet my life on that fact."

She moaned as I moved my hands upward, welling a drop of pre-cum on the tip of my dick. "You think that's the evidence Jenko spoke of?"

"The very evidence the rat planted before calling him, yes." I didn't hesitate to answer.

"Someone really wants to take you guys down, huh?"

I considered her question for a few seconds while working the muscles along her spine. Satiny skin... I breathed deep, inhaling her spicy scent deep into my lungs. "It would seem so. Once the boys are released, we're going to have to figure out a way to flush this rat from the club."

"They'll be out soon. I only left because I couldn't keep my eyes open and Jonny insisted I come home."

I continued working the muscles of her back until she grew lax, her breathing heavy—unlike mine, hers came from slumber.

Swollen and dripping, my cock demanded attention. A voyeur through and through, I lay on my back and palmed my dick while watching her sleep. I didn't even give a fuck if she woke up and called me a creepy fucker—I jerked myself to thoughts of my cock sliding between her parted lips, burying myself balls deep between her creamy thighs, and memories of her gasps and cries while coming.

With a grunt, I shot my spunk over my contracted abs and chest, spurts of white roping over my skin. Release, but far as fuck from the satisfaction of sharing the release with her.

Helina didn't stir.

My phone dinged, pulling me from deep sleep a few hours later. Somehow, Helina and I had ended up tangled together, her top sheet wrapping us up like a cocoon.

I worked an arm free and grabbed my cell off the bed stand.

Jonny: **We're out. Get to the club.**

A quick reply of a simple "K", and I glanced back at sleeping beauty to find her eyes blinking open. More green than brown, her catlike eyes focused on me.

I pressed my lips to her forehead as my semi-morning wood took note of her lace panties rubbing against my length. With a groan, I pulled back, fighting to untangle myself from the sheet. "I have to get to the club."

"They were released?" she asked, rolling to her back.

"Yeah."

I yanked on my clothes I'd left on the floor, taking note of the pre-dawn darkness around her blinds. Running a hand through my hair, I turned to find her studying me. One knee on the bed, I leaned over her, putting my face in line with hers, but not too close my breath would make her pass out.

"I can't thank you enough for what you did last night. Agreeing to help my brothers…" I shook my head.

"I hope you realize my doing this shows how much I trust in you—in your ability as a lawyer."

She nodded, still staring up at me, and fuck if I didn't want to rip off my clothes again and wrap myself around her body.

"I know that it puts you in an awkward position to defend us and our lifestyle you don't agree with," I said, forcing thoughts of her softness and warmth from my head. "Thank you."

She shrugged. "I'm desperate for clients."

Her honesty struck like a knife to my chest, and I backed off the bed without kissing her like I'd planned on doing. While I hadn't expected an "I did it for you," I'd hoped for something similar, something along the lines of revealing she cared about me beyond a mere wham, bam, thank you, sir.

"I gotta go." I turned and left without another word.

Struggling to deal with the knife in my heart, I dialed Jonny on the way and real vague-like let him know that Sweetie had found and disposed of some shit. He cursed the fact that she might have already destroyed the evidence, but I hadn't known about one of his secret contacts who could pull and run fingerprints. He growled for me to hurry the fuck up before cutting off the call.

Doubly feeling like shit, I drove the rest of the way in silence, wishing like fuck for a cup of coffee.

The club's main room was packed when I walked through the door. No music blared from the overhead speakers, simply a din of low voices filling the area.

I stood along the back wall, arms crossed, and nodded at Jonny when his gaze landed on me.

He raised his hand, and everyone quieted. "A few brothers won't be here for another hour or so, but I'm not waiting." His dark gaze scanned the room, and even I felt a shiver of fear lick down my spine at the determined glint in his eyes. "For those of you lucky enough to miss out on Jenko's hospitality overnight, I'll give you the short and sweet. Someone planted a box of narcotics here in the club and called the police."

Deadly silence lingered as he, Hawk, and Digger looked over the men, probably waiting for a guilty tell to pass someone's face. Even though I was a complete innocent, I still shifted as Digger's gaze swept over me. Had I not known, I never would have thought we'd shared women dozens of times. Cold-hearted bastard seemed ready to rip someone to shreds with the anger in his eyes and the veins and bulge of muscles in his crossed arms.

"Even though I'm tired as shit and pissed to fucking hell and back," Jonny said a few seconds later, "I'm in a forgiving mood."

Hawk scowled around the toothpick lodged between his teeth. Digger muttered a few curses.

Jonny ignored Digger and continued to study the unmoving, silent group before him. "If you're a rat, step forward now, and I'll end you quickly with a bullet between the eyes."

I swear I heard a fucking pin drop.

"I find out later it was one of you," Jonny continued when no one confessed, "and I'll smile over every scream to pass your fucking lips as the limbs are cut from your body. I'll feed your chopped off, shriveled dick and heart to the fucking sharks."

Digger actually grinned, a wildness in his eyes that sent a second shiver through me.

"Take the bullet," Hawk said, once more scanning the room.

No one stepped forward. No one so much as shifted—both those standing and sitting.

"No?" Jonny called out. "Last chance."

The club remained quiet another full minute.

"Okay." Jonny relaxed his shoulders, but his gaze remained piercing. "There's going to be some changes happening around here, first off being no more whores."

A few grumbles broke out.

"Not my problem if you can't get someone to suck you off outside these walls," Jonny said, quieting the men again. "But, if a single one of you gets picked up for being with a prostitute, or gets busted for propositioning an undercover cop, your colors are mine."

My eyebrows popped up.

"While I hate to even thinking one of you planted shit and ratted about it, I know it's possible. Every fucking one of you is going to sit down and have a little chat with the three of us," Jonny said, motioning to Digger and Hawk at his sides. "If you're loyal, you've got nothing to fear. I know this will piss a few of you off, but after being grilled by Jenko and the assholes working with him, I don't give a shit. It's time to clean house."

A few men nodded, glancing around as though trying to sniff out who might have turned on their asses.

If anyone dropped off the radar without telling the Gldiers' leaders, I wouldn't be surprised. Fuck knew, if I were the guilty party, I'd want to live. Only way to do that would be to get the hell out of dodge. Quick as fuck.

Helina

I shouldn't have felt guilty billing Jonny Hayes, President of the Fallen Gliders, but I did. Only a week after representing him and the dozen other Gliders at the police station, I sent a statement to the email address he'd told me to. He'd promised the Gliders paid in full, always on time—by wiring directly to a bank account—since they preferred to never owe anyone anything.

I imagined his owning the club free and clear must be nice. No bills hanging over the Gliders' heads.

With the rent due on my office, and my funds dwindling, I couldn't hold off on billing them. I had the money in the bank, but anxiety got the best of me. I sent the damn email, the word "desperate" ringing in my ears, but at least I hadn't charged him for the couple of times we'd spoken on the phone concerning club business and his cluing me in on things I needed to know.

Capone never called me. I never called him.

The way he'd walked out, the pain I'd seen in his eyes when I'd said I was desperate for clients, tore me up. I should have said something different, but unlike Capone, I'd never been good about sharing how I felt, especially the butterfly-type emotions toward a man that I'd never experienced before meeting him.

"For the best," I muttered to myself what I'd been saying since the morning he'd walked out. If only my heart would get on board with my head.

Blowing a breath between my lips, I dug back into my cousin's divorce file, needing to prepare for the upcoming court date.

Less than an hour later, I received a notification of the wire transfer.

Jonny had added a zero onto the bill.

"Mr. Hayes," I said when he answered. "This is

Ms. Bodnar."

"Did you receive the payment?" he asked, straight to the point as always.

"Yes." I frowned at my computer screen—at my bank account. "But it appears you added a zero onto your payment."

"I did." I opened my mouth, but he cut me off from arguing. "It's not a bribe," he said. "I'm not trying to grease your pocket and buy you off."

"Then what is all that extra money for?"

"For a job well done. For showing up at the drop of a hat without knowing jack shit about the Gliders and their business."

"I've been desperate for clients," I heard myself say again.

"Capone has had nothing but great things to say about you personally, and the track record you have... Well, I would like to keep you as the Gliders' lawyer—if you're willing."

A motorcycle gang president trusted me enough to hire me on for their future. They might be lawless, but I needed to recognize them as I had pointed out to Deputy Jenko—men who took care of their community in need. The YMCA's renovations they had helped fund. Our elementary school's special education department had monetary needs, and the Gliders had stepped in with a large enough donation, no further fundraising had been needed for two years. Countless other donations over the past forty years had helped those in need within the community.

I actually smiled as my thoughts eased. "I *am* willing."

"Glad to hear it," he said. "And one last thing."

"Yes?"

"About Capone."

"What about him?" My tone remained even, thank God.

"You hold his heart in your hands. I hope you realize what a treasure it is."

I found my lips twitching although my gut clenched. "Mr. Hayes, I never would have taken you for a romantic."

Jonny huffed. "I'm not." His gruff reply didn't change my thoughts, though. "Don't hurt him, Ms. Bodnar."

My lips flatlined, but I didn't take offense at the clear threat. "I believe I already did."

"He's been a miserable bastard all week, and to be honest, I'm fucking sick of it."

I didn't know what to say, so I kept my trap shut.

"He's loyal to a fault," Jonny continued. "One of the most generous, kind men I know. Soft as a squishy grape." He chuckled at the last word.

"He is, isn't he?" I asked, running a fingernail along the edge of my desk.

"He would lay his world at your feet if you told him to."

My smile returned at his choice of words. "Told, not asked?"

"He's submissive by nature, but that doesn't make him any less of a man."

I considered his words long after we hung up.

Capone

Helina: **My day sucked ass. Any chance you want to come over and cheer me up?**

I stared at the text a full two minutes. Did she want to get laid or did being with me actually make her happy? She had no qualms about voicing her wants or desires while fucking, but other than that? Other than pissiness, the woman didn't know how to communicate what she felt toward me.

Heaving a breath, I considered her invitation. Go to her place and have my heart ripped apart even more when she tired of me, or take advantage of every second she offered, every inch of skin she allowed me to touch and taste?

Fuck. I groaned as my cock swelled in my loungers.

I'd been fucking miserable since I'd walked out of her apartment. Miserable with the unrest in the club, my sole reason for being. My life was a waste. I had zero ambition to do anything beyond cooking since Helina had knifed me in the heart.

Having found that ball and chain—*love*—for that sure as fuck had to be what I felt for Helina, I didn't want to live my life without it. Wasn't fucking worth the effort.

Comparing her to a drug might not be what she wanted, but that's what she was to me. She'd entered my bloodstream with a blast of energy and life I hadn't realized I'd been missing.

When, I finally texted back, needing one more hit, regardless of how I might feel afterward.

Fucking drugs. We needed to stop dealing…

Helina: **I'm attempting to cook, so say six-thirty? You bring dessert.**

Oh, I'll bring dessert, all right, I mused to myself while texting back an affirmative. The woman was in for a special treat, the kind that just might show her how fucking perfect we were for each other.

****

Butterflies made my hands shake, and I scrubbed a hand through my hair before pressing the doorbell beside Helina's front door. She must have seen me coming—or was waiting—because the door swung inward.

Pink tinged her cheeks, her catlike hazel eyes meeting mine with a sparkle of light I hadn't expected. "Hey."

"Hey back," I said, soaking in every inch south of her smile. Deep cleavage I could get lost in. A little pink dress with the cutest damn apron of yellow and blue flowers. Didn't match worth a shit, but tied tight around her waist, the rounded bit of material accentuated her curves. "Damn, woman..." Legs bare from the knee down, including feet with pale, pink polish. "You look good enough to eat," I said, finally lifting my gaze to her face again.

Her smile brightened. "Thanks," she half-purred, all breathless and siren-like. "Come on in."

I stepped past her, fighting the need to adjust myself as her perfume swarmed over me.

"What sweet treat did you bring me?" she asked, reaching for the bag I held.

I pulled it back from her grasp. "Food first."

She rolled her eyes, her lips in one sexy pout I wanted to kiss away, but she turned before I made a move. "I hope it's okay..."

"What'd you make?" I asked, following her back the short hallway to the kitchen.

"You mean what did I *attempt* to make?"

I chuckled and set the bag on top of the island.

"A baked chicken, but I failed." She pulled a couple tins from the stove. Even the mitts on her hands made me want to bend her over the table—screw the place settings and single candle flickering between. "I got takeout from Diane's."

Biting back another chuckle, I moved toward the bottle of red and wine opener she nodded toward. "Can't go wrong with Diane's," I said.

"Don't laugh."

I let it fly. "Can't cook worth a shit, but you sure look sexy as fuck in that housewife get-up."

She snorted and put the bolognaise on the table. "Thank God I chose the type of career that will afford me a cleaning woman and takeout."

I wanted to offer my chef services on a daily basis, but still unsure of how she felt, I poured the wine and offered her a glass as she pulled up beside me.

"Cheers?" I asked, raising my glass.

"To my landing a new client," she replied, clinking hers against mine. "Thank you." Her voice had lowered along with the corners of her lips. "I know it was your doing."

I shrugged and sipped the room temp red.

"I've never had a man believe in me the way you do."

"Then they're blind. Or, just plain stupid."

Her smile returned along with the twinkle in her eye as she lifted her glass.

"Thought you had a bad day?"

Helina's smile widened, and she turned away, her ass swaying while walking to the table.

I let my groan out and followed to pull out the chair for her.

"Thank you." She tugged the chair forward, and

unable to help myself, I pulled her hair across to one shoulder and pressed my lips against the one I'd bared. Her head tilted to the side as she sighed, and I allowed myself a few more tastes of her neck, breathing her in so deep that my dick ached.

I stepped away, and she let out a huffed exhale. "If I wasn't so damn hungry," she said, "I'd tell you not to stop."

Grinning, I settled across the table from her. "I thought lawyers needed to be good liars," I said—same as I'd done before.

"What'd I lie about?" she asked, one eyebrow raised while dishing out the pasta.

"The bad day."

"Oh." She smiled and finished plating our food. "About that." Wineglass once more in hand, she twirled the stem between her fingers, her gaze on the red liquid inside. "It was bad in that I was disappointed in myself."

"For?"

"For the judgment I'd placed on you since we met at the wedding." She sipped and put the wine back on the table. "You offered forgiveness the other morning over breakfast, and I never even apologized."

"You were right to think the way you do." I twirled some pasta onto my fork, not meeting her steady gaze I swear I could feel on my face. "I've chosen a lawless lifestyle, one known for its violence and disregard for manners."

"But..."

I shoveled the forkful into my mouth, finally lifting my attention to her face. She watched my lips while I chewed. "But?" I asked once I swallowed.

"But the group you've aligned yourself with also is known for its generosity. Its support of the local people."

"Doesn't make our wrongs right."

A small smile tilted her lips upward. "No, but everyone—lawyers included—have, shall we agree, unsavory bits in their lives."

"No one's perfect," I agreed, twirling another forkful. "So, no more judging?"

"No, but there's more."

I raised an eyebrow, waiting.

"I want to apologize for calling you out and embarrassing you in front of your brothers. For assuming you're an alpha asshole like the bikers in my past. For using you for sex."

I grinned. "I'm ready and willing to be taken advantage of in that way *any*time, 'Lina."

She bit back her smile. "I won't apologize for my dominate nature—"

"It's sexy as fuck."

"—but my means of communicating my emotions could definitely use some work. Can you find it in yourself to be patient with me?"

"I *could*."

Helena narrowed her gaze. "Will you? Please?"

"I'd love to."

Both of us smiling, we ate in earnest, filling the holes in our stomachs while chatting about our childhoods and narcissistic assholes.

I stood beside her, drying the dishes she washed, wishing like hell I could do the same thing every damn night.

"More wine?" she asked, once we finished.

"How about dessert instead?" I grabbed the bag, and when she made a noise of agreement, I pulled out a Tupperware container, my back toward her.

"What is it?" she asked, trying to lean over my shoulder as I pried off the lid.

Container in both hands, I turned, my gaze gluing to her face. "A taste of what we could be."

"My weakness…" She breathed the words and jerked her gaze up from the homemade Rice Krispie treats.

My pulse fucking raced, but I needed to throw it all out there, get the broken heart over with if that's what lay in my future. "We're a perfect fit, Helina Bodnar. All that snap, crackle, and pop—your fire, your strength … I want it all."

"No man has ever supported me like you do," she whispered. "No one has edified me the way you have."

"They're blind," I said again.

"They're not real men," she replied, a twinkle in her eyes.

"Not man enough for you, no."

"Are you man enough for me, Jeremiah Caldwell?"

I cringed at the use of my full name. "I'm the only man for you—and you know deep down that I speak the truth. Tell me to stay, Helina."

She picked up one of the gooey squares. "Don't go." Half of the treat disappeared between her lips in one bite.

"You couldn't just say what I told you to, could you?"

"Get used to it."

I all but tossed the container back onto the island behind me, grinning like a fucking fool. "Yes, ma'am," I said, grabbing hold of her waist and yanking her against me.

She tasted like the most divine slice of heaven. My heaven, my ball and chain.

The End

DEDICATION

For those who stayed too long but finally found the courage to leave.

FALLEN GLIDERS MC: VOLUME TWO

JONNY

Fallen Gliders MC, 5

Lynn Burke

Copyright © 2019

Jonny

"Not a goddamn fucking thing."

Digger's words dropped like a rock in my gut, and I grimaced. "No leads? Nothing?"

He shook his head, and I glanced at Hawk. Toothpick between his teeth, he, too, shook his head.

"Fuck." I pressed the heels of my hands against my eyes and leaned back in the old office chair I had inherited from my father when I'd taken over as the president of the Fallen Gliders MC. It'd been pretty much nothing but a major shitstorm since.

A still-unknown snitch, one of my oldest brothers and best friend handing in his colors, Digger himself shot and almost beaten to death, arrests because one cop refused to be paid off … and no woman had gotten me off in long enough I couldn't remember the last time.

Never mind the sliver of jealousy eating away at my gut over the fact three of my brothers had fallen hard in love over the previous year, claimed their old ladies, and become changed men whether they knew it or not.

"I need a fucking break," I grumbled, dropping my hands to my desk. A bottle of Hennessey and a shot glass sat ready and willing to offer what a good, hard fuck should have—relaxation and a quiet brain. Downing one burning shot didn't help. The second, at least, had me sitting back in my chair and heaving a steadier breath.

Digger and Hawk watched me, unshifting, their faces closed off and unreadable. Both men had all but interrogated every single club member in an attempt to find out who was the rat trying to shut us down from the inside out. I'd expected a couple men to get pissy over all the questions and take off, but no one had handed in the colors since the arrests almost two weeks earlier. If anything, our club felt more tightly knit. Camaraderie, bro hugs, and all that bullshit. Should have settled my mind, but it didn't.

As president of our club, it was up to me to make decisions, but my fucking brain was about fried from stress I usually had no issues dealing with. I needed to get my fucking rocks off. Hard and thoroughly. "What the fuck do we do next? What *should* we do at this point?"

Digger shifted, glancing over at our Sergeant at Arms. "Hawk?"

Dark, hazel eyes peered at me, eyes that only revealed a hint of emotion when talking about or hanging with Janie. Hawk shifted his toothpick to the other corner of his mouth with his tongue. "If it wasn't one of our brothers—and we're sure as shit it wasn't," he said, "then it's gotta be one of the whores. Bring them back into the club."

I'd kicked them all out after spending the night in jail, putting the club on lockdown until we got the shit figured out. Hawk definitely had a point. "Consider it done."

Hawk glanced at Digger. "I'd tell you to tie them up one by one and work the truth out of them, but I don't think Maci would go for other women being wrapped up in your ropes."

The hint of a smile twisted Digger's scarred lip into what looked more like a scowl than a grin. "Tying a woman up doesn't have to be sexual. Say the word—" he turned toward me, "and I'll get whichever bitch it is to squeal."

I glanced at his clasped hands and the veins popping along his thick forearms, but shook my head. I refused to be like my father who had used his fists on whoever pissed him off—my mother and his countless girlfriends after her death included. While I wanted answers, I wouldn't lay a hand on a woman with the intent to hurt—unless we agreed beforehand on a little pain play and safewords. "We'll bring them back, but just keep an eye on them."

"We could set them up one by one," Hawk said. "The bitches like to talk, but if we do something discreet, we might catch the one leaking our secrets."

"Feed them false information." Hawk nodded as I clarified what he meant for my own tired brain.

Digger nodded, too, turning toward me, elbows on his thighs as he leaned forward. "We'll catch them, Jonny. I'll catch whoever it is red-fucking handed and take care of the problem."

A shiver licked down my spine, and not the pleasant type. I'd seen Digger "take care of the problem" a handful of times. The man was cold-blooded and cruel, regardless of the teddy bear Maci claimed him to be.

Loyal and fucking fierce, and I wouldn't have him any other way. And knowing Hawk would be beside him, assisting in whatever way necessary ... I was thankful as fuck for both of them.

"We still have to lay low on the drug trafficking," I said, drumming my fingers on my desk, determined to focus on the other issues battling in my head.

"Shouldn't be a problem," Hawk said, moving his toothpick around again. "The rental properties more than cover the club's expenses."

I nodded, but my thoughts turned toward where they often did when it came to the club making money—going legit. We fed the fucking drug epidemic in New Hampshire, and it had been our shit that Nicky's sister had OD'd on, swaying him to hand in his colors the spring before. I'd lost my best friend because of how we chose to make money.

"I'm considering going legit," I said, glancing from one man to the other.

One of Digger's eyebrows shot up, but Hawk didn't flinch.

"With marijuana legal as of yesterday in this state," I continued when neither spoke, "I'm thinking we ought to open a couple lounges—like a bar, but for smoking pot. With how sales have been going according to the news..." I let the thought die off and waited for their thoughts.

"Capone said something about going legit a few weeks ago," Hawk said, peering at me, but his expression didn't reveal jack shit of what he actually thought.

"And ever since, I've found the idea more appealing with each passing day and every fucking problem we encounter."

"Digger?" Hawk glanced over at the blond, non-jolly giant.

Digger shrugged. "Doesn't matter to me. I'm here for my brothers—and none of us do the shit we deal, anyway. Capone grows weed, most of us smoke it on occasion—actually makes sense to clean up our image.

Stay out of jail and out of trouble." His mouth twisted again. "Not that I wouldn't miss that last part."

I found my lips twitching, threatening to smile. "You could always be the head of security detail at the lounges."

"Doubt there'd be any need for skull bashing with a bunch of high, laid-back customers who laugh at everything and think unicorns shit fucking rainbows."

Hawk actually chuckled. "That must have been some pretty good shit Capone gave you last week."

Digger scowled at Hawk. "Fucking unicorns... You're not going to let that one go, are you?"

My lips definitely tugged upward. "I'd suggest keeping your pot-induced dreams to yourself, Digger. Your image is safer that way."

A snort huffed through Digger's lips as he sat back, arms crossed. He opened his mouth, but a light knock sounded before Capone poked his head in the office door. "Your burgers are up," he said with a grin and twinkle in his eyes. The club's pretty boy was one hell of a cook and had landed a badass woman who happened to be a lawyer—and a damn good one who I kept on retainer. One who'd painted up our image with Deputy Jenko, the asshole cop who had it out for us. Sure, we'd donated to charity a shit ton more than my father had since I'd taken over, but that wasn't enough to make some look away for when we didn't.

"Be out in a few, Capone," I said. "Thanks."

"Beers for you guys?" he asked, turning toward Hawk and Digger. Both men nodded, and Capone shut the door behind him.

Digger grumbled something about loose tongues while Hawk stood, stretching his back out.

"We can talk more on the future of our club over the burgers," Hawk said, his face deadpan, all business once more. "And Digger and I will make a plan to trip up whichever club whore is spilling our secrets."

"Good, because I don't think I can handle any more fucking problems—"

Capone opened the door—without knocking—and the twinkle and grin on his face had disappeared. "Hawk, there's a woman here looking for Janie. She's ... uh ... beat up pretty bad."

"Send her in," I said, my protective nature on auto-pilot when it came to women getting hurt.

Capone dipped his head and turned, motioning someone beyond the door into my office. "Go on in, darlin'."

My dick swelled for the first time in a long-ass motherfucking time as she walked over the threshold. The woman shuffling into my office had more than enough curves to fill a man's hands, long, highlighted blonde hair perfect for yanking on, and the most alluring blue-green eyes—surrounded by purplish bruises. Full lips, split and scabbed.

Gorgeous and battered, a fucking problem I didn't have the time or energy for even if my dick actually wanted to get wet.

"I-I'm looking for Janie..." The woman glanced at Hawk.

"And who the fuck are you?" he asked, towering over her by a good foot.

"Alexa. I'm a friend of hers—" She glanced at me. "From New York."

New York and Janie... "Did a Demon do this to you?" I heard myself ask through the sudden ringing in my ears as my dick fucking shriveled back to its usual limp state.

Alexa swallowed and dipped her head once, clasping a small purse against her stomach.

Fuck it all to fucking hell.

"Hawk, get Janie over here. Now," I said, pouring myself another shot.

A Silent Demon, our arch rivals, had beat the shit out of the first woman to grab my attention in over a year. Could my life get any fucking worse?

Alexa

The man behind the desk pebbled my skin the second his dark, piercing gaze landed on me. Already a nervous wreck from walking into the Fallen Gliders club that smelled like the Demons'—like tobacco, booze, and sex—I fought the need to fidget. Swallow against rising nausea.

Coming here was my only option. Reminding myself of what I'd been saying the entire drive from New York didn't lessen the tension stringing my body tight even if it was true.

The cops from back home didn't give two shits about a Demon's ex-wife and the countless restraining orders I'd attempted to get in order to protect me from Scott's fists. Enough money lined their pockets they looked the other way when told to.

Seeking asylum with the one group of men who wouldn't be swayed by the Demons had become my only option since everywhere else I'd tried to disappear to over the previous few months had been found out. My latest facial discoloring came thanks to a cousin I thought I could trust.

"Who did this to you, Alexa?" the man with the piercing eyes asked, his palms on his desk as though resting. I swore, though, that tension locked him up tight, same as me.

"My ex." I cleared my throat. "My ex," I repeated, a bit louder. "A-a Demon." I glanced at the other two men making the office feel much smaller than it was. One tall and dark, a toothpick between his lips and hazel eyes that seemed to read into every damn word I managed. He wouldn't believe a word I said.

Neither would the blond standing to his feet. Easily over six foot, he, too, peered down at me, muscled forearms crossing his chest. A ragged scar twisted the corner of his lips and lay beneath the beard on his jaw up toward his left ear.

"Why come here?"

I turned back toward the man behind the desk, and an actual tingle of awareness of his being a hot as hell man shifted me on my feet. "The Demons can't reach me here. They don't own you."

The blond snorted. "Fucking far from it."

"Hawk, call Janie," the man still sitting behind the desk said.

The hazel-eyed man pulled a cell from his back pocket, but strode out of the office before speaking.

"Have a seat, Alexa."

The low voice rumbled through me, sending another tingle through my body and settling between my thighs. Thighs bruised from Scott taking what he thought he still owned. I sat on the edge of the chair facing who must be the president of the Gliders' club—Jonny Hayes.

"Th-thank you for allowing me to come in."

Jonny's gaze slid over my face, probably taking in the bruises I hadn't bothered trying to hide with makeup. I figured pity might get me through the front door—and it had by a gray-haired man named Sniper manning the front door. Jonny's focus lingered on my mouth, but I fought off the desire to lick the sudden dryness from my lips.

Knowing sex might also help me get into their club—if the men liked bigger girls—I'd opted for a lower cut tank top, one that spilled enough of the girls out to snag a man's attention. The tank top also revealed the bruising teeth marks Scott had left beside my collar bone—and the fact Jonny's perusal hardened my nipples.

"Fuck." Jonny muttered the word, his gaze once more sliding back up to my eyes. "The motherfucker should be behind bars."

"He would be," I said, sounding more breathless than I'd have liked, "if the Demons didn't own the cops down there."

"Fuck," he muttered again, scrubbing a hand down over his face.

Hawk came back through the door. "Janie will be here soon. She's actually right down the road with Maci."

A shuddering sigh rippled through me, and I slouched back in the warm leather the mountainous blond behind me had vacated. "Thank you," I whispered again, my throat tightening and eyes welling. Any normal person would have feared relaxing with the three men covered in tatts and ripped like they made out with gym equipment more hours of the day than not, but they didn't carry the same ... energy of the Demons.

While they were big and intimidating as hell, for the first time in a long while, I felt safe.

Lips pursed, Jonny dipped his head and motioned the other two from the office. "Go eat your burgers," he told them. "When's the last time you ate, Alexa?"

"Lunch. Yesterday."

"Tell Capone to throw another burger on the grill, Digger."

"Will do." The low, rumbled reply of the blond shivered over my skin, but far from a sexual way. His tone spoke of bottled anger. Restrained wrath. Probably the Sergeant at Arms...

"Shot?" Jonny asked, pouring a glass full from the bottle on his desk.

"Yeah." I swallowed back another surge of nerves and the damn feminine interest that had gotten me in trouble with Scott in the first place. "Sure." I would never let another man touch me again. I would never be a possession to any man, ever again.

Jonny slid the shot glass across his desk, and I leaned forward to take it from his grasp.

His warm fingers closed around mine, but it was the darkness in his eyes that caught my breath rather than the electrical charge sliding up my arm and straight down to my clit. He didn't say a word—his gaze said it all: Fuck with me or my club, and you'll wish you'd never been born.

I dipped my head in acknowledgement, knowing I had nothing to hide, and he released my hand.

A heavy breath left his lips as he sat back in his chair, bottle still in his hand. "To better days, Alexa," he said, lifting the bottle toward me.

"To a better life," I said, lifting the shot glass. The burn, so fucking sweet, slid down my throat.

"You look like you could use another, but you should eat first."

"Yeah." I sat the shot glass back on his desk. "Yeah, I should."

"How long have you known Janie?" he asked, tipping up the bottle for another swig.

"About ten years."

"How long were you married to the asshole who did this to you?" He motioned toward my face, a glint in his eyes.

"Too damn long," I whispered, my throat tightening again, "but I didn't have the balls to leave, you know?"

"Yeah." He swigged and put the bottle down on his desk. "I do know. My mom hung out too damn long, too."

Our gazes snagged again, and my breaths sounded heavy even through hints of the eighties music from the club filtered through his closed office door.

The latch sounded, and I jumped, turning. "Janie!" I hopped up, and she hurried toward me, her face pale.

"What the fuck, Alexa!" She held out her arms, and I went willingly, the tears I'd been bottling up for over forty-eight hours letting loose. "Scott?" she asked against my ear as I soaked her shoulder.

I managed a nod.

"My father and the goddamn cops didn't do a damn thing, did they?"

"No."

"Motherfucking asshole deserves to die a slow fucking death."

I couldn't have agreed more, and as I rested my cheek on Janie's shoulder, my tears drying, I couldn't help but notice Jonny's gaze lingering on me. My skin pebbled again, but I turned away, shutting him out and mentally nailing down the "on" switch his dark eyes flicked inside my body with every glance.

Jonny

I couldn't get the image of Alexa's battered face out of my mind. Long after I collapsed on my bed later that night, I stared at the dark ceiling, my ears buzzing from the silence. The mattress beneath me lumped like never before, making for one hell of an uncomfortable night, never mind the unrelenting hard-on Alexa had talked my body into raising.

Damn dick had issues, the kind I'd actually gone to the doc for. Little blue pills had gotten the job done for a short while, but didn't bring back the desires I'd felt as a much younger man. Only in my forties, and my dick felt like it'd been halfway in the grave.

But Alexa...

"Goddamn." My mutter accompanied my hand sliding down over my abs to grab my aching length. I should have been happy at the steel-like rod, but the fact it'd sprouted up because of a fucking Demon's ex kept my brow furrowed.

"Fuck it."

I jerked myself, smearing the oozing pre-cum down my length and back up, my hips rising to meet my hard grip. Teeth clenched, I gave over to the need to blow my balls empty for the first time in a long-ass motherfucking time.

Imagining Alexa's blue-green eyes gazing up at me as I slid my slickened cock between her plump breasts had me groaning and spurting shots of cum up over my chest in a matter of seconds. Rope after rope of sticky white, hot as fuck, landed on my skin as my body spasmed, mouth gasping, head tilting back while my forearm flexed to milk myself dry.

One last spurt, and every muscle in my body went limp. My mattress hadn't ever felt so damn good. The buzz in my ears was overtaken by my thumping heartbeat. I breathed easy, my mind empty—for all of about ten seconds.

A cool evening breeze slid over my skin, and I heaved a sigh. While I didn't feel like moving, I didn't want my spunk drying and making a scratchy mess on my skin.

I groaned and rolled off the bed, intent on another hot shower and, I hoped, a good night's rest.

****

Bleary-eyed and tired as fuck, I stopped by Hawk's bike shop rather than head straight to the club. I'd already downed almost an entire pot of coffee before leaving my house, but the stress of bullshit hanging on my damn shoulders had me on the verge of curling back up in bed and calling it a day before nine even rolled around.

"Morning," Hawk called as I stepped through the door, a blast of heated air and the scent of grease and gasoline hitting me in the face.

I dipped my head and shoved my hands in my pockets, checking out the late model Harley's exhaust he attempted to replace. "Digger not in yet?"

"He's rarely in before ten anymore." Hawk grunted, arms flexing as he fought to loosen one of the bolts holding the flange onto the head.

I stood and waited for him to finish up, glancing at the bike Digger had been working on for me. Couldn't blame the man for taking his good old time. If I had a woman like Maci in my bed every morning, I wouldn't be so quick to leave either.

"What's up?" Hawk tossed the nut into an old coffee can and grabbed a rag.

I shrugged.

He peered at me while wiping his hands. "I saw

the way you looked at her the entire fucking time she, Janie, and Maci sat at the bar yesterday."

A muscle ticked in my jaw. "How's she doing?"

"Seemed more relaxed this morning, but Janie is full of piss and vinegar." Hawk moved toward the small office. "Coffee?"

"Sure."

He grabbed two Styrofoam cups and poured from the old-as-shit pot on the corner of his paper-covered desk. Piping hot and bitterly strong, the brew burned on its way down to my empty stomach.

"Janie wanted me to invite you over to dinner tonight."

My brow shot up as I sipped again. "What?"

"Dinner." An actual twinkle lit Hawk's eyes. "As in she cooks, you visit, and the four of us sit at my kitchen table and eat together."

I narrowed my gaze. "Is this some kind of matchmaking game?"

Hawk huffed a chuckle. "Guess Alexa was asking about you while they chatted last night."

"What'd she want to know?"

He sipped, his gaze steady on my face. "If you had an old lady. Shacked up with anyone. That sort of shit."

"Fuck."

"I told Janie to let it lie, but you know her when she's on a high."

"Yeah." I heaved a sigh. My sister dealt with the same bi-polar problems that afflicted Hawk's woman.

"So you coming?"

I snorted a laugh, my mind falling straight into the gutter.

One of Hawk's eyebrows shot up as he lifted his cup.

"She's gotten under my skin," I admitted, my lips still tilted up.

"Well, fuck. Now you have to show up."

"Can't fucking get involved, Hawk."

"Why the fuck not?"

I stared at him in silence for a few seconds, knowing he wasn't a dumb fuck. "Seriously? A Demon's ex?"

"I claimed the damn president's daughter."

He had a point. His and Janie's hooking up had almost caused an all-out war between the two clubs.

"They've been divorced for almost a year," Hawk said, sitting down behind his desk and propping his feet up on the corner. "She hasn't stepped foot into their club for almost double that time."

I sank into the chair across from him, but leaned forward, my elbows on my knees, steam rising from my coffee to waft up my nose. "Anyone know she's up here?"

"Alexa didn't tell anyone where she was headed when she packed up all her belongings and lit out yesterday morning."

"Family? Friends?"

"Not much family to speak of. It was a cousin that ratted her out to her ex this last time she tried to run and hide from him."

"Fucker."

Hawk nodded, the glint in his eye revealing the same anger stirring in my gut. "Fucking family turning her over to the bastard."

I shook my head, fighting the desire to crush the fragile cup between my hands. "Why come up here?"

"Alexa looked out for Janie when she first started going to the club—kind of like an older sister—and they've been in touch ever since. Janie told her about the kind of men that make up our club."

One of my eyebrows shot up. "Meaning?"

"Big teddy bears."

I snorted over the stuffed animal both Janie and Maci compared us to. "Alexa knew we would protect her."

"Exactly. So, dinner?"

I narrowed my gaze again as that damn twinkle lit in Hawk's eye.

"She's the first woman to catch your eye in years, Jonny."

"Fuck."

"Nothing wrong with feeling things out a bit."

I wanted to feel out things, all right. Every inch of her pale skin, every swell and indent from her toes to the tips of her blonde hair. My dick twitched just thinking about it.

"I don't need any more trouble," I said, although every part of my body except for my brain climbed aboard the "let's do this" train.

Hawk stared at me, gaze unwavering. "She's good for you, Jonny."

"Why do you say that?"

"'Cuz I know just about every fucking thing there is to know about you."

"True."

"She's the softness you're looking for. The kind of woman who would lay her life down for the man who loved her the way she needs. Loyal. Honest." Hawk shrugged, but I didn't second guess his read on her. The man hadn't gotten his Sergeant at Arms badge for nothing. "She's submissive, too. I'd bet money on it."

I scrubbed a hand down over my face, muttering a few curses. It was no secret in the club that I had a heavy hand when it came to women's asses. Most of the whores over the years had sported my handprints for days on end.

"It'll probably take a lot of fucking patience and tenderness on your part before she'll let you lay a hand on her in that way, though."

"Is she a danger to the club?" I asked rather than delve into the kink that used to grab hold of my mind and dick.

"I doubt her ex would come traipsing up here to our territory where he has no sway over the law."

I chewed the inside of my cheek, contemplating.

"I'm confident enough that I told her she's welcome to stay in my spare room for as long as she needs to."

Hawk made the decision an easy one for me, and I dipped my head while standing. "She's welcome in the club, then."

"Dinner?" Hawk called as I turned to leave.

My dick twitched again. "I'll come."

Hawk's chuckle followed me out the door.

Alexa

Thank God for concealer. I moved my head side-to-side, tilting my head this way and that in the mirror, pleased to find hardly any trace of bruising on my face. I'd slept like the dead in Hawk's guest bed, feeling safe for the first time in years.

I hadn't told a soul where I'd taken off to, and no one had followed me all the way from New York. There was no way in hell Scott knew where I was. I'd left my boorish job as a secretary, without giving a two-weeks' notice, months earlier when first taking off in attempt to escape him. Not that my old asshole boss didn't deserve it. A lawyer with pockets lined by the Demons, I'd realized too damn late he'd been the one telling Scott my every move.

"Bastard," I muttered, stowing my concealer stick back in my small makeup bag. Jobless and homeless—and I'd never been more at ease. I'd used the last of my savings to fill my gas tank in the old beater, but it had gotten me to a place I felt sure would be safe.

I peered into the mirror one last time, butterflies flitting around in my stomach.

Janie had invited Jonny for dinner. The Fallen Gliders president, a stern alpha-appearing man who sent all kinds of delicious shivers down my spine even if Janie said the club rumors whispered he liked to get rough in the sack. While Janie had sung his praises and claimed the man was a big teddy bear like Hawk, I couldn't help my hesitation over getting to know him better.

I didn't need another biker in my life. I didn't need another dominant asshole thinking he could control my life—or use his hands to enforce what he wanted for or from me.

Dinner, I told myself by way of a pep-talk. *Make friends, the kind that will help me rather than rat out where I ran to.*

I blew an exhale past my lips and let myself out of the bathroom. The scent of baking potatoes grumbled my empty stomach. I hadn't eaten much—or well—since I'd basically been on the run, and even though I'd lost ten pounds of the excess weight Scott had always complained about, I still struggled with insecurities about my figure.

Never a skinny bitch, I had curves to spare. Double Ds and hips made to bear children I'd wanted when first hooking up with Scott. He'd been heavy-handed from the get-go, but I'd been so enamored with his good looks, that I thought I could help mellow him out. Change him for the better—or at least learn to like the pain he assured me would lead to pleasure.

It never had.

I'd gotten an IUD not long after we'd married. He'd wanted kids, but there was no way in hell I would give him one until he changed his ways. That didn't stop the fucker from trying to plant his seed in me every chance he got, even after I'd divorced him and attempted to keep him away with restraining orders.

New beginning...

The heaviness lifted from my chest as I meandered into the kitchen to find Janie, pink-cheeked and wearing an apron. "Hey, Suzie homemaker."

She laughed, her green eyes bright. While on her high, her love of life proved infectious to everyone around her.

"What can I do?" I asked, sidling up to her at the counter, smiling.

"Want to chop some carrots for the salads?"

"Sure." I grabbed a knife from the knife block in

front of me, and Janie slid a cutting board my way.

We'd talked until close to two in the morning, and while I'd taken a nap after lunch, she'd tackled repainting the third bedroom to make into her office. The woman had more energy than the pink bunny in those battery commercials while on the high side of her rollercoaster.

I'd seen her crash, though, and the fact she'd found a man who loved her beyond her issues, according to her, sent an ache through my chest. A pang of desire for the same—a man who would love me for me, allow me the freedom to just *be*—almost made me want to give up my determination to never let a man lay a hand on me again.

My throat thickened, and Janie hip-bumped me. "Excited?" she asked.

"For?"

Janie huffed a low laugh and grabbed four bowls from the cabinet above our heads. "To hang out with the man who has your panties in a twist."

"My panties are not twisted, thank you very much."

"Liar."

I glanced over at her, brow raised as she tossed a handful of spring greens into the salad bowls.

"You were full of questions last night—and over lunch. Don't pretend you aren't interested in Jonny."

"Is that why you invited him to dinner?"

She giggled and hip-bumped me again. "Hawk said you're the first woman to catch Jonny's attention in months."

I hated that a thrill shot through me. "Meaning?"

"Meaning," Janie drew the word out while opening the silverware drawer, "that none of the club's skinny bitch whores have been able to get him up *or* off in a long-ass time."

"Sheesh. Is there anything you and Hawk *don't* talk about?"

"Nope." She popped the "p" and giggled again while pulling out some flatware.

Even though the thought he found my curves sexy set butterflies alight in my stomach, I rolled my eyes and went back to chopping the baby carrots I'd lined up on the board. "Kind of private info there, don't ya think?"

She shrugged and spun toward the table behind us. "Hawk said it's no secret Jonny's been jammed up the last year or so."

"What makes Hawk think I caught his eye?" I glanced over my shoulder, watching as Janie danced around, setting the table.

"He knows the man almost as well as he knows himself. He thinks you're good for Jonny, too."

"Hawk doesn't know me from Adam."

"He's an excellent judge of character."

"I'll bet you told him all about me," I muttered, turning back around.

"I may have said a few things—all good, promise."

I gnawed on the inside of my lower lip while thinly slicing the carrots. For the first time in longer than I remembered, the idea of having a man between my thighs didn't turn my stomach. To find a man who wasn't a prick, an unselfish lover…

The memory of Jonny's dark, piercing gaze dampened my panties.

It had been a hell of a long time since arousal had hit me in such a way, and I couldn't decide if I liked the warmth spreading through me or not.

I never wanted to be called wife or belong to a

man ever again, that was for sure, no matter how sexy or hot said man might be. Jumping in the sack with another biker even just to scratch the sudden itch Jonny had caused might give him ideas of making it out to be more than I would ever allow.

Hawk came through the front door, and my breath caught at the sight of the man behind him.

Damnit. My heartbeat kicked up a few notches, and my panties were done for, but my head. My head screamed *retreat* loud enough I questioned the wisdom of making "friends".

Jonny's gaze landed on my face, and I felt the scrutiny of his intense eyes across the kitchen.

Janie threw herself into Hawk's arms, legs wrapped around his waist as she attacked his mouth.

Jonny glanced at the two of them sucking face, and turned back toward me, one eyebrow raised.

I found myself laughing beneath my breath and shrugging. "Guess they kind of like each other," I said, my voice a little shaky.

"Guess so." He slipped his leather jacket off his shoulders, and my mouth dried.

Nothing sexier than a ripped man in a tight, white t-shirt. While Jonny probably had a handful of years—if not ten—on me, the man sure as hell took care of himself. A few lines lay at the corner of his eyes, and gray hinted in the dark hair above his temples, but beneath his neck? He could have been taken for a twenty-something with the hard dips and valleys of his body. Black leather pants clung to every inch of him from the waist down, including the bulge between his thighs.

Saliva rushed back to coat my mouth, and I swallowed while ripping my gaze off him to focus on the carrots. My hand trembled, and I put the knife down, deciding there were more than enough carrots chopped for four salads.

"Hope you boys are hungry," Janie said, a little breathless. "Want to go fire up the grill with me, baby?"

"Hmm." Hawk hummed his agreement and grabbed a couple beers from the fridge.

I busied myself putting the carrots on top of the four bowls of lettuce Janie had readied.

"Be right back!" Janie giggled and scooted out the door once more with Hawk.

Jonny stayed behind, beer in hand, focus on me. "How are you?"

I had to swallow again from drool and nerves alike. "Better than yesterday," I said, trying for a smile.

"Get some sleep last night?"

"Finally, yes."

"Hawk told me you're going to stay with them for a while."

I nodded and moved toward the table to put the salads by each plate. The weight of Jonny's stare kept my heartbeat thumping, my skin tingling.

"You're welcome at the club."

My attention shot toward him even though Hawk had already told Janie as much over the phone earlier in the day. Jonny swigged from his bottle of beer, dark gaze on my face while swallowing.

"Hawk says you're good people, and I trust him above everyone else."

Sudden tears filled my eyes, and I turned away to put the final salad on the table.

"Hey." The warmth of his touch on my elbow stilled me. "You okay?"

A mere foot from me, the slight scent of soap, hops, and mint clinging to him weakened me in the best way possible. "Y-yeah," I managed to say, but didn't pull away from the first man's touch I'd experienced without cringing.

Jonny glanced down to his hand still cupping my elbow and lifted his focus once more to my face, a question in his eye.

Temptation to lean into him, to accept the comfort he offered, played with my mind, and I stared up into eyes darker than the smoothest chocolate. Sexual energy charged between us, making it hard for me to breathe.

Jonny's gaze flitted down to my lips, and I realized I'd licked the lower without meaning to.

His bottle clinked on the table as he set it down, and my breath caught again as he lifted his hand and brushed my hair back over my shoulder, his fingertips feather-light over the skin of my neck.

Goosebumps spread down over my entire body, and I shivered, completely trapped by his gaze and torn between wanting to close the distance between us and scurrying away to find a hole to hide in.

"You and your gorgeous curves are one temptation I don't need right now," he murmured, his focus dropping to my lips again, "but I sure as hell *want*."

Good Lord almighty, the man didn't waste time or mince words. Tell him ditto or pull away?

The door opened, deciding for me, and I stepped away as Jonny's hand dropped from my elbow.

Janie smirked at me and flounced over to the canister she kept cooking utensils in beside the stove. "Don't mind me." She winked, grabbing the tongs and marinating steak off the counter before hurrying back outside.

Jonny chuckled and sat down, beer once more in his hand, his legs spread enough I found my attention drawn to his bulge again.

Janie hadn't been lying, I realized, my face going hot. I'd gotten him up, all right, but his hard length, trapped behind black leather, lay along his right thigh, thick and long instead of attempting to tent his leathers. Mouth watering, I tore my gaze away.

Jonny

Alexa smelled like ripe peaches, and the mere brush of my fingertips against her skin had swelled my dick to the point of aching within seconds. Her parted lips and the tongue that flicked out to lick the lower had me biting back a groan.

I'd wanted nothing more than to pull her into my arms, crush her curves against my body, and devour her mouth, but the tenseness of her shoulders, the hesitancy in her eyes kept me in check.

The last thing the poor woman needed was a horny bastard wanting to ravish every inch of her lush body.

Thank fuck Janie came dancing through the door when she had, because the temptation to taste Alexa, regardless of her fears, almost had my self-control caving to desires I hadn't experienced for longer than I remembered.

Alexa had haunted my dreams the night before and the daydreams as the hours passed at the club while waiting for dinner. The woman had gotten under my skin after a few hours at the club the day before, and I wasn't sure what to make of that fact.

Spewing out what I had about wanting her had been a mistake. Alexa didn't once meet my gaze while we ate dinner. The two times I brushed close to her while the four of us cleared the table and went outside to sit by Hawk's small firepit, she shied away from me.

Alexa had been hurt, both physically and emotionally, and keeping those facts in the forefront of my mind became a necessity. The last thing I wanted was to intimidate or scare her.

The slight bruising hidden beneath her makeup drew my gaze time and again, twitching the muscle in my jaw and twisting my stomach. I wanted to rip her ex's head from his body with my bare hands. Saw his dick off with a dull knife. Drink down his screams as I swung a hammer to crush the fingers he'd used to bruise Alexa.

I'd never been an advocate of abuse in any form, and before leaving for the night, I promised Alexa she would be safe with the Gliders. Walking away, my chest aching almost as much as my balls, I vowed that I wouldn't pursue her in any way. I would keep my hands to myself, my thoughts on how much I wanted her, too.

****

The whores started trickling back into the club over the next week. Digger and Hawk set up a plan to entrap whichever bitch felt the need to plant the drugs my cousin Sweetie Jane had found before the cops just happened to show up with a search warrant—and spill secrets whoever it was had no right knowing. The two men made a list to cross off as the whores cleared themselves by not misbehaving and taking the bait my brothers laid out.

Rather than sludge our way through them one by one, however, Digger said to leak secrets to a few at a time—knock down the list faster.

The first handful to sit at the bar got an earful of bullshit I'd told Capone to toss out about an opioid shipment arriving Friday morning at one of the apartment buildings I owned.

On the morning of the fake delivery, Digger, Hawk, and I sat in a car a few blocks away from the apartment complex. Two other brothers pulled in with the truck like Capone had said they'd do, but no cops, no Feds sped in to make an attempted bust.

Four whores off the hook.

That night, the club rocked, and the Gliders partied in celebration of having the easy pussy back. A handful of old ladies and other women—Alexa along with Janie and Maci—tore up the floor, shaking their asses.

Digger stared at Maci and Hawk at Janie while I tried to talk over the eighties music blasting overhead. I gave up, poured myself another shot of Jack Daniel's, and decided to drink up my fill of Alexa while sipping my whiskey.

Goddamn, the jeans she wore clung to her body like skin, every wiggle of her hips and shake of her damn ass tingling my hands with the itch to redden every inch.

"Jonny."

I felt the brush of breath against my ear and leaned away, peering up at one of the club whores who'd been around the longest. "Shelly." I dipped my head in greeting and dismissed her from my mind while turning back to watch Alexa.

Shelly didn't take the hint, but she rarely did. She slid onto my lap and grabbed my dick through my leathers before I could blink. A smile tilted her lips as she found me hard. "Well—"

I lifted her off me before she could say another word. "Not interested."

She glared down at me, hands on her hips. "The fuck, Jonny?"

I glanced back over at Alexa to find her scowling at the whore. My balls tightened, and I lifted my gaze once more to Shelly. She glared across the club at the woman who'd snagged my attention. "Who's the fat skank?"

My blood fucking boiled in a split second, and Hawk tensed beside me. "She's not a club whore like you," I all but spit. "She's a goddamn goddess and Janie's friend—therefore, she's my friend."

Still frowning, and without a word, Shelly spun

on her heel and flounced away as though uncaring a woman beside her had managed to turn me on.

Not that she had in a long, fucking time, anyway.

"Fucking jealous bitch," Hawk muttered loud enough I heard him.

Jaw clenched, I turned back toward the dancing women.

Alexa's focus stayed on Shelly as she walked away, her brow furrowed, until Janie hip-bumped her, drawing Alexa back into dancing.

Hawk elbowed me, and lifted his beer up as though saying "cheers". Digger glanced from the women, to me, to Shelly, and back again, his brow raised.

I shrugged and downed another shot, my head pounding from the thumping bass. A few seconds later, the song ended, and a slower one began.

Hawk and Digger left me alone to grab their women. Janie ended up wrapped around Hawk's waist, Maci's mouth plastered to Digger's.

Alexa slid onto the vacated seat beside me, and I slid a shot over. "Drink?"

"Thanks." She actually met my gaze, but her smile wobbled. I hated that fear of me made her unsure.

She tipped her head back and swallowed, and I tore my stare off her smooth throat. "They're really in love, aren't they?" she asked, sliding the glass back in front of me.

"Yep." I poured another and offered it to her, but she shook her head. "They're lucky."

I expected she hadn't meant for her murmur to reach my ears, but it did, and I couldn't have agreed more. My two best friends held their women close, lost in each other.

"Ever been in love?"

Alexa's question caught me off guard, and I

glanced over to find her peering at me, her gaze vulnerable for a change. "Not like that, no. You?"

She heaved a breath and glanced back at the dancing couples. "I'd thought so once, but Scott turned out to be a different man than I thought he was."

"Men like him deserve to be castrated and thrown into a pit of snakes."

Alexa turned back toward me, her eyes searching my face. "Janie said you threatened to take a Glider's colors if he hurts a woman outside of consent."

"I'd do more than that," I said, praying like fuck she believed me. "Not every man on this earth is an abusive asshole."

A smile flirted at the corner of her lush lips, and my dick leaked inside my damn leathers.

"I would never hurt you, Alexa."

The smile faded as she peered into my eyes. "I believe you." The half-whispered words barely reached my ears, and even though I had vowed to myself to leave the woman alone, I found my hand lifting toward her hair.

Silky strands slipped between my fingers as I toyed with the ends on her wavy tresses, close enough to her breasts I could have brushed my knuckles across the nipple pebbled beneath my stare.

I dropped my hand back to my lap. "The last thing I want to do is push you, Alexa. And I told myself I wouldn't pursue you, but…"

She stared at me, lips parted, pupils dominating the blue-green of her eyes.

I didn't know what else to say. Spout off how much I wanted to sink into her body, taste her mouth? Spank her round ass red and fuck her tits?

"Fuck." I scrubbed a hand down my face. "Sorry."

"You don't have anything to apologize for."

I shook my head. "The last thing you need right now is a man trying to get in your pants."

"All I see is a man trying to fight and win against lust."

I lost myself in her eyes. Fucking gorgeous eyes, lined with smoky liner and fringed by black, curly lashes. "Janie said you would never hurt me."

"I would cut off my fucking hand first."

Her gaze flitted over my face as though weighing the truth of my words.

Fuck it. I held out my hand.

Lower lip between her teeth, she peered into my eyes long enough I doubted she wanted me as much as I did her.

She slipped her cool palm against mine, and I pulled her sideways onto my lap. "Tell me to stop, and I will."

"I don't want you to," she whispered, and I leaned in, brushing my lips over hers.

I moved slow and gentle, going lightheaded from the softness of her mouth, the sweetness of her breath. One taste, and I knew with a certainty, I would never be the same again. Alexa grasped at my shirt, pressed into my body, lighting a fucking fire in my blood. Every muscle in me tensed with the need to take, but I held myself in check, keeping my hands on her waist rather than roam like I wanted to.

The tip of her tongue flicked over my lips, and I groaned, allowing her to lead even though I wanted to plunder. Unable to help myself, I grasped the nape of her neck and tilted her head, deepening a kiss I never wanted to end.

Alexa melted against my chest, and I lost all train of thought, all awareness of our surroundings while drowning in her softness.

A bump against my elbow brought me back, and I tore my mouth off hers to find Hawk and Digger had returned to the table, their women hanging on them.

My heart thudded in my chest as Alexa blinked at me, lips parted and pulse thrumming beneath the skin of her neck.

The music blared once more, but no one made a move to go dance. My thumbs rubbed in circles on Alexa's hips as I fought to get my head atop my shoulders to work, dominate the one between my legs.

"We're heading out," Janie half-hollered over the once more blaring music, and Alexa tore her focus off my face and nodded, but I didn't let her get off my lap when she tried to push up.

"Stay," I said when she glanced back at me.

She worked her lower lip between her teeth.

I held her gaze, praying like fuck she saw the truth in my eyes—that I wouldn't hurt her, just like I'd claimed.

"Okay." I read her lips more than heard her, and she relaxed into me once more.

Satisfaction—happiness—settled inside of me, and I slid my hand down her thick as honey thigh to squeeze her knee.

Digger and Maci left not long after Hawk and Janie, and I realized I didn't want to hang out at the club either.

I tugged Alexa close once more, my nose beneath her ear. "Want to get out of here?" I asked, my heart thumping, actual butterflies wrecking my insides.

She nodded, and I took a few seconds to breathe in the peach scent of her skin, taste the softness beneath my lips. A shudder trembled her in my arms, and I pulled back, searching her face. "My place or back to Hawk's?"

Ball in her court, I waited.

"Yours," she finally answered, and I didn't waste any time setting her on her feet, clasping her hand, and striding toward the front door.

Capone gave me two thumbs up from behind the bar, eyes twinkling and grin all but splitting his face.

We needed to talk about his thoughts on going legit with marijuana, but that could wait.

I needed to show Alexa how gentle a man could be.

Alexa

My heart beat in my throat, and although my head second guessed the decision I'd made, my pussy throbbed with the need to be filled. Heading back to Jonny's meant sex, of that I had no doubt, and although I should have been scared or at least hesitant to move so damn fast, I couldn't help myself.

Stupid? Probably, but the need coursing through me didn't give two shits.

I wanted Jonny, fuck the consequences. He'd initiated the kiss we'd shared, but he let me lead, let me control the pace. And, God, could the man use his lips. Like a bird in flight, my mind had emptied, shivers licking my skin as he'd tasted me, his gentle tongue sweeping into my mouth, melting every inch of my body.

Jitters trembled through me as I climbed onto his bike behind him and wrapped my arms around his waist. Hot and hard... *God.* I laid my cheek against his back, breathing in the scent of his soap, his body heat soaking into my front—and soaking my panties. The fact a gun was tucked in the back of his waistband didn't stop my body's desire.

The bike rumbled to life, and we pulled out into the night, wind whipping at my hair. Eyes closed, I smiled and mapped out his abs rippling beneath my hands. Scott would have grabbed my hand and shoved it between his legs, but Jonny only tensed beneath me, letting out a few curses as he slowed for a stop sign.

It took all of maybe five minutes, but it felt like forever before we pulled into a driveway beside an old two-story Victorian lit by a far-off street light. The garage sat back a bit farther than the house, its door automatically rising as he rumbled toward it. Once inside, the engine cut off, and I stood on shaky legs, wiping my palms on my jeans as Jonny climbed off his bike.

I stepped back outside to take in the old mansion-like place. The house could have been a bed and breakfast place—huge, beautiful, and immaculate. Manicured lawn, herb garden, and flowers perfumed the night air. Not what I expected at all. "This is your house?"

"Inherited it from my grandparents."

"It's beautiful."

Jonny unlocked the side door, stepped back, and motioned me inside. "It's a work in progress, so ignore the mess."

The kitchen hadn't been updated like the outside. An old green stove looked well-used but clean, and the linoleum floor creaked as I walked inside.

Jonny shut the door behind us and tossed his keys on the butcher-block island on wheels in the center of the room.

I faced him fully, yet unsure of how to proceed—it'd been so damn long since I'd *wanted* a man.

He held out his hand, same as he'd done at the club, and the second I slipped mine into his, he pulled me in, wrapped his arms around my waist, and held me, chin resting on the top of my head. "I want you in my bed, Alexa, but if it's too much, too soon, we can hang out in the living room."

I eyed the old stairs against the far wall thinking I wanted nothing more than to be spread out across his bed, his hands and mouth on me. "The bedroom's upstairs?"

"Yes."

I stepped back and laced my fingers through his. "It *is* too much, too soon, all things considered, but I haven't felt this kind of need in so long ... I can't even remember feeling this kind of want before." I swallowed against my nervousness. "But it can't be more than this, Jonny. I'll never be a possession again—no man's old lady. Just tonight, okay?"

Jonny squeezed my hand, the fire in his eyes lighting one in every cell of my body. Without a word, he led me across the creaking floor, up the equally creaking stairs and down a hallway leading toward the front of the house. Three other doors lined the carpeted hallway, but he pushed in the fourth, drawing me in behind him while flicking on a lamp by the door.

A wrought-iron frame, two old bureaus...

That's all I caught sight of before he cradled my face in his hands and claimed my lips.

Heaven. Home.

The two words flitted through my brain, but Jonny's kiss, his sweet breath, and gentle hold wiped all thought from my brain. I simply felt ... the softness of his lips, the heat and wetness of his tongue searching out my mouth, his warm palm on my cheek, the other snaking through my hair. He didn't tug—but I felt sure he wanted to with how the tension in his body hummed against me.

I clung to him, unable to get close enough. Wrapping one leg around his waist and grinding my throbbing clit against his hard length was absolute torment. Too many clothes, too many feels.

My whimper had him stepping back, his brow furrowed while searching my eyes. "All right?"

His low tone rumbled through me, and I clenched my thighs together. "That noise escaped because I want more, not because I'm afraid."

Lust flared in his eyes, and he ripped his t-shirt off overhead.

My breath caught at the sight of the muscles I'd

explored while on the back of his bike. Ripples flexed down over his abs, and the V of his hips and the dark, happy trail disappearing beneath his leathers watered my mouth.

Jonny pulled the gun from his waistband and stuck it in the bed stand, turning once more toward me.

Swallowing, I reached out and ran my hands over his prominent pecs, down those hard ridges and indents, straight to the bulge straining for release.

Hands fisted at his sides, he let me explore at my leisure.

I made short work of the clasp and zipper keeping me from what I wanted. He groaned as I reached in, wrapping my hand around his hard cock.

"Fuck." He grabbed hold of my hand. "It's been a long time for me, Alexa."

His confession surprised me—what biker bad boy would admit to such a thing? "Me, too," I whispered, squeezing beneath his hold, peering up into his dark eyes.

Silence settled over us except for the heavy breaths we shared. Jonny slowly slid my hand down his length to the root of his cock and back up, his jaw clenched, but pulled our hands away before I could smear the pre-cum at the crown down over him.

Cock sticking straight out from the opened leathers, he reached for the hem of my shirt, a question in his eye.

He likes your curves…

Still battling insecurities over how I looked naked, I nodded and lifted my arms, helping him rid me of the constricting clothing keeping us apart. I kicked off my shoes as the cool air kissed the lace of my bra and bare skin. My fingers fumbled at my jeans button, and he once more closed his hands over mine, helping me.

Jonny pushed my jeans down over my hips and

sank to his knees while sliding the denim to my ankles. Hand on his hot, hard shoulder, I tottered on one foot then the other while stepping out of the jeans.

"Christ, Alexa." He ran his hands over my thick calves. "You're so fucking gorgeous."

He kissed my knee, my thigh, and I grabbed hold of his head as he bypassed my pussy to kiss my belly button. All-too aware of the softness around my middle, I bit my lower lip, but he brushed his stubbled cheek across my belly, his eyes closed while palming my ass and squeezing—not hard enough to hurt, but again, I felt sure he wanted to and held back.

"So soft," he murmured against my skin, dragging his lips down over the front of my satin panties. Nose buried against my clit, a rumble sounded from his chest. "So damn sweet." He tipped his head back and peered up at me, and my knees trembled at the desire on his face. "I want to taste you."

My head jerked up and down on its own, and still holding my gaze, he slipped his fingers alongside my hipbones and pulled my panties down past my knees where they floated to the floor on their own. He leaned in, and my teeth found my lower lip … the tip of his tongue sliding up through the seam of my pussy lips pulled a moan from me, but I couldn't look away from his face.

No man had ever made such noises while lapping up my arousal. No man had ever held my gaze, letting me know with his face, his eyes, what he thought of my pussy, my flavor. I couldn't fill my lungs. Couldn't control my trembling.

Jonny latched onto my clit, gentle flicks of his tongue setting off the telltale tingles in my toes that led to climax.

"G-going to come," I gasped, and he rocked back

on his heels, his lips glistening in the lamp's light.

Without a word, he stood, reached behind me and unclasped my bra.

My too-large breasts spilled out, hanging heavy, nipples pebbled. He filled his hands, finally tearing his focus off my face. "So beautiful…"

"Too much," I countered, my eyes rolling back into my head as he thumbed over the aching tips.

"They're perfect," he said, his tone brooking no argument.

He bent at the knees and lifted me up, and I squealed, my heart in my throat. The strength in his arms, the ease with which he carried me to his bed clicked something inside me—woke some strange, unnamed emotion I couldn't place, but I'd never felt more feminine, more beautiful in my life.

The softness of his comforter slid along my skin as he laid me down.

Soaked, trembling, and stomach a mass of jitters, I clutched at the blankets beneath me while he stepped back to kick off his boots and push his leathers down.

Gloriously naked—beautiful, thick cock, jutting straight toward me, leaking pre-cum from the slit. Ready to plunder.

I licked my lips and stared as he bent and retrieved a condom from the back pocket of his pants. He took his damn time rolling the rubber down his length, his gaze eating up every inch of me as I lay there, waiting … needing with an all-consuming lust.

"Hurry," I heard myself whisper.

Focus on my face, Jonny crawled onto the bed, prowling toward me like a tiger, all fluid grace, a predatory glint in his eye.

He held himself in check, I realized for certain while I clasped his rock-hard shoulders as he planked over me and kissed my lips with a gentleness that stung my eyelids.

"Don't hold back," I whispered as he trailed his lips down the slope of my neck and my hands found purchase against the muscles of his back. "Please ..."

He lifted up and held my gaze, the muscle in his jaw ticking, the tense energy radiating off him rushing arousal to my pussy. "I promised I wouldn't hurt you."

I cupped his cheek. "You won't."

The muscle ticked again as he shook his head. "Wrap your legs around me."

I'd already begun to do as he asked and pulled him close enough his cock brushed along my pussy. Jonny slid up through my wetness, once, twice, and angled to notch his crown inside me.

My breath caught on a moan, and he slowly pressed into me, stretching me, filling me entirely until the head of his cock brushed against my womb.

"Goddamn, Alexa." Jonny growled and leaned down to tip his forehead to mine, his sweet breath caressing my face as he trembled atop me. "You feel so fucking good around my cock."

I squeezed my inner walls, and he groaned again, flexing his ass to nudge a tiny bit deeper, pulling a gasp from me.

He cursed and backed out, only keeping his crown inside me. "*So* fucking good," he whispered while sliding back in. "Fuck." His mouth found mine, and the gentleness disappeared as he began to rock in and out of me, lips, tongue, and teeth devouring my mouth, my breath.

I writhed beneath him, my body teetering on the edge of climaxing. So close, so damn close.

"Need you to come," he panted against my lips, his hips plowing into me, his cock brushing against my womb over and over. "Need…"

He ground his pelvis against my clit, and I bowed beneath him, euphoric tingles racing up through my body and detonating inside me. My pussy clamped down on his thrusting length, and I cried out, my hands and thighs clutching at him.

Moans and groans passed between us as he fucked in and out of me, prolonging my climax. "Let go, Jonny," I managed between gasps, and he wrapped his arms around me to grab hold of my ass, thrusting with abandon and pushing me along his mattress, his face buried in my neck.

His cock swelled, and one deep thrust landed him against my womb where he groaned and shuddered.

God, how I longed to feel the hot spurts of his cum deep inside me. Coating my still-pulsing pussy. I wanted to milk every drop from him…

He stilled, his body a steel cage around mine. While he'd given over to his body's need to fuck me, I wondered how much he still held back.

I released my grasp from his shoulders and ran my hands down his spine. His ass flexed beneath my hold, and I let out a shuddered sigh, a huge smile on my face.

"Did I hurt you?" he murmured against my neck.

Eyelids fluttering up, I moved my hold to the sides of his head and lifted him away enough I could see his face. "No." Cheeks pink, lips parted, and eyes satiated, the damn man had weaseled his way right into my heart.

Too soon, my mind whispered, but I swallowed against the fear. *A kind, gentle man, one needing release as much as I did … nothing wrong with a little consensual sex.*

I tried for a smile, but Jonny kissed the attempt

away until I shuddered once more, a heavy sigh sinking me into his mattress.

"I know you said it couldn't be more than tonight, but will you stay?" he asked, pulling back, those dark orbs once more seeing right through me.

Too soon.

"You sure?" I asked instead.

"Wouldn't ask if I wasn't."

I found myself smiling again even though my head screamed for me to get the hell out. "Okay."

Jonny Hayes actually grinned—and my heart absolutely melted.

Jonny

Her ass fit perfectly in my hands—and I wanted nothing more than to smack the flesh, watch it jiggle. See my handprint bloom to life on her pale skin. I wanted to pull her hair, sink my teeth into her tits until I covered them with my marks.

Alexa fucking wrecked me, but in the best way possible. Stark, naked honesty shone in her gaze as she'd laid it all out there for me. She held nothing back, didn't hide behind walls. No games, no pretenses.

Talk about fucking refreshing—and her declaration about it being just the one night, a mere fuck, wasn't going to stand. I didn't believe in love at first sight, but I sure as hell needed her in my life.

One last kiss on her swollen lips, and I backed out, groaning as her pussy clenched to keep me inside. "Don't move," I said, climbing off the bed. I cleaned up in my bathroom and returned to find her still sprawled on my bed, and fuck if I didn't get all poetic in thinking she lay where she belonged.

Poor woman just escaped an abusive asshole, and I wanted to stake a claim. She'd needed release as much as I had, but there was no way in hell she looked to hook up with any permanence even if we seemed to connect beyond mere bodies humping toward climax. The softness in her blue-green eyes suggested interest while I wiped between her thighs, but I flicked off the light without speaking my mind.

I pulled back the comforter, and she snuggled beneath.

I couldn't remember the last time I'd invited a woman to share my bed for the night. Hell, I couldn't even remember the last woman I'd brought home.

Alexa curled into me without hesitation the

second I lay down, her lush curves fitting against me in all the right places. I'd called her perfect, and I hadn't been lying. Physically, she was everything I could want—and I closed my eyes praying like fuck the rest of her would prove to be the same.

Not one for pillow talk, I kept my silence, and relaxed when she sighed, her breathing regulated in slumber within a matter of minutes.

Not a chatter bug. I found myself smiling at nothing in the darkness of my bedroom. I hoped the morning would bring more evidence of ways we clicked and her agreeing to more than being mere fuck buddies.

****

The scent of coffee pulled me out of the deepest sleep I'd had in months. I sniffed. Sniffed again, wondering what the hell.

"Hey." Alexa's low, raspy morning voice tented the blanket over my hips, and I blinked open one eye.

She sat on the edge of the bed, my white t-shirt hiding her perfect tits, her blonde hair a rumpled mess. Lips still swollen. Shoulders relaxed, and makeup smeared around her bright eyes.

"You're gorgeous," I muttered, fisting my cock.

She glanced down at the movement beneath the comforter, her cheeks tinging pink and nipples pebbling beneath my shirt. "Want some coffee?" she asked, her voice more breathless than a few seconds earlier.

I pushed the blankets down over my body, thrusting into my hand while baring my cock. "I'd rather have you ride me."

She swallowed, her gaze flitting to my face as the pulse leapt in her neck.

"But coffee's good," I said when she didn't speak or make a move.

"You held back last night."

I nodded, still lazily stroking my cock.

Alexa licked her lower lip, glancing once more at my dick. "Do you ... like to hurt women in a sexual way?" she asked, her voice quiet.

"Only if they want me to."

"Spanking?"

I bit back my groan at the memory of her plump ass. "Yes."

"Pulling hair? Biting?" She met my gaze once more, her eyes flitting from one of mine to the other as though hoping to read the truth of my answer.

"Yes, and yes," I said, my hand stilling. "But not without consent or safewords,"

She nodded and climbed atop me, lifting my shirt so her bare pussy rested against the top of my hand and my cock.

"Christ." I breathed out the word and released my hold on myself to grasp her bare hips lightly beneath the shirt.

She ground her pussy against my aching length, slickening me with her arousal. "I-I'd like to try all that with you," she whispered, staring into my eyes, "but right now, I just want you to fuck me."

So more than just one night. *Fuck, yes.* "Condom?"

"I want you bare—if that's okay?"

"I fucking hate rubbers," I muttered, my dick jumping at the thought of feeling her pussy against my skin. "Birth control?"

She nodded and shifted her hips, notching me against her opening. "Clean, too."

"So am I."

I flexed as she moved back, and we came together in one rocking motion.

"Fuck." I clenched my jaw, the wetness of her

heat clasping me. "Never gone without before," I said between my teeth, fighting to keep from digging my fingers into her hips and taking what I wanted.

Alexa slid forward along my length and sank back down, her lower lip between her teeth.

"Take off the t-shirt," I said. "Touch those beautiful tits for me."

Red infused her cheeks, but she did as told, her small hands lifting the heaviness of her breasts.

With a heave of breath, I sat up and latched onto the pebbled nipple of one she held, breathing in her sweet, peach scent, the desire to bite rather than lick racing through my blood.

Her breath caught as she lifted and lowered over my cock, her wetness leaking down over my balls, pussy clenching with every gentle scrape of my teeth over her hardened nub.

"Harder," she whispered, and I thrust up into her as she sank onto my shaft again. I went for a small nibble, and she moaned, her back arching, pressing her tit into my face. "Yes…"

Her whispered word fucking thrilled me, and I nibbled again, thrusting up into her as her pussy clamped down on me.

"Oh, God." She whimpered and gasped while moving against me, her body a fucking vision of motion, swaying and grinding.

I slid a hand around her backside, my fingertips trailing up and down her ass crack while she moved on me. As she lifted, I gathered moisture off my dick and slid a fingertip over her asshole as she fucked down onto me again.

Her breath caught, and she stayed impaled, circling her hips in time with my finger rimming her ass. I released my mouth from her breast with a pop. "Like that?" I asked, pressing lightly.

She whimpered and nodded, eyes clenched shut, pulse thrumming in her neck as she ground against me.

I thrust with my hips and slid my finger past her ring of muscle.

"God." Her breath left in a rush, and she tipped her head back, her neck an offering I couldn't pass up.

I latched onto the softness of her skin at the base of her neck, and she began to rock on my lap. "More," she whispered, her hands grabbing hold of my head to keep me close.

Teeth, or finger in her ass, I wasn't sure which she meant, so I went with both, nipping her flesh with my teeth in open mouth kisses and finger sliding in and out of her tight hole while she rode me.

"God, yes." She gasped and shuddered, her fingernails digging into my scalp. "Fuck, yes." Her pussy spasmed. "Jonny!" She cried out my name a second time as her inner walls clamped down on my thrusting cock, and I captured her mouth, swallowing every whimper and moan of her climax while shooting my cum deep inside her.

Nothing fucking compared to erupting in a woman's body without the strangling hold of a damn condom. Nothing. Fucking perfection, and I wasn't about to give up what I'd just found—fuck the Demons, and fuck her ex. I just needed to show her I could be the man for her.

Alexa

Euphoric tingles raced over my skin as Jonny washed me in the shower. Gentle hands, caresses, and kisses worshiping my curves—I'd never felt so cherished. Falling for Jonny came easy, regardless of my body and mind's warring. Falling in love would be the same if I allowed myself the freedom to try again.

Scott had seemed nice enough in the beginning, though, too.

But Jonny, even with the roughness he'd admitted to liking, didn't seem like the kind of man who would abuse a woman. Atop the good things Janie had told me about him, the honesty of his words, the tone of his voice, his lack of hesitation when answering my questions about his sexual preferences led me to believe he was nothing like my ex.

Only time would tell—if Jonny even wished to pursue something beyond a few casual fucks. It hadn't even been twelve hours that I'd spent alone with him, and I'd mentally gone back on my "fucking only" thoughts from the night before.

He dried me off and pulled one of his clean t-shirts down over my nakedness, a smile curving his lips. "You look good in my shirt."

"You look good on *me*."

We both laughed, and I pushed away the insecurity Scott always made me feel over the weight I'd gained since we'd first met. In my late thirties, I no longer had the body of a twenty-something young woman who loved her yoga and green, gag-worthy smoothies.

Twice while heading down the stairs for the coffee I'd made while Jonny still slept, he grabbed my ass and rumbled his approval in his throat.

Scott had been the first to fuck my ass—and I'd hated every second of it. Even though I told him I preferred not to, sometimes while fucking, he'd pull out of my pussy and shove into my ass "by accident". He'd stay there, though, not bothering to apologize while thrusting until he came.

Bastard.

Jonny's probing finger had lit a fire in me that my ex never had. I *wanted* Jonny's dick in my ass. I wanted him to fill me, brand me with his cum.

All hot and bothered again, I poured two mugs of coffee and turned, handing one to Jonny who had crowded up behind me.

"Thank you." The twinkle in his eyes and slight smile heightened my pulse further.

"So." I sipped, finishing the *now what* in my head.

"I've got to meet with my brothers this morning. I can drop you off at Hawk and Janie's."

I fought to keep my smile in place and nodded. Tired of me already? He'd had me, so he was done? Or, I realized, my heart dropping further, he wished to stick to the "fucking only", just like I'd said.

"Do you have plans for tonight?" he asked, raising his cup and wiping the thoughts away.

My smile came easy enough. "No."

"Can I take you to dinner? Say, six?"

"I'd love that."

****

"So, did he get it up and get off?"

"Janie!" I jerked my head toward her the second I set my purse on her and Hawk's kitchen table.

She giggled. "Never mind. Your face says it all."

Heat had flooded my cheeks, so I glanced away, moving toward the coffeepot for another cup.

"He any good?"

"Seriously?" I pulled a mug from the cabinet overhead and thumped it on the counter. "Kind of personal, don't ya think?"

"You *are* walking a little bow-legged."

"Oh, my God." The heat in my face traveled down through my body, and I poured myself some coffee.

"I'll take that as a yes." Janie giggled again. "Want to go shopping? Hawk handed me a couple hundred this morning and said to go have some fun."

"Your fun while on a high and your pockets full, if I remember correctly—" I sipped my coffee, "is buying a bunch of junky trinkets that you'll only end up tossing out later on."

"True." Janie blew a breath between her lips. "Shoes." Her eyes lit up again. "Let's go splurge on a new pair of shoes for both of us! A cute little wedge-type heel for summer."

"It's not yet warm enough for open toes."

"Come on! It'll *feel* frivolous and scratch my itch to waste money."

I found myself smiling while walking toward the guest room, Janie hot on my heels. "Okay. Cute heels, and maybe I'll fill out some applications while we're out."

"Awesome!" Janie squealed and rushed into her room, leaving the door open. "Let's wear something extra sexy and head over to the club for lunch, too!"

The new life ahead of me seemed so promising, I didn't think anything could bring me down, but within two hours, I found myself, heart pounding in my chest, crouched low in the front seat of Hawk's truck Janie and I had borrowed for our outing.

"Sure it was him?" Janie whispered even though

no one would hear us inside the truck's cab with its door and windows closed.

I clenched my eyes shut, fighting to keep from hyperventilating while the profile I'd seen seconds before flashed across my mind. Long blond hair in a low ponytail, crystal-clear blue eyes, and full beard carefully groomed... "It had to be Scott." My voice shook.

"How the *fuck* would he find out you're up here?"

Eyes still clenched shut, I shook my head. "He knew we were friends ... lucky guess maybe?"

"Fuck." Janie shifted, and I finally opened my eyes to see her lifting up and shoving the key into the ignition. "Stay down." Her head swiveled side to side, looking for the man I'd seen as we'd exited the mall. Our sprint across the parking lot had winded my out of shape body and my thumping heart to the point of pain.

"I don't see him."

"He's in jeans and a long-sleeve black shirt." I swallowed against the adrenaline pumping me with the need to flee or fight.

"Don't see him," she repeated. Frowning, she pulled out of the parking spot, but kept the speed to a minimum, her head swiveling from mirror to mirror.

"Anyone following?" I asked, shifting as the floor mat started to dig into my knees.

Lips pursed, she shook her head. "Not that I can tell."

"Take a few wrong turns."

Janie nodded, and I remained on the floor as she drove for a few minutes, the silence of the cab ringing my ears.

"Nothing, Alexa."

I finally pulled myself onto the seat and glanced in the side mirror. A few cars littered the road behind us, but none that I recognized. Blowing a huge breath between my lips, I forced myself to settle back and pull on my seatbelt.

"It's not lunchtime yet," Janie said, "but I think we should head to the club whether the boys are done with their meeting or not."

"Okay." My voice sounded like a mouse squeak, and I wanted nothing more than to hide in a house's wall from the big, evil cat wanting to eat me alive.

Jonny

Capone had done his homework—even without knowing I'd been considering his idea of going legit. It probably helped that he had a not-too-busy lawyer in his bed every night. Lucky bastard. Besides beautiful, Helina knew how to take a project by the balls and dig to find the what and how of every aspect.

He'd already finished up the application and permits process to open a retail store for the edibles he had planned—and the lounge I'd secretly been considering. Helina had helped him draw up a business plan for his own retail place, but they'd also done one along with a business corporate structure to present to me in the hopes of talking the Gliders into going legit with a couple of lounges opening over a five-year period.

Papers spread over my desk, I sat, stunned, taking in the hours of work the two of them had given. Capone sat sprawled on one of the three chairs across from my desk, Digger and Hawk to his left.

"All we need," Capone said, "is to find the funds to clean up that empty warehouse the Gliders own on the corner of Main and Delaware. It's the perfect spot. High traffic, close enough to downtown to draw people in."

"Damn." I cleared my throat and glanced at Hawk. "What are you thinking?" I asked since his face didn't reveal jack shit.

"I wouldn't mind going legit since the thought of Deputy Jenko getting something to stick enough to land our asses in jail—away from our women—would be fucking hell."

"Digger?" I asked, turning my focus on him.

"Make me the head of security, and I'm in."

I snorted a laugh. "Any chance to break some bones."

"Fucking right."

"Yes, you'd be head chef, Capone," I said, knowing that was one of the main reasons he wanted to push the lounge idea with its full menu—which he also had printed out, pricing and all.

He grinned.

Sitting back, I found myself internally relaxing for the first time since assuming the role of President. "We're going to put this before the entire club for feedback. Members and prospects alike. I think it's only fair since they're either paying membership fees or working their asses off to join a brotherhood that's currently focused on its outlaw ways."

"We could probably get the bulk of the club in here within two or three days," Hawk said around his toothpick.

I nodded. "Make it happen."

A knock sounded on the door. "Yeah?" I hollered.

Rucker, my tech guy and part-time bartender for the club, pulled the door open. "Janie and Alexa are here. Wasn't sure you wanted them to wait out here?"

Janie pushed past Rucker before I could answer, her hand clasping Alexa's and pulling her in behind. Both women's faces seemed a bit pale, Alexa's eyes wide and full of fear as her gaze landed on me.

I stood as Hawk did, but he reached them first. "What happened?" he asked, holding Janie's forearms.

"Alexa saw Scott in the mall parking lot."

A shudder rippled through Alexa's body as I pulled her against my chest. I held the back of her head, seeing fucking red. "You're sure?"

She nodded against me, letting loose a muffled sob.

"Fuck."

"He knew we were friends," Janie said from her place snuggled against Hawk, "but I doubt he drove all the way up here on a guess."

"Fucking snitch," Digger grumbled, cracking his knuckles.

I let out a handful of curses, stroking my hand up and down Alexa's back as she sniffled against me. She'd been hanging around the club for a week, and pretty much everyone had to know she was friends with Janie. It was possible someone connected the dots to where she'd come from and dropped a word to our enemies. "We need to end this shit."

"Toss the whores out again," Capone said.

While I wanted to agree, we needed to find out who the fuck talked. The next three on the list had been set up for the following morning with a false drug drop off same as the first group.

Alexa trembled in my arms, and more than anything, I wanted to get her home, away from people and the racket of the club. "Capone, bring my truck to the back door. I'm taking Alexa to my place."

He grabbed my keys off my desk without a word and disappeared out the office door.

"Digger, Hawk, make sure tomorrow's drop is all set to go. I probably won't be there."

"Done," Hawk said as Digger dipped his head in agreement.

****

Alexa insisted on slouching on the passenger seat where she wouldn't be visible from the outside of my truck while I drove us home. She filled me in on the details of what had happened while she and Janie were out shopping, and assured me the man she had seen was her ex. While the man hadn't made eye contact with her, she'd been married to him long enough she recognized his profile from a decent distance.

"It's possible he didn't see you," I said, squeezing the hand she hadn't released since scurrying into my truck and grabbing hold.

"If he had, he'd have come directly after me, I'm sure." She let out a huge sigh, her weariness all too evident.

"When we get to my place, I'll pull into the garage. No one will see you enter the house from there."

"M'kay."

"Then you're going to eat some lunch and sit in the tub for a nice long soak."

"Thank you, Jonny." Her whisper sounded tearful, and I glanced down to find her eyes welled.

"I won't let him near you. I won't let him hurt you."

"I believe you."

Such faith in me—and we'd only just met. My heart actually ached with an unfamiliar emotion, but I liked the feeling.

Within a half hour, Alexa had eaten a few bites of a sandwich and sat submerged in my tub, a glass of wine in her hand. I didn't have any bubbles or bath bombs to murk the water, so every inch of her body was on display.

I'd planned on giving her complete privacy, but she wanted me near, so I'd kicked off my boots, put my gun in the bed stand, and pulled a straight-backed chair into the bathroom beside the tub.

My dick, squashed in my leathers, wasn't too happy with the arrangement, but I focused on the words pouring from her full lips, the stories she'd started to unload and couldn't seem to stop.

I nodded on occasion to let her know I followed, but more often than not, my jaw clenched over some of the shit her ex had done to her in the past. The fact she didn't have a shit-ton of baggage toward men surprised me. She opened up, baring her soul to me, another biker, one she hardly knew.

"I wish I'd gone to Sturgis with Janie and her friends last summer." Alexa swallowed down the last of her wine, water droplets falling from her forearm.

"Why's that?" I reached for her empty glass and set it on the counter beside me after she handed it over.

"Maybe I'd have gotten lucky and met you."

"The timing wouldn't have been right."

"True." She sighed. "I wouldn't change anything in my past, though," she said, peering up at me, her head tipped against the back of the tub.

"Why the hell not?"

"Because of where it led me. If my ex hadn't been an asshole, I never would have left him. I never would have run north. I never would have met you. By sight," she said, "you'd most likely be judged as being just like him, but that's so damn far from the truth."

I wanted to fish, wanted to know what she thought, so I pushed. "What is your perceived truth about me?"

"You're kind. You want to do the right thing. You're loyal. Giving."

I found myself trying not to grin like an idiot. "Keep going."

"There's nothing perceived about the fact you're hot as hell. Sexier than any man I've ever laid eyes on. You're also one hell of an unselfish lover that I wouldn't ever grow tired of."

The room thickened with instant sexual tension, and I slid my gaze down over the pulse in her throat to the budded nipples below the water's surface.

"Water's getting kind of cold," she said, her voice

low, husky, "but you're welcome to join me."

I stood and ripped my shirt off overhead, shoved my leathers and boxers to my ankles, and climbed in behind her in a matter of seconds.

Alexa settled against my chest, and I wrapped my arms around her, one hand cupping a breast, the other sliding over her pubic bone and straight into her hot pussy.

"Oh, God." She arched against me as I thrust two fingers into her and rolled her nipple between my fingers. "Make me forget today, Jonny," she whispered, digging her fingernails into my flexing forearm as I finger-fucked her.

I released my hold on her breast, wrapped my arm around her waist, and easily lifted her in the water, lining my dick up with the back of my other hand. I pulled my fingers free, grabbed my throbbing length, and notched into her. Releasing my hold on her waist allowed her to sink onto my body, and she pushed down until her pussy swallowed every damn inch of me.

"Fuck." I growled in her ear, nipping at her lobe.

"Mmm." Her husky agreement jerked my dick against her womb.

"You feel so fucking good around my cock, Alexa." She lifted and lowered, my thrust meeting her halfway. "So fucking good."

Water sloshed over the tub's edge as we set a steady pace, but I didn't give a fuck. I filled my hands with her breasts, pinching her nipples enough to draw gasps and groans from her.

"Touch your clit," I said in her ear. "Come for me."

She did as told, her pussy clamping around my length, her body spasming in my arms.

Teeth gritted, I continued to fuck into her,

drawing out her climax until she relaxed in my arms.

"What about you?" she whispered as I lifted her off me and stood, cradling her against my chest.

"I'm not done with you yet." Soaking wet, I strode into my bedroom and laid her on my bed. "On your belly."

With a sigh, she rolled, and her gorgeous ass ensnared my gaze as the early afternoon sun shone through my blinds, lighting up her entire backside. I leaned down and kissed each cheek, and she parted her thighs. Her puckered hole begged for my tongue, and I obliged, licking, her musk oozing pre-cum from my dick. She lifted toward me, fisting the blankets beside her as I ate her ass, dipping into her pussy, and returning to rim her hole.

"Fuck, do I want you," I said, my face buried between her ass cheeks while I squeezed them with my palms.

"Take me, Jonny," she half-whispered, half-panted.

"I don't want to hurt you."

"You won't. Please." She lifted her ass higher. "Take my ass—show me what it's supposed to be like."

I groaned and fisted myself to keep from blowing my load. "I don't have any lube."

"Cooking oil will work," she whispered.

I hopped off the bed and moved down the hallway, down the stairs into the kitchen, hell bent on grabbing the oil and high-tailing it back to her before she could change her mind.

A bulking shadow by the back door pulled me up so damn quick I almost stumbled. "The fuck!"

I felt the rush of air more than saw a fisted gun swinging my way and ducked, weaving back on instinct. Finding my footing on the balls of my feet, I rushed forward, slamming my shoulder into the bastard's middle. We crashed into the island, sending it along with the two of us to the floor.

Something hard as fuck—the gun I vaguely realized—clobbered me against the side of my head, ringing my ears, but I clung to consciousness, pummeling my fists into the body beneath me, uncaring of my nakedness. I needed to protect Alexa.

Grunts sounded in my ears as my fists flew, and the fucker landed a few more of his own, but red hazed my vision. We grappled on the floor, and I finally pinned him, our tangled forearms across his neck, my other hand tight around his wrist holding the gun.

"Goddamn motherfucker," I growled and pressed down on his neck, wishing like fuck I could have both hands wrapped there, slowly choking the life out of him.

Fucker wasn't much bigger than me, but he must have been high on coke—a fucking relentless, untiring machine—

He kneed me in the spine, and I bowed with a curse, his arm slipping away from his neck as my hold loosened.

"She's my fucking wife." He spat and slammed his fist into my temple, dazing me again.

"Ex, you fucker," I growled, landing another lucky punch to his bleeding nose.

We rolled, crashing into the overturned island, both of our hands on the gun. Teeth gritted against pain and fear for Alexa, I held tight with every bit of strength I had, but the fucker was stronger. He pried my fingers off the gun, and roaring, hit me in the head again, dazing me to the point I went limp long enough he could shove me aside.

I groaned, trying like fuck to focus, needing to protect Alexa like I'd told her I would do.

"Thought you could fuck my old lady, did you?" His harshly whispered words barely registered. "I'm going to put a bullet in your head," he continued, his blue-eyed gaze narrowed, filled with rage. "Then I'm going to go upstairs and fuck her just like you planned on doing. It's my name she'll be screaming, you motherfucking—"

A shot sounded, and I blinked, wondering at the lack of pain ripping through me.

Alexa

I knew. The second Jonny's raised voice reached me, I fucking *knew.*

Scrambling off the bed, I ripped his bed stand drawer open. *Thank fuck.* My hand shook as I grabbed his gun and sprinted down the hallway on light feet, uncaring of my nakedness.

The crash of something in the kitchen and following grunts had my heart in my throat, lower lip between my teeth to keep from screaming. Scott had been the one to teach me about guns, and his doing so would be his downfall.

He wouldn't have come empty-handed, I knew, and although the two scuffled as I crept down the stairs into the kitchen, I expected he already had his gun palmed. Sure enough, Scott stood a few feet from Jonny's sprawled form, gun trained on him. He started spewing shit, calling me his old lady rather than ex-wife, and halfway down the stairs, I lifted Jonny's gun, aiming for his heart.

My hand shook, and I pulled the trigger, cutting his words off and spinning his body away from Jonny.

"The fuck!" Scott shrieked, grabbing his right arm, the gun still dangling from that hand. He jerked toward me. "The fuck, Alexa!"

"Drop it." My voice sounded calmer than I felt while keeping Jonny's gun trained on Scott's face. "Now."

He hesitated, blood running down his arm to drip on the floor. I didn't dare look away from him even though I longed to check on Jonny.

"Drop it," I said again through gritted teeth, "or I swear to fucking God—"

"Or what, Alexa?" Scott sneered. "Gonna shoot

me? Hmm? Kill the only man who could ever love your worthless, fat ass?"

I tightened my grip on the gun as he glanced down at Jonny.

"You would let this asshole fuck you? He's nothing." Scott spat on Jonny, and I knew what I had to do. I knew how to protect both me and Jonny for the rest of our lives.

"His dick is bigger," I said. "Thicker." Scott's focus whipped toward me, the afternoon sunlight pouring through the kitchen windows washing across his scowling face. "Jonny is ten times better in bed than you could ever dream of being. I've screamed his name so much in the last week that I lost my voice."

Scott raised his bloodied arm, but I squeezed the trigger first, his bullet slamming into the stair below me. His arm dropped to his side. He glanced down at the blood soaking his black t-shirt. "A-Alexa?" Wide eyes, blue as a clear sky lifted, rested on my face and glazed over.

He fell backward.

"Jonny!" I breathed out his name and rushed down the last bit of stairs, dropping to my knees beside him.

"You're so badass." He grimaced, and I pressed a hand to his bleeding temple.

"Are you okay?" I asked, as the adrenaline pumping through my blood crashed into me.

"Yeah."

Trembling from head to toe, I stood and grabbed a handful of paper towels to press against his head.

"Scott?" he asked, lifting up.

"He taught me how to shoot."

"I meant is he out cold?"

"More like for good."

Jonny snorted a laugh, and I found myself smiling, too, even though the situation certainly didn't warrant it. "Best go throw some clothes on—and grab my boxers. We need to call the police."

My heart lodged in my throat again. "Don't you have guys who can clean up this mess?"

"I do," Jonny said, struggling to sit, "but we need to clean this up the right way—protect you from repercussions from the Demons. Everything about this scene will scream self-defense to any detective who walks in here, and if we do things law-wise, it'll cover your ass."

"Okay." I glanced over at Scott's unmoving form, but couldn't stomach going any closer to look at his face.

"My cell was on the island."

Gaze flitting around the kitchen, I noted the overturned island and the scattered papers he'd kept atop it. *There...* I grabbed up his cell and met his gaze.

"Call, Alexa." His voice soothed me. "I promise it'll be okay."

****

Just as Jonny had said, the detectives who showed up and questioned us for a couple hours while the crime scene technicians did their thing—and the coroner took Scott's body away—claimed there wouldn't be any charges pressed against me.

With my prints on the gun and the powder residue on my fingers, their tests would confirm that I'd been the shooter. Take into account the bullet from Scott's gun on the stair beneath where I'd stood, and the police said self-defense. As for the first bullet wound in Scott's upper arm, I told them I'd done it to keep him from shooting Jonny, which was the truth.

He shook Jonny's hand before leaving. "While it's pretty cut and dry to me, I'm sure Deputy Jenko will be sniffing around. But with the victim being a member of the Demons, it's possible they'll want to retaliate—self-defense or no. I'd ask that you contact us to deal with the problem rather than take matters into your own hands if they *do* show up."

Jonny dipped his head, and the detective left, finally leaving us alone for the first time in hours.

I stepped into Jonny's arms as soon as he shut the door behind the cops and rested my cheek against his chest. "I'm not sorry."

"You goaded him on purpose, didn't you?"

I pulled back enough to gaze up into Jonny's dark eyes. "Yes. I needed to be free of him. Free to move on without fear for my life. Right or wrong, I would do the same thing again ten times over."

He caressed my back. "You do realize the Demons are going to want to talk to you even if it isn't their own justice they're after."

My head jerked in a nod. "I'll tell them the truth and keep my fingers crossed."

The muscle in his jaw ticked. "They aren't going to get within fifty feet of you."

I chewed the inside of my lip. "Do you think I should call Janie's dad outright? Explain what happened?"

"Might be best."

Heaving a breath didn't lessen my sudden nerves.

"I won't let them hurt you, if that's what you're worried about."

"I'm more afraid they'll come up here, the whole lot of them, like the detective said, and attempt to take out as many Gliders as they can."

"They could try." A darkness shadowed his eyes as he narrowed his gaze.

"What are you thinking?"

"I'm thinking I need to make a phone call before you put one through to Janie's dad and possibly open a can of shit."

I raised an eyebrow, waiting.

"Janie," he explained. "She has a way of taking down the Demons for good, so I'm thinking that maybe the Gliders ought to indulge in a last bit of sinning before going legit."

Jonny

Later that night, it was my turn to throw a dinner party, but the guests included quite a few more than Hawk and Janie, who'd I'd spoken to that afternoon. Digger and Maci, Capone and Helena, and Rucker all arrived, curious as hell over why I'd called a short-notice meeting outside of the club.

We hadn't yet met with the other brothers to discuss going legit, but beyond that, what I had planned needn't involve anyone else—and I wanted secrecy for what we would do. Every single person to file into my house could be trusted, of that I had no doubt.

Rather than cook, I had a few pizzas delivered, and we all chowed down before sitting in the living room in a circle of chairs, everyone's gazes resting on me.

I nodded at Janie, and she pulled out a stack of papers I'd asked her for but had yet to read. She handed them to me.

"What I have right here," I held them aloft, "is enough evidence to bury the Demons for good—and finance the first Gliders' Lounge."

Helina's eyebrow popped upward and Maci's mouth dropped open, but Digger, Capone, and Rucker didn't twitch.

"Janie?"

She wiped her palms down her jeans. "My father—" She cleared her throat and started again, "My father is in deep with a New York mafia family. Sex trafficking."

"Sick bastard," Helina muttered, and Janie nodded.

"We can take them down from the inside out without their knowing."

"That's where Rucker comes in," I said, taking

over and laying out the plan Hawk and I had discussed over the phone earlier while Janie had downloaded to her computer and printed out the pictures she'd taken with her phone of the secret papers of her father's.

Hacking into email accounts of those in deep with the Demons and anonymously demanding payment for our silence would be a breeze, Rucker assured me, and I continued on with my thoughts on sending the information Janie had obtained about the Demons' dealings to the proper authorities—ones who hadn't been bought by our rivals.

"How do we know who has or hasn't been bought?" Digger asked, leaned forward, elbows on knees and hands clasped.

"There's a listing in there of men whose pockets he's greased," Janie replied.

"What a moron," Helina said with a snort. "Sorry, Janie."

Janie's smile appeared forced, but she shook her head. "He's not the smartest man on the earth, and this time, I'm thanking him for it."

Digger eyed the papers I'd placed on the floor between my feet. "What else is in that pile?"

"I haven't read through them yet, but we're going to do that right now," I said. "See what kind of ammunition we have, who all we can extort building funds from. See what kind of a shitstorm we can stir up to wipe out other assholes like the Demons."

"Why are you offering to do this, Janie?" Maci asked. "I know you've made a new life here being Hawk's old lady, but this is your father we're talking about."

"If you knew half the things he's done, half of the things he's allowed to happen, the things he has ordered others to do..." She glanced at Alexa, her brow furrowing. "What happened to Alexa isn't just the norm with the Demons—it's encouraged to keep the whores and old ladies in line. Teaching them their place, my dad says. Almost the entire club is made up of narcissistic, sexist assholes who only care about getting drunk and getting laid."

Helina snorted, glancing at Capone. "You're lucky the Gliders like strong women and allow them a voice."

"I'm the luckiest son of a bitch alive, darlin'," Capone said with a grin, squeezing her knee.

"Pass those papers, Jonny," Helina said, fire glinting in her green eyes as she held out her hand. "Let's see all the skeletons in Don Taylor's closet."

I took the top couple and passed them clockwise. Silence settled except for the crinkle of a turned paper as we perused the evidence to put the Demons away.

The first few pages listed the Silent Demons in alphabetical order. Looking for two names in particular, I scanned toward the bottom half of the alphabet, my finger sliding from one name to the next.

"Digger," I said, checking one last time to be sure.

He grunted, and I lifted my head. "I have a listing of Demons. Your two friends aren't on there."

He nodded, and not needing to discuss their murders, we returned to our papers even though Maci murmured, "Thank God."

Before doing away with the two fuckers who had attacked him and Maci, I'd made sure to check their IDs. Memorized the names of the two men who thought to kill my brother and rape his woman.

Nicky had helped to do away with the two men, and I knew I could rest easier knowing they *hadn't* been Demons like we'd originally thought.

"Fuck *me*," Rucker muttered five minutes later, sitting back in his chair, stare on the paper in his hand.

"Pretty sure all the whores would take you up on that," Capone said with a chuckle.

Rucker lifted his gaze and glanced at the men one by one. "Whores … I found our rat, brothers."

"What?" I stood and strode across our small circle and took the paper from his outstretched hand.

A listing of names—first and last—ran down the left, and a town and state listed directly across from each.

"Number seven," Rucker said.

Michelle Stevens. I raised an eyebrow, not getting the correlation even though she was listed as living in our town.

"Michelle," Rucker said. "Shelly."

"Holy fuck." The words left my lips on a harsh growl as others around the circle muttered similar sentiments. "Motherfucking whore!"

"She went through my bag at the camping trip," Janie said, sitting up straighter.

"And called your father after learning who you were to tell him you'd been kidnapped." The anger lacing Hawk's voice sent a shiver down my spine.

"She's got to be the one who called Scott, too," Alexa half-whispered. "There's no other way he would know I was here."

"She planted the fucking drugs," Digger said, his tone level and seemingly unfazed. I knew better. "She told the police about the goddamn shipment that got nabbed." He cracked his knuckles. "Say the word, Jonny."

Maci slapped his arm. "You will *not* hurt that woman!"

Digger jerked toward her. "She's a fucking snitch, Maci! A goddamn, loose-tongued bitch of a liar who needs to be silenced!"

Voices rose in agreement with both Digger and Maci, but I lifted a hand, shutting them all up in a blink. "Did you know her, Janie?"

"I didn't meet Shelly until coming here, but I do know the name Michelle Stevens. Wish I'd put it together before, but Michelle used to ride with the Demons years ago, when I was a kid. She ran into some trouble and ended up owing my father a lot of money. Rumor had it he had her taken care of, but I guess that's not the case."

I frowned. "She pays him back by whoring herself out to his enemies, stealing information, and trying to set us up."

"Say the word, Jonny," Digger repeated, his voice low.

Maci smacked him again.

I heaved a heavy breath, considering. "I don't condone violence against women." A glance at Alexa showed her face relaxing, a small smile tilting her lips. Faint bruising still colored her face, exhaustion lying heavy beneath her eyes. It had been one long-assed motherfucking day—for both of us.

"You can't just kick her out and let her walk away," Hawk said, leaning back in his chair, white-knuckled grip on the papers in his hands.

"No, we can't. Suggestions?"

"As your lawyer," Helina said, staring me down, "I insist you tread carefully here, Jonny. I will look the other way when it comes to extorting bastards who made money off sex trafficking, but I can't defend men who plot murder in front of me."

"Bitch deserves to die," Digger muttered, ignoring Maci who glared at him, arms crossed.

I tended to agree with Digger, and the old me, the

one my father had hoped I'd become, itched to put a bullet between her eyes—after slicing out her tongue. "We'll give her the choice."

Digger cocked his head to the side in question, but Hawk didn't move. Both Capone and Rucker, hearts softer than the other two brothers, shifted in their chairs.

Helina's eyebrows rose. "Meaning?"

"Give her the option of a slow, painful death—"

"That's what I'm talking about," Digger growled.

"—or a bottle of pills," I finished, pretending Digger hadn't spoken.

Hawk nodded his agreement immediately, and although Digger scowled, he dipped his head.

"And I suppose Digger will stand over her, gun trained on her face until she swallows them all down," Helina said.

"Until she fucking breathes her last," he added with a slight smirk that pulled on his scar.

I scanned the circle, one person at a time. "It wouldn't be by our hand. It would be *her* choice." No one argued or offered another option, our lawyer included, and I faced Alexa fully. "The Demons are going to come looking for Scott."

She nodded. "Without a doubt."

"Then we need to get this shit to the authorities now." I turned toward Rucker. "How long?"

"We don't even need to access emails or hack for a damn thing, with this kind of evidence," he said, glancing at the papers we all held. "If Janie can get me copies, I'll have this to the local FBI in a matter of minutes. If you think they're trustworthy, Jonny."

"I do."

Hawk pulled a thumb drive from his pocket and tossed it across the circle to Rucker.

"Sweet." Rucker's eyes lit up. "Let's do this."

"Contact the FBI first. Extortion second—of every single bastard involved in selling sex slaves. Hack their bank statements—demand it all."

"You got it, Jonny."

Seeing as how he'd been in on a few other extortion deals for the Gliders, I trusted Rucker to know what to say to get the job done. I tipped my head toward the door, and he hopped up, hurried through to the kitchen, and slammed the back door behind him.

"While I'd love to take care of the Shelly problem tonight," I said, "I'm fucking exhausted."

"I can go alone," Digger offered, but I shook my head.

"You, Hawk, and I will go tomorrow night."

"What if the FBI come down on the Demons before then, and Shelly gets tipped off?"

I scrubbed a hand down my face, so damn weary, I couldn't think anymore.

"We'll go in the morning," Hawk said. "Meet at the club at eight?"

I nodded, and Digger muttered his agreement.

"That's it, then," I said. "Everyone, go home. Lock up. Get some sleep."

Helina pulled Alexa aside, and I stood close enough to catch some of what passed between them. I knew Helina had yet to find herself a secretary, and she'd heard through the grapevine that Alexa used to work as one down in New York. They exchanged numbers, and I found myself smiling. Alexa planned on staying in the area—and I couldn't have been happier over that fact.

Alexa

Jonny held me in his arms, but he breathed heavy in sleep long before I could fully relax. Scott had found me, and if Shelly had been the one to phone that information in, Don Taylor would also know. Scott would have come on his own since he never involved any of his brothers in our problems—made him look like a pussy, he'd told me often enough, his old lady running off and divorcing him.

No, Scott would have acted alone.

But Don Taylor would send someone up here sooner than later to find out what had happened to him.

I slipped from beneath Jonny's arm, gathered my things, and snuck out of his room. Each footfall on the stairs creaked, and I bit my lip, praying it wasn't loud enough to wake him. Once in the kitchen, I dressed in the dark and made a quick phone call.

Jonny had weaseled his way into my heart so damn quickly—and I wasn't about to put his life in danger until things with the Demons got resolved. I chewed my fingernails to nubs while waiting for my ride. I'd considered calling Janie, but that's the first place the Demons would look when they came up to find out why Scott had disappeared.

"He's not going to be happy," Helina said, bleary-eyed and dark hair a tangled mess as though she'd just been thoroughly loved.

"I know, but I can't put him in danger."

"He's going to think you were kidnapped," she muttered, pulling away from the curb.

"That's why I left him a note on the kitchen island."

Helina huffed a breath. "Did you tell him where you would be?"

"Yes, and I asked him to stay away."

She snorted. "Jonny's not like my soft marshmallow, so he won't."

"Marshmallow?" I asked with a small burst of laughter.

"Capone is nothing but a softie," she said, smiling over at me. "And I happen to enjoy his submissive nature. He lets me be in control—most of the time."

I shook my head, gaze glued to her profile. "The Demons would *never* allow a woman like you or a man like Capone in their club."

"Their fucking loss, then, isn't it?" Her green eyes glinted in a streetlight we passed by.

"Definitely."

****

I turned my cell off and eventually drifted off to sleep on Capone's couch. His automatic coffeepot started dripping at six, waking me up from an arousing dream of Jonny's face between my thighs.

Unable to help myself, I grabbed my cell off the coffee table and lay back down, powering it up to check how many times he'd called.

Just once, and tears hazed my vision at his recorded husky morning voice, telling me he wished I had discussed leaving with him first. While he didn't like that I'd left him, he thanked me for showing him how much I cared.

"I'm falling hard and fast for you, Alexa." His voice sent an ache through me as I listened a second time. "And when this is all behind us, I hope you'll let me in."

"Fuck." I swiped a tear from the corner of my eye, and needing to change my mind's course, I clicked on my messages.

Hawk had sent me one, telling me Janie had

crashed, wondering if I could go be with her while he, Digger, and Jonny went to take care of business.

"Goddamn it." I shot off a text letting him know where I was, threw back my blankets, and pulled my clothes on.

Turning over evidence to put her father away for life—it was no wonder she'd spiraled into a depressive mood. What person wouldn't?

Hawk: **Be there in five.**

Capone and Helina still hadn't crawled out of bed, so, same as with Jonny, I left them a note telling them where I'd gone.

Seven minutes later, I climbed into the cab of his truck. "How's she doing?"

"Not good. I fucking *knew* this was going to happen."

I'd expected anger or disappointment in his eyes, but the pain I found while clicking my seatbelt brought the damn tears back to my own eyes.

"She's been doing so damn good, too," he continued, speeding back the way he'd come. "I hate seeing my little butterfly like this. Fucking wrecks me." His voice broke, and his beard twitched as though he clenched his jaw to keep his emotions contained.

"I love her so goddamn much," he whispered a few seconds later, his voice gruff.

Janie had told me how Hawk loved her—his unconditional loyalty to her regardless of her issues, but seeing it firsthand sent that pang through my chest. "I'll stay with her," I said. "And I'll make sure she eats, too."

"Thank you." Hawk glanced over at me.

"Of course." I tried for a smile.

"I hate that I can't be with her when she needs me the most."

"I'm sure Jonny would give you a pass on this

whole Shelly business this morning."

"He would." Hawk nodded. "But as the Sergeant at Arms this is my duty."

I nibbled on my lower lip a few seconds, studying his profile.

"What?" he asked without glancing at me as though he'd felt my stare.

"The brotherhood comes first for the Gliders, doesn't it?"

"Not for all of us, and the only reason I'm leaving her right now is because you're here. Because I can trust you to take care of her."

My chest ached anew at his kind words.

"The Gliders aren't anything like the Demons." He glanced over at me. "Jonny would cherish you every second of the goddamn day if you'd give him a chance."

The damn tears stung again, and I clutched my purse tight on my lap.

"Just because he's a biker, a gang's president, doesn't mean he's an abusive asshole like the one from your past."

I nodded, and glanced over at Hawk again.

"Your mind is working," he said, without looking at me.

"Can I ask you something personal?"

"Go ahead."

"Janie likes to talk. A lot." I shifted on the seat and cleared my throat. "Especially about sex."

One of his eyebrows lifted as he glanced over at me. "Go on."

"Well ... she told me ... God." Heat flooded my face. "This is so inappropriate."

"Spit it out, Alexa."

"Okay." I blew a breath between my lips. "Janie told me that you like to spank her and that she enjoys it."

His whiskers twitched again, but I felt sure it was from fighting against a smile. "That's true."

"So, I'm wondering … how is your spanking her ass not abuse? I mean," I angled toward him, "it's got to hurt, so why does she even let you do it?"

"Because the pain morphs into pleasure—if the right man is the one giving it to you."

I chewed on the inside of my lip. Janie had all but said the same, but to hear it from a man's perspective…

"Jonny told you he likes to get a little rough while fucking?"

"Yes."

"He would chop his own damn hand off before hurting you. I've known him most of my life, Alexa. The man will not let loose on you unless you ask him to." Hawk pulled into their driveway, and turned the key, but didn't climb from the cab. "He wouldn't ever treat you like property, either, I can promise you that. And since you left him last night to protect him, I'm thinking you care a hell of a lot for him, too."

I nodded.

"Then think about what he wants to do to you. Imagine it happening, and I'm sure your body will answer the questions battling in your head."

My face heated again, and I scurried from the truck, needing to focus on something other than the rush of heat between my thighs. The thought of Jonny slapping my ass while *taking* my ass revved me up beyond any fantasy I'd ever imagined.

Answer given, my body declared.

The sound of a sob met me as I walked into Hawk's kitchen, wiping away all thoughts of Jonny and sex.

"Go on back," Hawk said from behind me, keys in his hand. "I'll pour us some coffee quick before I have to leave for the club."

I started across the kitchen, but pulled up short, the memory of why I hadn't come to them the night before flitting across my brain. "Hawk, if the Demons come looking for me, this is the first place they'll show up."

He nodded and pulled his cell from his back pocket. "I'll send over a couple guys to watch over you both."

"Thank you," I whispered and turned, intent on wrapping my arms around my friend and offering her the support she'd given me since arriving in New Hampshire.

Jonny

My chest felt like a knife lodged through the breastbone, twisting its serrated edges through flesh and muscle, ripping me to shreds. Fucking hurt.

I'd crumpled Alexa's note after hollering her name like fifty times and sprinting downstairs butt-assed naked upon finding her missing. Actual fucking tears had stung my eyes as her written words, their deeper meaning, slithered into my consciousness.

She cared about me. Deeply enough to sneak away in the night to protect me—because she had to know I wouldn't have let her go.

"Fuck." Scowling and yet thrilled inside from the hurt in my chest, I climbed on my bike and took off for the club.

Hawk had called me right before I'd left, filling me in on what had happened with Janie and his calling a couple brothers to watch over them both while we took care of business.

Fucking hated it, but I didn't have a choice about leaving Alexa and Janie. Shelly had to be dealt with before Taylor had a chance to get in touch with her.

Rucker's text stating all the goods had been sent to the FBI had waited on my cell when I finally thought to check it. That had been at two in the morning.

"Should have taken care of Shelly last night," I grumbled into the wind blasting my face. Usually when riding, I experienced a sense of freedom, a deep-seated happiness of being right where I wanted to be.

Not that morning.

I wanted all the shit to be gone, Alexa in my bed, gazing at me with so much more than lust in her eyes. I fucking wanted it all.

Digger already sat in his truck out front of the

club, and I parked and climbed into the cab. I quickly filled him in on what had happened.

"Fuck." He stared down the road Hawk would be arriving by. "It's gonna take a few extra minutes for him to get here if he's waiting on some brothers at his place."

I nodded and finally texted Rucker back, asking if he'd gotten word from the friends we'd sent some paper goodies to.

Rucker: **Nothing yet. Will let you know asap.**

Hawk pulled in a few minutes later and hopped in the back seat of Digger's cab. "Let's get this done."

Digger pulled out, and I turned in my seat. "Who'd you call to watch over our women?"

"Sniper and Damon."

I nodded and turned back around. Both men had been patched members for over twenty years and were also two I would trust with my life. Sniper had gotten his name for the years he'd spent in the Marines behind a big-ass scope, taking out assholes one by one from distances I couldn't even begin to think of shooting. Damon was built like a brick house, same as Digger, and had proven to be almost as mean. Both would do nicely as bodyguards.

Pushing aside thoughts and concerns over both Alexa and Janie, I focused on the woman about to get a surprise visit.

Shelly had been around from my dad's days. She'd been with the Gliders longer than any of the other club whores.

"Shelly ever introduce any new whores into the club?" I asked, searching my brain for the answer.

"Not that I know of," Hawk said as Digger shook his head.

"That bitch keeps to herself, but I'll gladly threaten to smash a couple fingers to find out the answer."

While the idea satisfied the darker side of me, I decided against it. "We can't leave any trace of our being in her place behind. None. Not in her apartment, not on her body. That means gloves at all times, too. Understood?"

Digger shot me a scowl. "I really want to fucking bury her."

"And you will. By giving her these." I pulled the unlabeled prescription bottle from my pocket. While I didn't condone drug use in the club and we'd been laying low, I still knew where to get shit without anyone knowing.

"Sure they're enough to do the job?"

"The mixture of pills in here will shut her body down within an hour."

"Too damn easy," Digger muttered, shaking his head.

Shelly answered the door in a tattered robe, her face paling the instant she found the three of us on the other side. "What's up, boys?" she asked, her voice small.

I pushed into the tiny kitchen, Hawk and Digger on my heels as Shelly backed away from me, swallowing and wringing her hands. A glance at her coffeepot revealed she'd yet to have a cup.

"Brought you a little something to go with your coffee this morning, *Michelle Stevens*."

Her gulp was fucking music to my ears. "P-please, Jonny…"

Digger pulled out one of the two chairs at her table and motioned for her to sit with the gun he held in his free hand.

Her makeup-smeared eyes twitched along with her blonde, straggly hair as tremors took over her body.

She sat, her eyes huge while staring across the table at me.

"Hawk, get the lady a cup of coffee, would you?"

I pulled on my own riding gloves one at a time, keeping my face void of all emotion while peering down at her. "I know who you are, Shelly."

"I'm so fucking sorry, Jonny." Tears raced down her cheeks. "I didn't have a fucking choice, I swear to God! I didn't—"

"Shut the fuck up, Shelly."

I lifted my gaze from Shelly to Digger as he towered behind her, death in his gaze as she heeded his command.

"Don Taylor is going down, too," I said, returning my attention on Shelly. "The entire Silent Demons chapter in New York is about to get an early morning visit from the FBI."

Hawk set a steaming cup in front of her, but she didn't touch it.

"Digger."

He'd already wiped the pill bottle clean of prints before coming up to Shelly's floor. He reached over her shoulder, and she jerked away with a squeak, but he simply set the bottle beside her coffee.

"Now, you *do* have a choice, Shelly," I said as Digger backed off again. "You can either spill your secrets and swallow down every single one of these fucking pills, or I'll let Digger's inner demons loose on your ass."

A shudder rippled down through her, and she grabbed up the bottle without hesitation. "Thank you, Jonny. Fucking thank you." A single sob ripped from her as she popped the lid and palmed the pills that would ship her off to the hell she deserved to burn in.

"Spill your guts first," I said.

She stared at the handful of white tablets. "I-I used to be one of the Demons' whores." Her voice barely escaped her trembling lips. "Hard up for cash, I stole from one of the brothers, and Taylor gave me an offer I couldn't refuse."

Tears coated Shelly's eyes when she finally lifted her head to meet my unfeeling gaze. "The Gliders have been nothing but kind to me, and I'm so fucking sorry for everything I've done. Everything I've shared with your rivals. I-I know I'm a piece of trash—"

"Got that fucking right," Digger muttered, his flinty stare on the top of her head.

"—and I don't deserve your mercy."

"Why'd you tell Taylor Janie had been kidnapped?" Hawk asked.

Shelly swallowed. "I thought that starting a war would get me out from beneath Taylor's thumb. I-I didn't want to hurt anyone, really, but living like this for the past twenty years..." A shiver slid down over her, and she closed her fingers around the pills.

I couldn't rouse a single ounce of pity for the bitch. "You planted the drugs and tipped the cops?"

Her head dropped again as she nodded.

"Ratted out that last shipment we sent north?

Again, she nodded.

"Alexa's ex?"

"I called him," she whispered.

"Jealous bitch," Hawk muttered.

She pressed her lips together.

The muscle in my jaw ticked, and temptation to let Digger have at Shelly flitted through my brain. I wasn't in the mood for a mess, though. Best just to get it the fuck over with. "Anything else you need to get off your chest before going?"

She opened her mouth and slammed it shut. A

quick jerk of her head side to side let us know she'd rather take the rest of her sins to the grave.

"Down the hatch, then," I said, nudging her coffee closer to her with the back of a gloved knuckle. "You're going to sit right here until those little pills kick in," I said, letting her see the satisfaction of her impending death on my face. "And Digger will stay with you to send you off."

Another shudder rippled through her, and she closed her eyes and tossed those damn fuckers right down her throat.

****

"Should have fucking let me smash every one of her goddamn fingers," Digger muttered as he climbed into his truck. "Fucking sucked having to sit there in silence, waiting for the damn pills to work. When they first started to kick in, she was high as a fucking kite, laughing her ass off, but it didn't last long. She ended up on the floor, choking on her own fucking vomit."

"You check her pulse?" I asked.

"Dead as a fucking wrench."

"Good." I nodded, beyond thrilled to have that piece of shit off my brain.

"Anything from Rucker?" Digger asked.

"He received a reply to the anonymous email he'd sent Janie's papers from. The agent thanked him and asked to know his identity. Rucker wiped out the email account without replying."

"Asses covered," Hawk said, having as much confidence in Rucker's computer hacking abilities as I did.

"Now we wait for the news to explode." I found myself smiling, and glanced at my phone again. No word from Alexa, Sniper, or Damon. "It's still early, but I'm going to grab a drink at the club and make a few arrangements before heading to Hawk's and claiming my woman."

The safest place for Alexa until the Demons rotted in jail was the damn club—and I should have realized that when she'd first shown up. While the fucking rooms on the third floor weren't all lavish and well-stocked with anything other than condoms and lube, at least a queen-sized mattress, clean sheets, and blankets sat ready for use.

I hoped it wouldn't take much to convince her to come with me. Stay with me—even after she felt safe enough to take up Helina on that offer of a job she'd given and start her life over.

Alexa

I launched into Jonny's arms the second he walked in Hawk's door. A sob ripped from me, and I buried my face in his neck, apologizing over and over for leaving and making him worry like I'd done.

Hawk left us for the bedroom where Janie still lay, but at least she no longer cried. I'd even managed to entice a smile from her while talking about spanking and butt plugs.

Jonny cradled my head in his hands and claimed my lips, emptying my head and flooding my panties with wetness. The adrenaline from the previous however many damn hours weighed me down with exhaustion, but I needed him.

"Take me home," I whispered against his lips the second he let me up for air.

"I'm taking you back to the club." He stepped back, and my heart squeezed, insecurities lashing at me from every direction even though he caressed his thumbs down my cheeks. "It's the only place I know you'll be completely safe."

"Will you stay with me?" I squeaked out the words, not wanting to fish but needing to just downright know.

"Ten thousand fucking horses wouldn't be able to pull me away from you, Alexa."

He dipped down and kissed me again until I forgot my anxiety, my name.

He sent Damon and Sniper on ahead, and I climbed onto the back of his bike a few minutes later, Janie resting, Hawk thanking me again for watching over his butterfly.

An older woman with soft-looking gray curls met Jonny and me right inside the club's front door. After leaning up to kiss Jonny's cheek, she smiled and held out her hand toward me. "You must be Alexa."

I nodded and glanced at Jonny, but he smiled with tenderness at the gray-haired woman.

"I'm Sweetie Jane," she said. "Jonny's cousin and the Gliders' adoptive mother."

"Oh." I smiled and shook her hand. "Nice to meet you."

"And you as well, young lady. How is Janie?"

I shrugged. "Been better, that's for sure, but Hawk is there with her now." As though my words said it all, Sweetie Jane nodded while turning her gaze up at Jonny.

"The room at the end of the hall is all set up. I'm assuming this is the lovely lady who will be staying there?"

"It is."

"Well." Sweetie Jane smiled again, her blue eyes twinkling as she let out a soft chuckle. "I won't keep you."

She pushed out through the door, and I raised an eyebrow at Jonny.

"My cousin. She's the club's maid."

I snorted. "I hope you pay her well. Cleaning up after a bunch of horny men."

"She's well taken care of, don't you worry." He motioned toward the stairs, and I started across the quiet club. Without the eighties music blaring, the place really had a cozy, man-cave feel. No one had shown up yet to start partying for the day, so we had the place to ourselves.

Jonny pushed open the door at the end of the hall on the third floor, and motioned me in. "Isn't much, but it's the safest place for you right now."

I moved into the room, glancing around. Sterile,

like a hotel, but safe. "It's perfect."

"You'll only be here until the Demons are all behind bars," Jonny said, shutting the door and taking my purse.

"And then?" I asked, my heart suddenly thumping.

Jonny set my purse down on a chair by the door and took my hand, pulling me against his hard, tensed body. "Then you're coming home with me."

I smiled, tilting my head back to better see his face. "Is that a fact?"

"It is."

"And then?" I asked, raising an eyebrow.

"Then you'll start your new life—by my side."

His words shot a thrill through me, and the confidence with which he spoke quieted whatever insecurities thought to linger. "You sound pretty sure of that fact."

"I've never been surer about anything in my goddamn life." He kissed me until my knees weakened, until I squirmed against him, trying to rub my throbbing clit against the hard length down his right thigh.

He devoured every inch of my mouth, his body looming over mine like a wire stretched tight, ready to snap.

"I want you, Alexa." His whispered words against my lips as a shudder rippled down through him pulled a whimper from me.

"Then take me."

"I want to mark your ass so damn bad." He half growled the words while sweeping me up into his arms.

"Then do it," I whispered, my body so on board with the idea I knew my jeans had to be soaked through.

He set me on my feet beside the bed and ripped his shirt off overhead.

I didn't wait, but followed suit, stripping in a matter of seconds, uncaring of the sunlit room revealing every inch of my skin.

Jonny's heated gaze slid down over me, and another rush of warmth settled between my thighs. "Safewords." He lifted his focus to my face, peering intently into my eyes. "Green means go, yellow is slow down, and red means stop."

I nodded.

"Say it back to me."

I did as told, managing only a whisper, my skin pebbling beneath his stare. Fear of his hitting me should have had me running for the door. Fear of pain without the promised, possible pleasure should have had my pussy dried up, but wetness leaked down my thigh.

"On the bed," he practically croaked. "Knees."

Knowing I was beyond words, too, I did as told, putting my ass on display, my cheek on the bed.

He groaned. "Goddamn, woman."

"Please," I managed, unable to keep my need quiet.

The bed dipped behind me.

Smack!

"Shit!" I shrieked the word as a searing sting raced across one ass cheek.

"Tell me you're okay, Alexa," Jonny said as though through clenched teeth, while rubbing his palm over the sting.

"Green," I said although tears leaked from my eyes.

He landed another swat, and I bit back my cry.

"Alexa?"

"I-I'm good," I whispered, the sting lessening enough I realized my arousal level hadn't diminished one damn bit.

"Tell me to stop and I will."

"Green, Jonny." I wiggled my ass, chasing what Janie had promised the right man could bring.

Three more swats, and I relaxed, the pain buzzing straight into my already throbbing clit. *Oh, yes ... this.*

"You look so good with my prints on you," Jonny said, smoothing a hand gently across my backside, and I pushed into his touch.

"Need you," I managed past my dry lips. "Please."

He dipped two fingers into my sopping pussy and groaned. "Fuck me, are you soaked."

I whimpered as he finger-fucked me, taking me so damn close to climaxing that I clenched my eyes shut. "P-please, Jonny."

My pussy sucked on his retreating fingers, but he slid them up over my asshole, and I bit my lip to keep from crying. "Need you so damn much," I whispered, clutching at the blankets balled in my hands.

"Here?" he asked, easily sliding a finger past the ring of muscle in my ass.

"Yes." I groaned. "Fuck, yes."

Eyes clenched shut against the climax ready to lay waste to me, I listened as Jonny opened the bed stand drawer.

Cool liquid slid down through my crack, and I arched my back, lifting my ass in offering.

"So fucking gorgeous." His low rumbled tone shivered goosebumps across my skin. The slide of his cock up through the lube between my cracks had me whimpering again. "You're mine, Alexa."

"Mmm hmm," I agreed, pressing back as he placed his crown against my hole.

"Say the word," he said, his voice strained.

"I'm yours."

He pressed in, and I gasped as he breached my muscles. "Fuck. So goddamn tight." A little nudge pushed him in further, and I groaned, arching my back again and pressing toward him.

Hands clasped on my hips in a bruising yet luscious grip, Jonny shoved in, stuffing my ass full of his dick. I fucking loved it.

The second he started to back out, my body detonated, and I shrieked his name, cursing and begging him to fuck me.

With a growl, he plowed into me over and over again, cursing and calling me his, beautiful, perfect ... his words garbled, breathless.

He buried deep and lay atop me, his cock pulsing, shooting cum deep into my ass.

I fought for breath as euphoric waves swept over me, knowing I'd finally found what I hadn't even realized I'd been missing.

Epilogue
Jonny

Ten months later

Digger looked good all cleaned up, his beard clipped, and wearing nice slacks and a button-down shirt. As head of security at The Gliders' Lounge, he took pride in his station beside the black, half-circle couch of the VIP area on the establishment's dais along the backside of the dance floor.

Alexa snuggled against me, giddy from too many champagne toasts, her warm fingers snaking between the buttons of my shirt.

Opening night, and the club hopped. I'd given into Hawk's insistence on music other than eighties, and even though enough joints lit the room to give the casual guest a slight buzz, a few dozen souls danced to the low music with its strobing lights overhead.

Grinning, I glanced around those seated with me in the dimly lit VIP area.

Janie sat by Alexa—on Hawk's lap, the baby bump rounding her belly not hindering her from grinding away at my best friend's dick trapped beneath his black jeans. Their mouths remained fused as though they didn't hear the lot of us telling them to head upstairs to a private room.

Helina, all prim and proper in a little black dress, her legs crossed, leaned against Capone, eyes for only him even though he wore chef's clothing and smelled like food. Having gotten through the initial rush of orders swamping the state-of-the-art kitchen I'd insisted on setting up for all of his hard work—financed by all those wonderful bastards who paid to keep their anonymous extortionists silent—he slumped down on the couch to join us. He'd grabbed the bottle of bubbly off the glass, circular table in front of us and took a long pull.

His blue eyes twinkled, and he grinned like a fool as though the world lay at his feet. A big-assed rock sat on Helina's left ring finger, so I expected he *did* feel that way.

Maci sat beside them, her smile soft as she gazed at the man looming to my right. She'd officially become Digger's old lady, insisting he ink her with a tattoo declaring her his property.

Digger's chest had puffed out for weeks after marking her, not that I could blame him.

I gazed out over the lounge, almost completely content.

The Silent Demons chapter in New York had completely disbanded, most of its members behind bars, a few, even, found dead by their own hands— supposedly. I expected the mafia family they'd been in with neck-deep, might have had something to do with it.

I'd sat down with the police department—the asshole Jenko included—and told them that we were going legit. I told them whatever it was they thought we were into would no longer be an issue between us, and I also promised to take the colors of any brother who didn't comply with our new ways.

Considering what our at-the-time-approved lounge would be serving, I doubted there would be too many fights or need for their presence. I'd promised to provide security inside and out, and I had also shaken every single fucking hand before leaving.

And Alexa …

I squeezed her against me, and she lifted her gaze from my chest, her blue-green eyes full of love. "I got you a present," I said, reaching into my pocket.

"What?" Her eyes twinkled as she sat up.

My hand fisted around the gift, I slipped onto the

floor, keeling beside her.

Her smile faded as her eyes shot wide open

"Alexa." I lifted my hand and opened my fingers. The diamond glinted in the strobe lights. "Will you marry me?"

"Oh, God!" She clasped her hands over her mouth as her eyes welled with tears.

Janie actually tore her lips off Hawk and scooted sideways. She squealed.

"Well?" I said, smiling up at the only woman to ever capture me in every way—heart, body, and soul.

"Yes." Tears streamed down Alexa's cheeks as she gave me her left hand, laughing and choking back a sob. "Hell, yes."

I slid the ring onto her finger, stood, and pulled her up into my arms. "I love you more than anything in this world."

"I love you, too," she whispered, her eyes shining through her tears.

I became aware of the hoots and congratulations being tossed out, but couldn't bear to look away from her. She grabbed my face and kissed me, and I thought, *now—now I'm completely content.*

"What the *fuck*!" The happiness in Digger's curse pulled me away, and I turned toward the entrance where he stared.

Nicky...

I grabbed Alexa's hand, and grinning like an absolute idiot, I hurried off the dais, knowing the others followed.

Fucking Dominic Nicky Landon stood inside the entrance, his little Mel hanging on his arm. His piercing blue eyes scanned the dim room, and landed on my face before I made it off the dance floor.

He dipped his head and started our way.

My face fucking hurt from smiling. Still clutching Alexa's hand, I pulled him into me with my free arm, smacking him on his back. "So fucking good to see you, brother."

We stepped away at the same time, and I pulled Alexa closer. "Alexa, this is Nicky. Nicky, this is Alexa. She just agreed to be my old lady."

Something like a smile lit Nicky's eyes as he held out his hand. "Never thought I'd see the fucking day. Congrats."

"Never thought I'd ever get to meet the old man these boys reminisce over every time we get together." Alexa's words twitched Nicky's lips, and Mel outright laughed, squeezing Nicky's middle.

"He's *my* old man, thank you very much," Mel said, her whiskey-colored eyes twinkling.

"Hawk..." Nicky's gaze flitted down over Janie and her baby bump. "The fuck?"

"I know, right?" Hawk actually grinned and yanked Nicky in, slapping his back. "Good to see you, brother." He introduced Janie, and Digger pushed forward.

"Let me through, man." He grabbed Nicky up and squeezed, lifting the old man clear off the floor. "Fuck, Nicky. Where you fucking been?"

"Listening to rumors about the Demons," he said with a chuckle as Digger finally set him down. "Rumors about the Gliders going legit. Opening a pot joint with all the funds they mysteriously came into."

Capone grabbed Nicky's hand. "Glad you could make it."

I lifted an eyebrow. "This your doing, Capone?"

"Shit yeah." He grinned, pulling Helina against his side. "Figured if we went legit, the old man might want to come back for a visit here and there. This is

Helina, by the way."

They exchanged pleasantries, and Digger swore, pulling Maci closer. "You remember Maci—she's now my property."

Both Mel and Nicky's eyebrows rose, Helina rolling her eyes, but Maci beamed, twisting so they could see the tattoo on her right shoulder blade.

Nicky actually smiled. "You're still putting up with this ugly brute?"

"This *ugly brute*," she said, leaning into him, "is the best thing to ever happen to me."

"Well, shit." Nicky scanned the lot of us, his arm pulling Mel once more against his side. "I leave, and you all fucking fall in love like a bunch of pansy-assed little bitches."

Hawk snorted and shoved a toothpick between his teeth. "You first."

"Come join us," I said, tilting my head toward the stairs once everyone's laughter died down.

Nicky and Mel settled beside me as we all took our seats again, their heads swiveling while taking in the place.

"So, what do you think?"

"I think it's fucking awesome." Nicky turned his gaze on me. "Never figured something like this would happen for the Gliders."

"Like Capone probably told you, it was all his idea."

"Best fucking idea the pretty boy ever had."

Nicky's words brought a huff from Helina even though a sassy smirk tilted her lips. "Best thing this pretty boy ever did was chase after *me*."

Nicky chuckled. "I'll give him that."

I flagged a waitress down. "Grab us a bottle of whiskey and some shot glasses," I told her as she drew near. With a nod, she hurried off again.

"I've still got your colors in my desk drawer back at the club, Nicky."

His gaze whipped toward me.

"The vest is yours if you want it."

Mel squeezed his hand. "Don't even think about saying no," she said.

"Been missing you boys this whole time," Nicky admitted, his gaze taking in the men around him. "And while I've been happy as shit with Mel, I'm needing my brothers, too." He held out his hand, and I clasped it tight. "I'll take that vest back as long as you don't expect me to be down here every day. Too damn old. Too damn in love with my woman to leave her alone for any extended period of time."

I squeezed his hand, never feeling so content, so full in my fucking life. "You got it."

"I want to dance." Janie stood and smoothed her hands down over her bulging belly. She'd been having more normal days than not ever since getting pregnant. Hawk's face fucking glowed as he stared up at her.

"I'm in!" Maci jumped up to join her, and Alexa and Helina stood as well.

"Go on, baby," Nicky said to Mel, smacking her ass as she stood. "Have some fun."

The ladies left us men, and the waitress arrived with our whiskey. I sat forward, closer to the glass table, and poured the five of us brimmed shots.

"To life," I said, grinning once we all held one in hand.

They all agreed, and we tipped back together, the burn sliding down my throat. I poured another. "To my brothers." I lifted my glass. "May the days ahead of us be many, our beds always warmed by our women, and the whiskey pour like fucking water."

We tipped back again, and Capone slammed his shot glass onto the table. "Check out those gorgeous women."

I turned … all five of our women shimmied their asses off, gazes on us. "Let's go get 'em, boys." As one, we stood and made our way across the dance floor, toward the women who had claimed our hearts.

Life couldn't get any fucking better.

The End

www.authorlynnburke.com

EVERNIGHT PUBLISHING ®

www.evernightpublishing.com

FALLEN GLIDERS MC: VOLUME TWO